'This is just a beautifully pow[erful novel.]
Pip Adam

'Funny, sharp, sad and profound, ... made me laugh,
think, weep and actually beat my breast. A masterpiece.'
Elizabeth Knox, *The Conversation*

'*Delirious* by Damien Wilkins is a beautiful work of fiction and
if it reduces you to tears then you will not be alone. . . .
The book of the year is all heart.'
Steve Braunias, *Newsroom*

'*Delirious* rearranged me. Utterly absorbing, moving, brilliant.'
Emily Perkins

'There's so much poetry and beauty in this book . . . I have a
very tender heart and it feels stronger for having read it.'
Gabi Lardies, *The Spinoff*

'I found it amazing that a book about traumatic events was also
so funny, and even at times whimsical. . . . I like it when a novel
reflects life so closely and this novel is so close to life it's almost
psychedelic with it: so much detail, and beauty
and harshness and weirdness.'
Claire Mabey, *The Spinoff*

'A charged book . . . *Delirious* is an accurate and sympathetic
study of change, age and growth. Set on the very edge of land,
the novel is poised between rational assessment
and the mysteries of the deep.'
David Herkt, *NZ Listener*

'Ageing may not be seen as the most glamorous topic, but this
smart and sensitive novel proves it to be rewarding, if rare,
territory. *Delirious* teaches us that there is always more to learn
from the past—personal, pre-colonial—and that
ageing is a perilous, precious privilege.'
Claire Travaglia, *Kete Books*

By the same author

Novels
The Miserables
Little Masters
Nineteen Widows Under Ash
Chemistry
The Fainter
Somebody Loves Us All
Max Gate
Dad Art
Lifting

Short Stories
The Veteran Perils
For Everyone Concerned

Poetry
The Idles

Non-fiction
When Famous People Come to Town

For Young Adults
Aspiring

Delirious

Damien Wilkins

TE HERENGA WAKA
UNIVERSITY PRESS

Te Herenga Waka University Press
PO Box 600 Wellington
New Zealand
teherengawakapress.co.nz

Copyright © Damien Wilkins 2024
First published 2024
Reprinted 2025

This book is copyright. Apart from
any fair dealing for the purpose of private study,
research, criticism or review, as permitted under the
Copyright Act, no part may be reproduced by any
process without the permission of the publishers.
The moral rights of the author have been asserted.

ISBN 978-1-77692-208-6

A catalogue record is available at
the National Library of New Zealand

Printed in Singapore by Markono Print Media Pte Ltd

*For my mother
and for my sister Miriam*

One

That year. *That year.* People always said, that year. It must have been the winter after that year when Mary borrowed a friend's funny old bach up the coast for a week. Pete didn't come with her. Go, he said. Go. What a great idea. She could tell he was hurt.

The bach had a turret room which overlooked a parking area and then on to the sea. The friend was replacing the fireplace with a wood burner, which sat under heavy plastic in the main room. The hole in the ceiling waiting for the connection was covered by a flappy piece of timber. At night the persistent wind slapped it around. Mary and Pete had sometimes stayed here in the summer when Will was little. It was a summer place. Now it refused to warm up. The two small fan heaters slaved away uselessly, scorching her ankles. Mary didn't mind much, moving around inside with her coat on and a daggy woollen hat she'd found in a cupboard. She went for brisk walks, nodding at the dog walkers on the beach. One day a small terrier was lifted off its feet by a gust of wind. It found itself on its back on the sand and lay there for a moment in total confusion.

Mary ended up staying in bed a lot, reading the crime thrillers she found on the bookshelves.

Each evening she went upstairs and watched the sunset, with a glass of straight gin from a bottle in the kitchen. *Help yourself to anything, Mare.* She'd never much cared for gin or drinking. The whole bach stay was an experiment, as she guessed everything was now. A series of firsts. She seldom went anywhere without Pete. It was the first time she'd been here without him. They'd had some wonderful stays. In summer the sky was often magnificent over Kāpiti Island, moving its shades of pink, red, purple. Sometimes it looked as if the edge of the sea was on fire. The dream of living here on this coast was born in those short visits. In winter it was hard to say when the day ended and the night began. The sea was grey, like some molten metal. She watched it all fade into darkness, the seams of water and sky disappearing. It looked like the liquid in which submarines would be suspended. A strange wartime sea.

Mary found a pair of binoculars. The room also had a telescope set up in it, pointing out at the horizon. The telescope had belonged to her friend's ex-husband. He was supposed to retrieve it, though he always put it off—his way of maintaining the relationship, the friend supposed. Mary had never really known how to look through a telescope. She could never get the knack of closing one eye.

On day five a woman parked her big black house-bus in the area in front of the bach. She was setting up camp, with her buckets slung over her wing mirrors and her fold-out chairs and mats on the tarseal, a blue tarp tied over the windscreen for privacy. She had a little yappy dog she carried under her arm on her way to and from the public toilets on the far side of the parking area by the boat club building. The woman had wild sculpted blondish hair and was about Mary's age. Could that be you? Mary said to herself. Caucasian female, mid-forties, five-foot-six. What series of events had led the woman to this situation? The paint job on the bus was homemade; it looked as though the wrong kind of paint had been used. It had almost a blackboard finish. Indeed, there were words on the side of the bus, phrases, mostly smudged and unreadable. One of them said 'Powered by the stars'. To be out there in the elements on your own was impressive and not quite impressive enough for Mary to walk over the little hump of dune and invite the woman in for a drink. The bus sort of ruined her end-of-day ritual.

That evening, before 5pm, she went up to the turret room, but instead of training her rapt gaze at the mysterious sky Mary grabbed the binoculars and started following the woman as she fussed about outside her bus and spoke to her dog.

She didn't know why she couldn't leave the woman alone. It was all legal. Her parking in full view was just tough luck. Mary had a kind friend with a bach she could borrow, so where exactly was her leg to stand on?

Then, as she was watching, a car pulled up alongside the bus and a man and woman got out. They spent a lot of time talking, the three of them. The man was in his forties, tall, in a dress leather jacket and neat jeans. He kept looking around as if checking for others or to see if they were being observed. Mary slunk down lower in her vantage point. The new woman was a carbon copy of the bus woman but stockier. They looked like they were trying to agree on something. Well, Mary surmised, drugs. Or sex. Next the man entered the bus with the bus woman while the other woman got back in the car.

Hello. The man didn't re-emerge for another twenty minutes. When he did, it was almost dark, and he got in the car and drove off with the other woman.

Mary was just about to abandon the turret to heat her packet dinner when the bus woman emerged, walking quickly towards the boatshed, where Mary saw a different car was waiting. She got into this car and it left. Busy lady.

Pete would ring every evening and they would have a short conversation about what they'd done during the day. He would speak about something that had happened at the library. *People asked such funny questions.* She would wait until he'd finished and then tell him about the weather, unusually detailed descriptions of the hourly changes. First it was this and then it was that, things got better before they closed in again. He must have been beside himself to hear her talk like this. With obvious painfulness they were attempting to piece it all together again, somehow return to each other. She felt guilty about this, but no matter how normal she tried to sound, she realised Pete would be worried that one day she could walk out of the bach and into the sea. Surely her strange new reporting on the weather was a prelude to some disastrous event? *No, she never mentioned anything like this or gave any indication she was heading towards it. We just talked about normal things.* Such an act was not on her mind, though sensing it was on his mind made her doubt herself. Maybe she was capable of it and just hadn't seen it? Each day she stared down the sea, as if saying, No, not today.

Mary was woken that night by the sound of the dog barking and howling. When she pulled the curtain she couldn't see a thing in the darkness. The dog kept it up for hours. The loose piece of timber on the roof banged away. She dozed and woke, looking at the clock on the bedside table every thirty minutes. She was locked into a pattern, deciding to get up, then drifting off to sleep again only to wake to the sound of the dog and the banging. It was as if she'd been thrown down a well and then all her furniture had been thrown down after her. At a certain point early in the morning she was aware of the silence. She was exhausted.

After breakfast, when she walked past the bus on her way to the beach for a stroll, the woman was there, sitting on one of her chairs, the dog in her lap. She caught Mary's eye and nodded a greeting. Mary should have kept moving. She was leaving that afternoon. She'd never see her again. The wind lifted the woman's hair into a tall accusatory pile, a column of spun stuff as if the woman was standing upside down.

'Quite a performance from the dog last night,' Mary called out.

'What was that hon?'

Mary came closer. The woman had bare feet, green nail polish. Mary pointed at the dog. 'Barking all night. I'm up there in the house, you know.'

The woman glanced towards the bach. 'Cool spot.'

'Yeah. Kind of wrecked my sleep.'

'Oh hon.'

Mary thought she was talking to her, but this was addressed to the dog.

'Dog seemed really distressed,' Mary said. 'And I was almost going to come over and see what was going on.'

The woman stared at Mary.

Picturing this, as she did for years afterwards and still did and was doing now, more than three decades on, as they prepared to move house again, Mary wanted to give her a fag but she didn't have one. The woman did have a smoker's reckoning squint though. Her eyes drilled into Mary. For the first time in ages, someone was looking at her free of any complicating feeling except fresh dislike made in the moment. The woman didn't have a clue about her. Didn't know Mary's son was dead or that she'd lost the job which defined her. They lacked any history except what was happening now. Mary felt alive, capable of an action she couldn't foresee.

'Were you hon?' the woman taunted. 'Were you going to come over?'

Mary half turned from her. 'Thinking of other people would be nice.'

The woman stood up and put her dog down on the chair. Her hands were now on her hips as she leaned towards her. 'Why. Don't. You. *Die*.'

It was strange, and it had always been the case, that without the police uniform on you didn't feel tough or even capable. It was all a trick. A trick that worked. Everyone said it. The cape of a superhero. Then nothing. A current of fear raced through her. She was aware that she needed to organise herself, prepare herself, yet she was failing to do this. Time sped up. Coming to the bach had been a mistake. Unless this was the real reason she had come. This person in front of her.

'Here we go,' Mary said, taking a step back.

'Seriously?' said the woman.

Mary was moving away now, turning to the bach.

'Seriously, you nosey bitch?' the woman called out.

Was she coming towards her? The dog had started to bark.

'Yeah yeah,' Mary said. She flapped a hand behind her. 'Whatever.'

'I know where you live, dumbarse.'

'I'm calling the cops.' *I am the cops.*

'Ha ha.'

'You can't do this.'

'Do what?'

'You know.'

'Look out for what's coming, lady.'

Behind her there was the sound of something clattering over the concrete. She flinched and kept walking. Maybe the woman had thrown a chair or a bucket, but Mary didn't turn around. The woman was muttering and cursing, her words carried off by the wind.

When Mary got back to the bach she was shaking. She stomped around swearing and packing her stuff. She was leaving right away. Then she thought, why? The plan was to leave in the afternoon. Stick with that, and stuff her and her ugly bus. But she found herself emptying the fridge, vacuuming, wiping the benches. She placed the viewing cap on the telescope and tidied away the binoculars and the books she'd read. She worked furiously.

She rang Pete and told him she'd be home a bit earlier. He asked if everything was all right and she said it was fine, just that the weather had packed in so she may as well come home. Okay, he told her, that's great.

She was on the road within the hour, still trembling.

Sometimes, thinking back to *that year*, Mary couldn't remember in any sort of detail the major things or the order in which they'd happened. Yet the woman with her black bus and her blue tarpaulin was always there. Mary could walk to that carpark now and be there within ten minutes. But she didn't need to. She could replay it all in her head, feel again the solidness of the dunes under her feet when she made it to safety, the stiff brush of the lupins against her damp jeans. She'd never told anyone about it. Yes, it was that year, when a pair of middle-aged women might easily have got into a physical fight in a deserted beach carpark in front of a small dog. What had Mary planned to do, grab her by that tall column of hair? It was the most obvious method of attack. She would have torn at it with all her might. She felt sure that the woman wouldn't have lasted a second. She felt sure that, had she managed to gain possession of the hair, source of her adversary's strength, she would have been able to return home renewed.

Two

At first she thought it was a wrong number. Couldn't even recognise her own name when it was spoken. Who? She was busy with all the jobs that had to be done ahead of the big move. And her phone didn't ring much anyway. Pete of course would call if he was out and about. *Did you say we need or didn't need potatoes?* His fingers couldn't manage texts and she'd need her glasses. Colin was a regular caller, though mostly at night. She remembered her mother would always say, Now who could that be? As if every phone call was remarkable, shocking. And her sister Claire would say, I think it might be the Prime Minister with news of Daddy's knighthood, the first man in a metalwork factory to receive the honour. *I think it's Mary's boyfriend!*

One of Mary's hearing aids had popped out and she poked it back in. Some days she didn't bother with them. On the phone the caller was asking again if he was speaking to Senior Sergeant Mary Brunton. 'Back in the day,' she said finally. She knew he was a cop. 'Senior citizen more than sergeant now,' she added.

'I hate to bother you. Have you got a minute?'

'I have many minutes.'

'Okay, good. You see, something's come up.'

The caller paused. Mary could hear voices in the background, then a scuffled sound as if he'd put his hand over the phone. She waited. Immediately she was back at the station, making calls herself, with people not caring you were on the phone, not interested that perhaps you had issues of great sensitivity to communicate. Difficult things. Impossible things. Or even routine things. It was all the same. Even if you found a quiet space, someone would burst in with news, with some urgent matter. Or just for a joke. Men on a mission, or just men. You were needed. Right now! Hey! Knock knock. Phones weren't real policing. *You ringing your hubby, love?* It was pretty awful. She missed it with a sharp pang.

'Call me Mary. And anyway, you've promoted me. I'd better come clean. I never made Senior. They got rid of me before I could put in for it. I had most of the exams under my belt.'

'Right. Mary. I'm Dave Monk, CIB Wellington. This matter, Mary, it's not really to do with the job. Not you and the job. Just to reassure you.'

'Okay,' said Mary. 'I feel better now. Do I?'

'We've had a development and I'd like to maybe sit down with you, Mary, and go over it. If you have some free spots.'

'All my spots are free, Dave.'

'Excellent. Then let's aim for next week. Friday? 11am?'

'What are we dealing with here, Dave?'

The scuffling muting sound happened again. It was definitely his end, not hers. Not her graunching stones. After decades of her thoughts moving against themselves, it seemed her brain was about to trickle from her ear and pool on the floor in a conical mound of fine gravel. At which point darling Pete would walk in and say, Never mind, love, let's clean up this little mess, shall we. Lately he'd been hovering near her, expecting something. She felt watched.

Then on the phone, ignoring her question, 'Yes, yes, good.

Friday, 11am.' Was she on speaker phone now, with Dave scribbling on a pad? The world of the station filled in behind them once more. She caught laughter. Dave said, from further away, 'It's a matter of some—'

'Sensitivity,' Mary supplied. 'Yes, but what sort of sensitivity? I'm so old, Dave, I might not be around next Friday to hear it. Give me a clue.'

'Ah,' he said, picking up the phone again, switching it off speaker and making his voice uncomfortably close, 'it's connected with your son.'

The phrasing was trapped in her ear for a moment, going around.

She was standing at the French doors of their bedroom, looking out towards the island whose bushy lower reaches carried all those amazing birds. The island was theirs, the birds'. It belonged to them. Within minutes of leaving the boat, there was a welcome or a warning zipping along overhead. She and Pete had done the overnight stay years ago. A kiwi had sniffed her boot when they lined up outside the lodge and waited in the dark. The Dutch woman beside her was weeping. They'd heard their first karakia, spoken by the lodge manager over their roast chicken. Funny what came back. Plenty of Māori battles had taken place there. Hand-to-hand, very bloody. Pete was a history buff. Imagine the surprise of the musket, he'd told her. In the olden days the island guarded the way south. Whales swam past and were slaughtered. Imagine the surprise of the harpoon, she'd said. None of it seemed likely the day they'd visited the quiet place, enjoying the birds and the views back to where they lived. Now the island rested, exporting kiwi, taking in tourists.

Pete had told her recently that he was weaning himself off

their bedroom view so that when they left he wouldn't miss it as much. He'd pass the doors with his head averted and she'd laugh at him. His strategy was wise and, for her, completely unworkable. Her eye was always drawn. She had to look at things. She wished she didn't.

Finally, the decision was made, the house was going on the market. Open homes starting soon. They had to cope with that in their own ways. They'd done it before. They'd come through. It wasn't the end of the world. It was only a chapter closing, Pete said. How long was this story, Mary wondered.

When her phone rang, she'd been sorting through old clothes, preparing a load for the hospice shop, a load for the recycling bin. One for the rubbish. Pete had jeans and trousers going back twenty years, more. He hadn't thrown anything out. *Good painting clothes.* She'd laid them out on the bed, as if inspecting the wardrobe of a man who'd died. All these former Petes. Her shirt collection was equally sad. It was not that she couldn't imagine wearing some of this stuff; it was that she could—and no one would notice or care. Somewhere along the line she had become a Lady with a Scarf, invisible, typical. Mary thought she would pass herself in the street and not even notice.

It's connected with your son. There was the echo of the last time such a phrase had sounded, almost forty years ago. Back then she chased crims in a skirt—she was in the skirt, not the crims, though in fact there'd been a few. A stiletto chucked accurately was no laughing matter.

And nor was this.

'What did you say?' She hardly wanted to hear the words again, but she felt she must, since these days she easily missed some bits when people spoke and got the wrong end of the stick. She needed to make another appointment with the hearing place. Jo. Nice woman. No judgement. The stuff she'd pulled from people. *Lovely!* she'd say, when it was the unloveliest thing in the world. Mary always closed her eyes as the suction probe started, and saw herself underwater, pressurised, obliterated. It wasn't terrible at all. She almost looked forward to it. It wasn't like the prickly and rasping invasion of the dental hygienist, with her questions. *How many times a day do you floss? Do you drink coffee or tea? How many times a day? What about snacks? Do you snack? Do you even care about your gums? Have you ever drowned a kitten?* Jo had no moral position. And when the roaring stopped, there was the amazing plug of wax, the stiff brown cartridge Mary had made simply by what had happened in her head. Lovely! She'd thought it into being, this repulsive undeniable part of herself. *See you next time, Mary. You will, Jo, you will.*

'William Paul Brunton,' said Dave Monk, Wellington CIB. 'Your son . . . died . . .' he was fishing for the bit of paper '. . . March fifth 1982, aged eleven years. From drowning . . . on a school trip . . . which I probably just need you to confirm, sorry I should have done this earlier, but I need you to confirm, Mary, that this is all correct and I haven't somehow found another Mary Brunton who was in the force.'

There'd been high-level meetings about whether a female officer could wear trousers. It went all the way to the top. The Minister had an opinion. A Very Important Man had spent time thinking about her legs. Mary used to borrow a pair of Pete's trousers to do late shifts in winter—and there were complaints from some of the blokes, jibes. *Hey, Morrie, come over here will you? Oh Mary, sorry thought it was someone else.*

'1982,' she said. 'How old were you then, Dave?'

'Me? I was born in 1980.'

'How incredible. Police these days, getting younger and younger.' Mary took a deep breath.

'So, confirming it's you.'

'Yes. Yes, Detective, you've got your man.'

After the call, she went down the narrow stairs one at a time, kicking the first big plastic bag of clothes ahead of her while holding on to its taped-up top. Probably unwise. Old woman falls down stairs. Hip fracture. Pneumonia. Curtains. You'd rather have the skull fracture and be done with it than drown in your own fluids. She'd attended a fatality just like it in her first week. A bone-cold house at the back of Karori. A neighbour had called it in. The ancient husband still in bed when they arrived, waiting for his breakfast. He'd thrown off the blankets and then he couldn't or wouldn't move. His entire narrow body encased in an ancient pinkish one-piece long john, like the first stage of mummification, with his oddly prominent scrotum a bulging pocket of folds as if a kitten or a soft toy was hiding there. Idly, he scratched himself and stared at Mary. *Who are you, girlie?* They brought him a cup of tea and he asked where the toast was. And the senior constable had told her what was she gawking at, get the toast. *Honey*, said the husband. You can't go calling her Honey, said her senior. Two men laughing and she was stepping over the body at the bottom of the stairs, with a cat watching from the top step, then following her into the kitchen. Forensics had been delayed. Young Mary was alone downstairs, opening the cupboard of the deceased woman, finding a jar of honey almost frozen solid. It was touch and go whether she would run from the house. The cat pressed its tail around her legs, and she was saved. You'll need feeding too, I guess, she told the animal.

Halfway down Mary knew she should have waited for Pete to come home, but now the bag was blocking her way and there was no option but to give it another kick. It was like kicking a bag of human organs.

It would have been better to throw all the clothes out the window.

Their great love for the house, built up over twenty years, now had an asterisk or two attached to it, these stairs being a major. Pete had a hip; she had an ankle, and a knee. It wasn't the only reason they were leaving but it was on the list. She still had to check in with Pete regularly: 'Explain again why we're doing this?'

The first time she'd asked, Pete had said, 'Because we're going to a better place.' And they'd both burst out laughing. It was now a routine. *The better place.*

The independent-living units at the retirement village ten kilometres up the coast were, objectively speaking, better. They'd scoped them out quietly. It wasn't quite confirmed yet. They were selling and would need somewhere to live. They had their names down. The little houses were nice-looking, tucked inside their neat low hedges, secure in their aluminium-framed windows, their all-round weather-tightness. The tidy paving everywhere seemed not so terrible. Weren't they sick of weeds? Certainly they were done with drains, with draughts and leaks.

For ages they didn't discuss it, not properly. They were afraid. They were proud. And they were not old old. They semi-resented her nephew Colin's not-so-secret scrutiny of their capacities whenever he visited, his educational anecdotes about elderly patients who'd waited too long. He was a GP. They weren't, Mary said, 'village people', and she'd done the 'YMCA' chorus, with her arms in the air, shaping the letters. She didn't really know how she knew this. Pete certainly didn't. He listened to folk and blues, mostly on the LPs he'd picked up when they were no longer needed by the library. It was now a large collection. If she had to think of him quickly that was the image which arrived: Pete bent over the stereo, blowing at the needle with pursed lips. And would those hundreds of records be coming with them? Surely not. Every move was a subtraction. You shed possessions until you were left with your pyjamas, after someone had stolen your slippers. She thought of Pete's mother.

'Do it while you can,' Colin told them. He was middle-aged, pale and rope-thin, and with his shock of white hair looked, Mary thought, like an unlit candle. They laughed about good old Colin—how decrepit did he think they were? In many ways they still thought of him as about twelve years old, bounding into their place like a big puppy. *Is Will home? Is he home?*

And again they were not old old. Not in their own minds. Yet people seemed unsurprised when they announced they were selling. This caused Mary and Pete to feel two things at once: that it was a good decision, and that they were older than they thought. She was seventy-nine and he was seventy-eight; she enjoyed it most, of course, for the three months they were the same age.

There was no crisis, Mary thought. Not until Dave Monk called—and what might that change? The worst had happened already.

The first bag of clothes tumbled free at the bottom of the stairs. It hadn't split open. Good. She paused. In the distance the sea percussively rinsed the sand. A flash of doubt passed through her. She knew how to wait it out. Why were they moving? Tell me again. Could they not rewind the last few months and set out on a different course? She was looking at the chimney of their wood burner. Had that been a significant moment in their choosing, in their dithering? The Day of the Sweeps, some months ago now.

The husband-and-wife team were into the living room with their tools before they had time to think, Oh yes, we booked them ages ago and finally they're here, good! In fact, Mary and Pete both felt it was, strangely, not good, yet they couldn't stop them. Once the drop cloth fell over the floor, it was as if the space had been solemnly claimed, like a sheet over a body.

The room instantly was not theirs.

The pair were filthy, their overalls covered in soot, smears of it on their faces. Before they'd even started! Mary had laughed, she couldn't help it. More from a sort of joy. It was like they were hosting the nineteenth century. Incredible to be so dirty. It was easy to imagine a small boy appearing—their son—and being shoved up the chimney, his little feet poking out the bottom, then disappearing. Yet here was the industrial vacuum cleaner with its telescopic brush.

'This will be pretty quick,' said the woman, whose name was Susie. She sounded uncertain.

'Pretty straightforward,' said the man, Chris, who was having trouble finding a plug. Pete pointed one out.

Mary and Pete were stunned into silence, like children whose game had been taken over by adults.

When the sweep sent the hose up the chimney, Mary recalled the colonoscopy she'd had a year ago. All clear. Chris's chimney hose was jammed, and he jiggled it, giving it a shove, then releasing it back down before a renewed assault. He puffed and muttered and smiled. Soot settled on the drop cloth and—as they discovered later—elsewhere.

Pete had noticed a bird's nest in the wire basket at the top of the chimney. He'd been about to climb the ladder to remove it, but Mary had stopped him. He'd got it in position when she arrived on the scene. 'What do you think you're doing?' She saw his body splayed out, his spasms. Ever since his heart diagnosis two years ago, flashes of his end came to her with a vividness which made her gasp.

If she found him and they were all alone in the dark house at night . . . She would cope, she knew she would. And if he came across her . . . ?

It had been ages since the chimney had been cleaned. They'd get someone in, Mary said, kill two birds—and their nest—with one stone. And this had turned into the need for a full replacement of not only that antiquated section but the whole flue since it was deemed 'a future problem'. Another man had come—the sweeps' boss—and tutted and grinned, saying that a flue like the one they had was really from the dark ages. They'd felt bullied but in a kind way. With the new set-up, the man said, they wouldn't recognise themselves. The wood burner's efficiency would dramatically improve. They'd be adding years to its life. And no more nests.

The chimney should have been someone else's problem, Mary thought. Like a few things around the house. The downpipes, the cracked retaining wall, the wobbly fence, the garage threatened by the deadish banksia which dropped its grenades under the lawnmower, dulling its blade and threatening Pete's shins. They'd let things slip a bit. The maintenance. Oh, the maintenance.

But there was no backing out of it. Susie and Chris were here, covered in someone else's soot, ready for action. Susie held the new section in bubble wrap in her arms, babying it, and studied the wood burner. It appeared then that they'd never done anything like this before, and Mary laughed again. Maybe they'd purchased the gear a month ago, watched a YouTube video, then dabbed soot on their faces. Crazy! Who were these people?

In the kitchen, Mary said to Pete, 'We'll pay them in shillings.'

He frowned. He didn't like her being satirical about working people. He was very sensitive on this issue, since he didn't believe he'd ever been a worker. Through some quirk of fate, he'd been allowed to live among books.

After Susie walked up the stairs there were black smears on parts of the wall where her side had brushed it. She carried the top section up and through the doors on to the deck. Chris followed her with a ladder, banging it happily and burping when he got to the top. It was wonderful how they worked in a wave of minor destruction.

Susie bashed at the chimney with a mallet while Chris steadied the ladder. Mary and Pete stared at them through the glass doors. It was common now to feel bullied. They gave in, believed other people, their confidence sapped by assertion. The world was full of these figures who knew what was right, who saw them and concluded they were more or less useless. Pushovers, said Mary. We're a pair of pushovers. We don't have a spine between us. Was that why the village beckoned? A sort of strength-in-numbers deal? Outsource our decision-making to the management, hide behind our hedge? On the other hand, the village were also experts at old age. They knew a thing or two about . . . Mary guessed it was called caring. She shuddered at the thought of underpaid and highly stressed strangers touching her, assisting her.

Surely she was getting ahead of herself. And Pete was really okay. You looked at him and you thought of self-control, and bicycles. He still biked to the shops. The indoor life of his profession had marked him with a certain quietness but it hadn't robbed him of basic physical competence. He could change a washer. He had a chainsaw and a pair of chaps which made him look like a cowboy in a musical.

Yet when Mary had ordered him not to climb the ladder, he'd agreed at once. She'd not been a police officer since 1983—thirty-five years!—but she could still summon it. The tone. Sometimes, she knew, she moved about as if she still wore a uniform. In a box they hadn't got to she would find her hat, her medals.

Finally, the chimney was reconstituted. In the living room again, Chris was wiping the new pieces with a rag soaked in spirits, while Susie on a step ladder stabilised the black cylinder with a pair of dirty gloves. When she stepped down, they saw she'd rubbed against the curtain, leaving black marks.

'Oh, don't worry about that,' said Mary. 'Easy to clean.' She wanted them gone then. She was sick of the show.

But Susie was already pulling at her gloves with her teeth to get them off, and then reaching up to unhook the curtain. 'No, no, that's my fault. I'll get it washed and back to you. No worries.'

'Mucky pup,' said Chris, flicking at her backside with a rag.

They watched again wide-eyed as this thing happened, their curtain gone.

Afterwards they sat in shock, full of resentment but also delight. It was something to tell Colin.

The window, lopsided when the remaining curtain was

pulled, sat strangely. At night people could stare in. Who? Their house was on a rise fifteen metres above sea level, surrounded by karaka trees whose glossy leaves caught the moonlight. No one was coming up the path to catch a glimpse of these two useless old people bumbling about.

A few days later they came home to find the curtain in a paper bag by the front door. When Mary put it up again, it was an inch shorter than its mate. The sweep had put it in the dryer.

Mary stared at the short curtain now. It said to her, It's time. Then she got on with her rubbish bags.

The night of Dave Monk's call Mary lay awake in bed beside Pete, her mind going, merging with the constant sound of the sea, like the ambient noise of a distant city, or a jug boiling in a far part of the house. I must go and turn that off, she thought. She grew convinced there was something she needed to do to stop the noise. In the next moment she knew again it was the sea. She went back and forth like this, unpleasantly, wishing it were later and that she could get up and start the day. On sleepless nights as a child her mother used to tell her, *Think of something nice.* For a while she shared a room with Claire and her sister would say, *Better not think of me.*

When Mary and Pete had first bought the house, it was all unbelievable. They'd walk to the end of the street, cross the dunes—the poor dunes!—and meet the sea as if visiting a giant in a fairy tale. It was always a surprise to come across it. In summer, lying on their backs, they'd be rocked in the giant's arms. She'd bought a wetsuit and entered the water even when daylight saving ended. Sometimes she would wave to an elderly couple—'elderly'—who also swam in winter. He was apparently a retired rear admiral. They were tall and fit and they always waved back. How strong and healthy she'd felt! Mightily, she and Pete wielded badminton rackets. The net was hooked up between trees by the garage. They swatted the shuttlecock in the warm evenings, drank beer on the deck with friends and were bitten alive as the sky went crimson. Those were the healing years, she thought, when some benign wave carried them forward and out of harm's way.

And though they'd known it was coming, here was a new wave, catching them unawares. Like the fantastical sweeps. And here was Dave bloody Monk with his development. How could she wait to hear what he had to say? It seemed a mercy not to put Pete through the same thing, so she hadn't told him. Simple. He didn't know and didn't need to. Not immediately. Not in his condition. She would carry it. This was her rubbish bag. Not that she was in tip-top condition. She'd had those months with a walking stick after her knee op. Embarrassing at first, then she got over herself. Her joints. Her weight.

She suddenly remembered with great vividness passing the physical exam at police college, scurrying up the wall, leaping fences, crawling and sprinting in the boys' school shoes she'd had to buy because there were no suitable women's shoes. This was a test which wasn't even required of female recruits back then—it was too unladylike—but which Mary had insisted she take. She needed to show them, the other recruits, her bosses, her family, her sister Claire, who'd doubted the whole enterprise and laughed at her. *Oh Mare, don't pout!* How hard she'd worked. Had almost given up a few times. And she'd pulled it off. Then, only a few months into the job, she'd been chasing a pair of offenders in Berhampore, reaching for the same branch they'd used to leave a property because why not? She was young and fit and the adrenaline was pushing her on. The baddies were getting away. The branch snapped, dumping her in a veggie patch, Mary ending up with the ankle which still gave her twinges and worse. It was dumb, humiliating. *How's the silverbeet, Mare?*

Now she told Pete to use the handrail. His hip probably needed to be replaced. They got a man in these days and Pete would tell him in his 'man's voice', 'I have a chainsaw if you need it.'

She knew she could get up any time, go downstairs and read her book—usually that knowledge took over and she was released without having to leave the bed. Tonight the trick didn't work. Instead, a memory came to her of Claire visiting in the days after Will had died. Her sister and Will were often paired in her mind. Lately they were there a lot, a double act she didn't know what to do with except watch them come and go, come and go, a bit like the two crims who'd taken the branch to launch themselves over the fence and into darkness. *Wait! Stop! Halt!* She gave chase and they always escaped. Here they were again.

Claire had arrived unannounced because Mary wasn't answering the phone. Pete was out on some ridiculous errand—getting rid of a bunch of stuff which had happily lain under their house for years to the tip. Frankly she was glad to see him go.

Now here was Claire, walking up the path to the front door, carrying a casserole dish, a dumb look on her face. Mary was at the window in the upstairs bedroom. She thought for a moment of crouching down and not answering the door.

Let her leave the casserole on the step. Claire was a terrible cook. The casserole would have stressed her enormously. She'd always considered other people's interest in the kitchen a monumental bore. If a recipe called for four cloves of garlic, Claire found another recipe. Mary watched as her sister stopped and walked back along the path, still with the casserole in her hands. She stopped after a few paces. Claire turned around and walked towards the door again. Mary saw that her sister's lips were moving. Claire was at the door but frozen, except for her mouth. It struck Mary that her big sister was rehearsing what she'd say. She was working on her script. How to speak? It was quite funny. Poor Claire.

Finally, Claire put the casserole on the doorstep.

Mary, brave police officer, experienced door-knocker and bringer of bad news, slumped against the wall and slid to the floor. It felt as though someone or something was pressing on the top of her head.

A few moments later there was a knock at the door. Mary peered out the window. Claire was back again, but this time she had Colin with her. He'd been told to wait in the car, or perhaps he'd refused to come with his mother. He was a sulky teenager, gangly and belligerent and competitively attached to his competitive mother. Sometimes it seemed they were more like siblings. They fought over the newspaper crossword and any puzzle. They read the same novels— murder mysteries—and compared how quickly they'd solved them. Did real murderers commit so many basic errors? Colin asked his aunt. Were they all so thick?

Mother and son demeaned Colin's father (Claire's ex-husband) with joint glee, vying for the most inventive putdown.

Colin also loved Will. He loved him with unabashed

sincerity, and was unfailingly protective of a boy who was always pleased to see his much older cousin and who somehow was a good influence—at least for the time they were together.

Her nephew loved someone and now he was gone.

The world was stunning. It stunned you. It collapsed on top of you like a wall of bricks.

They were here from kindness, she reminded herself. There was no language. Of course there was no language. Why would Claire even think she might be able to say something?

At the front door, Colin fell into her arms, almost knocking her down. Mary took the boy's full weight, the unsupported heft of his heaving shoulders, the hard stone of his forehead against her shoulder. He wailed and wailed. It was a hell of a sound. It bounced around the hallway, hurting her ears. Mary staggered and held on. He cried uncontrollably while Claire, behind him, held the casserole.

Mary thought, The boy is crying on behalf of both sisters. Claire had retrieved him from the car for this purpose. She sort of admired her sister then. In place of the opening speech, with which she was obviously struggling, Claire had delivered this—six feet of grief, raw and exposed and wet and loud. Unable to speak, she said, *Here you go sis!*

The tricky sisters were both bereft.

Colin was not bereft. He had this contribution to make. Mary felt thankful.

Then her shoulder began to hurt and she nudged Colin's shaking head a little. 'Hey,' she said. 'All right.' Her back was sore from his weight, and she shifted, causing him to straighten. He stood up again, his face gleaming with tears. He looked in confusion at his mother, perhaps uncertain if she disapproved. Had they spoken in the car on the way over to the house about how they were to behave, how they should be strong for Auntie Mary and Uncle Pete? No blubbering. Had he fallen short? It was difficult to tell, Mary thought. Claire was saying something almost under her breath. Finally, Mary worked out it was connected to the casserole, what was in it and what to do with it, heating instructions. She almost laughed at Claire then. She almost lost it. She nearly screamed, That casserole will taste like nothing because you couldn't be arsed putting any flavour in it!

Her sister was moving past them on her way to the kitchen. 'Once I have free hands,' Claire muttered, 'I'll be able to . . .' And then Mary lost the words. She was looking at her sister's broad back. As a girl, Mary had climbed on to that back. When Claire was in a good mood, she would look at her little sister and say, All right, pipsqueak, hop on. But it never lasted long, the ride. And Claire always dumped her with some force. If their mother saw, she would tell her off for it and Claire would say, It wasn't me, she jumped off. No, you threw her. I saw! And Mary would say, I don't mind, I don't mind. I like it. How she longed for her sister's approval, for her to become soft and yielding. You'd like anything, Claire would hiss at her, suddenly vicious, Mary's loyalty spurned. *Harden up.*

Poor dead Claire.

Poor dead William David Brunton, about whom there was a possible development.

Mary made a mental note to do something with Colin on Claire's next anniversary. They'd let the arrangement lapse. Lunch somewhere in town, just the two of them. Her treat. He always had a strong appetite, and they would argue about who was paying and who had paid last time. He was a bit pompous of course, used to being listened to, but he also knew he had to sing for his supper. He was indiscreet about his patients, seeing his aunt as so ancient she couldn't possibly do anything with what he spilled. He may as well have been speaking to his dead mother, which in a way he probably was.

Beside her in bed, Pete made a strangling sound, went quiet, and then resumed regular breathing.

Finally, Mary got out of bed and, using the light of her phone, made it down the stairs. More foolishness. Her bare feet clung greedily to the wooden steps. She was aware of her toes gripping. She found some old sandals by the back door and walked into the garden. It was a cool, still night after several days of rain and wind. The trees glistened as though coated in oil. She listened to the whistling tree frogs, louder than the sea. *Croak.* They were saying, *We are all going to croak.*

A while ago they'd taken a drive—which they said was just for fun—to check if the frogs could be heard in the village area. Because they would sorely miss their frogs if they left this place. They'd parked one evening just outside the village, winding down the windows and listening. Yes, the frogs were in the trees, with their hingey sound. They drove home happy, or if not happy then satisfied on that point. The frogs are coming with us!

It was a kind of game they'd hit on—What We Like About Where We Live and What We Would Miss. Continuing to enjoy the process, they could maintain a belief that it was all play and nothing was certain or decided.

When they got home, their frogs greeted them. Mary and Pete felt part of a broad community, keyed into a wider vibrating world. Noticing things was a way of being included, even or especially if those things didn't really need you. It was tremendously moving. Pete wept in the bathroom, turning on the radio to cover the sound, and Mary pretended not to hear him.

And what about the birds? Their house was on a flightpath. Tūī would zip up the steps, occasionally crash into the large window of the living room. So Mary and Pete made that reconnaissance trip also. One chilly afternoon, just for the exercise and the curiosity value and the game, they were walking in and around the village, and soon found themselves on the path that led through the wetlands to the estuary, crossed by little bridges. Some of the units looked directly on to this area, with picture windows and armchairs positioned for viewing. They could never see anyone sitting in these rooms. The interiors disappeared in shadows, or was it some special glass? Occasionally a small dog would wander forward and look at them.

Outside there was plenty of action. The usual array of black swans, ducks, pūkeko. Then a little shag raised itself on a rock in the water, extending its wings as if saying, Hold on, hold on there. They stopped and watched. The shag walked around a bit and then refolded its wings, as though putting away a piece of fantastical machinery. The bird looked so proud, Mary and Pete were both grinning.

The grass was spongy with all the recent rain. Wind channelled in from the sea, moving the tops of trees. Mary had the sudden desire to leave the world of the dinky bridges and the mallards and the picture windows and take a brisk walk to the sea's edge. The waves were brown and churning, matching her sudden disagreeability.

Pete stopped, tapped his chest. 'I have a pain.'

'Okay,' she said. It had happened before. 'Take it easy.'

She helped him to a nearby bench which had a plaque remembering that this was someone's favourite stop to watch the herons. The someone who'd died. No herons today. She took out her phone from her jacket pocket and held it up to him. Was it time to make a call?

Pete shook his head. 'Give me a minute,' he said.

His tachycardia was a tricky fellow. It plunged him into a bad mood. He was always so even-tempered.

'Sorry,' he said.

'Don't be silly.'

They sat for a while. A pūkeko high-stepped towards them, then veered off, flicking its tail feathers and showing them the white undercarriage.

Mary had driven them home from the village, and when she turned on the wipers instead of the indicator, Pete swore. He seldom swore. She didn't drive much anymore, finding her concentration wandering.

He would probably end up with a pacemaker, but he was trying to avoid that. Yes, Mary had said the first time he'd offered this, because if you get a pacemaker, you won't be able to take up arc welding or be a dentist and use descaling devices. She'd done her research, whereas he was less interested—this was also out of character.

In the car they proceeded in silence. He needed to concentrate on his heart, or forget it—she wasn't sure which.

She thought of the time she'd asked him where he'd like to go for his retirement. They were planning the overseas trip. Pete said, 'I would like to stand beside the lions outside the New York Public Library. Patience and Fortitude.' And that was what they did. 'It's us,' Pete had laughed, pointing at them. It had been so hot and humid in the city. She'd not enjoyed it much and felt doubly frustrated she'd been unable to hide it from Pete, whose birthday trip she was trying hard not to ruin. The day before, they'd had a little row which ended in her lying under a tree in Central Park for two hours while he went to MoMA. They'd made up; they always did. Making up always gave Pete a terrific lift, as if he'd been dreading some finality. In front of the lions, she said, 'I know which one I'm definitely not.' Then added, 'Am I either of them?' Pete had kissed her on the side of the head as an answer. He was immensely happy. He led her inside the library as if into a church, whispering and treading with sudden softness. She copied his movements. She had the strange feeling that in some sense he was walking inside her. He was still in a position of reverence for her, or rather for them.

Standing in the cold in her sandals and bare feet in the middle of the night, Mary remembered the final part of that trip to see the birds.

Walking slowly up their path, Pete in front, she had seen a rat looking at them from behind a nearby bush.

She'd had a sudden thought—more than a thought. The strong feeling of him being there with them. Will. In the rat? *How?* A rat was repellent, a predator. An enemy. Except Will had had a rat for a time. It had travelled on his shoulder, run up his arm, lodged in his pocket. Mary could hardly stand it. She'd felt it was a test. Can you cope? Thankfully, it wasn't around for long. It ran off one day and Will was on to something else. He tended not to dwell.

Pete was concentrating bitterly on the steps, fiercely alone. Surely he'd seen the rat and averted his look. Why? Because he was in discomfort and wanted to lie down.

Spirits.

The word meant little to her.

Who knew what a spirit required? Certainly not a long-retired cop. Anyway, the rat sped off. Gone.

This was not the house Will had grown up in. How could he be here? They'd moved when Pete had about five years left at the library, on the downward slope, he said. Mary was then contracting. She wrote risk-assessment reports for a security company which specialised in shopping malls. They'd seen the house in the paper and hadn't been to the first open home. Then, on a whim, they drove up the following weekend. Immediately it seemed possible. They liked the funny little porthole window in the upstairs bathroom, the circular stairs—the way to a cabin—and of course the sea. Waking up to that! They liked the trees and the birds.

Had Will been here all along?

Once nephew Colin had made an odd confession. They were having one of their lunches. They'd each had two glasses of bubbles. He said that for a laugh he'd joined a group of sceptics looking for ghosts. Getting spooked in old buildings. Bullshit photos of ectoplasm. But why did you join? she asked him. Just a giggle, he said. It seems like a lot of trouble for a laugh, she told him. Actually, he then said, in a funny way—not funny ha ha—I sometimes think I'm looking for Mum. He'd stared at her with defiance. He knew a boring GP shouldn't voice such an opinion. It was out of character for him especially. And, he said, I wouldn't be shocked to come across her. Somehow, you know.

Solid, sensible Colin with his GP manner of explaining things away, looking for his mama's ghost!

Listening, Mary realised this didn't seem fanciful or pitiable. Yes, she told him, it would be nice to see Claire again. They'd clinked glasses at that. Had gone on with some other topic. Hugged briefly in the usual way on parting. Hello to Uncle Pete. Never spoke about it again.

Mary knew the rat was not their son's spirit, just as it was important to remember their son had not come back as a bird-spirit and that the pīwakawaka who fed near their bottom fence, among the grass clippings and the mulch pile, were simply themselves. They followed you, looking curious and friendly, because of the insects you disturbed. How often she'd longed to find him in their darting shapes! But that was not him either.

Will had been a careful and precise boy, moving with caution, even grace. If he turned his head, it was in consideration and never with suddenness. He looked at the world with the sort of slowed attention a scientist might have. It could be infuriating, for sure, if you wanted him to do things, if you were in a hurry. He was never in a hurry. Their mini zoologist! On the sidelines of his primary school sports games—soccer or hockey—Will often lay on the grass and opened the little door of the box he'd made for his latest creature, a wētā, a mouse, a rat! To the coach's irritation, other children would leave the game and lie down beside him. When Colin came around, the older cousin would spend hours patiently helping Will construct the various dwellings he needed for his animals. Colin's freneticism, his manic quality, would dissipate. It was a sort of miracle. Will was like some kind of medication the other boy would absorb.

Mary had followed Pete inside the house and gone into the bathroom and suddenly couldn't stop shaking. It was strange thinking how they'd become a couple who used the bathroom in this way. They retreated and composed themselves, re-emerging to fill the jug, make tea. Her body was vibrating with sorrow and self-pity. Will was with her every day, of course—as a feeling, as a memory; he used to do this, he liked doing that. Remember when.

The rat had nothing to do with memory. It was out there in its body, alive. What was the connection? That Will had once had a rat? It went deeper, but Mary was faltering. She'd opened the door of the bathroom and gone upstairs to check on Pete.

Tonight she wondered if this was the Will who Dave Monk was also bringing back. Someone somehow alive. Her thoughts didn't make sense to her, but they were her thoughts.

A person couldn't sleep with all of this going on.

When she went back inside, she found Pete in front of the wood burner. He gave her a fright, standing in the dark. Like a ghost of himself. Turning to her, he said, 'You too.'

A reply caught in her throat. She'd been annoyed with him that afternoon. He'd questioned her about the stuff she'd sorted, all those old clothes. He didn't seem to understand the tasks they had. They'd agreed to sell the house and now he was slightly disconnected. It was as if, with the big decision made, he found the small things beyond him. And she'd had to take it all on herself.

She moved to him and put her arms around him. He still carried the warmth of their bed, a slight sour smell. She stepped away again. Now was the time to tell him about Dave Monk's call. But he was saying something about the wood burner.

Yes, yes, she agreed, immensely tired now and hardly listening to him and instead making up her own version of his words . . .

Whoever lit the fire now, whoever came to own this house after them, would see and feel how the air sucked the flames into quick life. Blessed be the sweeps.

Three

He borrowed Mary's pillow and propped himself up further, looking out to sea.

Today cloud covered Kāpiti. The island was still marvellous and it was almost as if looking at it was wrong or he was doing it wrong. With insufficient dignity. You shouldn't lie in bed and stare, especially not now, when they were abandoning it. He was supposed to have given up anyway—stopped looking. Gone cold turkey.

Mary was already in the shower and it had been a wakeful, rumpled night. Things were askew. Did either of them sleep anymore, really? You entered the dark and took your chances, and precious little was concerned with rest. Instead, how about hurled around by lines of thought which seemed promising before collapsing? How about visited by the dead who wanted to go shopping or eat at restaurants no longer in business? *What do you mean it's closed?* His mother was frequently there, talking about herself in a way he couldn't follow. How about pricked by alarming sensations in your bladder, your bowel, and made active by sudden desires—to answer a ringing phone, to turn off the oven, to register for a free gift, to look for the animal in pain whose cries came from downstairs. It was tiring being asleep, and they were usually glad when morning came. Mary would yank on the long cords of the bedroom blinds like someone hoisting a sail and finally catching a breeze. Yaa, she would sigh each time.

The blinds, running from floor to ceiling, were a weight. Yaa. Good exercise.

Pete continued to look out. On the horizon a pair of tiny blocks appeared stationary. Sadness summoned, was it? Ships at sea, going about their mysterious voyages. Less romantically, they were probably chugging off to China with a bunch of unprocessed logs. It struck him that he enjoyed the way Mary didn't do sadness. She did irritation, certainly. He could irritate her, he knew. It felt amazing that this had gone nowhere. Or rather that it had gone here—they were old together! But not like old shoes or whatever people said about old married couples. He valued their awkwardness still. Not conflict but—friction? Not nastiness. But—privacy? And withholding. Not everything shared, open. This, he felt, was a sort of freedom. You let the other person be themself. He'd never been complacent, he hoped. Was it all to justify some failing on his part? No, they seemed well matched. Now they were on the edge of a new phase. Thoughts crashed into each other. It was all to do with the house sale.

He feared her loneliness. Would being with him make her lonely? If he got sick, would she feel stuck? They saw so few people these days. He hoped his heart issues wouldn't ruin her life. He'd begun to catch her giving him looks, assessing him for his—resilience? The same kind of squint she'd have when she was checking a food item for its use-by date.

Why had she been standing outside last night?

He hated when they weren't in sync.

She took on more and more, not bothering to wait for him.

Even though they'd agreed she wouldn't attack the old clothes without his help, she'd gone ahead and done it. It was unusual. He was certain he'd lost things he meant to keep.

And she'd been dismissive, abrupt. What was he moaning about, she said. That was one less job they had now. She'd done it. Her tone was a bit wrong for Mary. She seemed angry about being asked a fair question, as though she saw its fairness and rejected it because she had other things to consider. What other things? If he remembered correctly, Mary had had the same hastiness and unreasonableness when they'd had to clear out her parents' house. Swift disposal was her modus operandi there too. Sentimentality was not in sight. She kept very few items: a green ceramic vase, a lemon squeezer (theirs was broken), some books (only because he insisted).

When Pete came down for breakfast after his shower, Mary was looking at the paper. 'What's been happening in the world?' he said. He asked every morning. He was interested. He liked to keep up. This morning the question felt flat.

She liked to get to the paper first and there were pills she had to take at least half an hour before eating which meant she was always out of bed before him. She followed two topics in the paper: gardening and crime. She barely knew anything about world politics and history unless it was assassinations. Local issues lodged only if a city councillor was up on charges in court or was accused of misconduct. He'd been shocked when they got together that she voted National. Why, he asked her, wouldn't she vote Labour? Because she'd always just gone with National. They supported the police, she said. Her parents voted National. Your parents? He'd laughed at that, but she was serious. They were cut from a different cloth. He'd wanted to leave his parents at the first opportunity he got, not that they were awful or anything. You just had to make that separating act. Yes, yes, Mary agreed. She and

Claire had schemed and schemed to escape—but always with a sense that they'd return. Mary, right up to the time they died, remained her parents' little girl. The pencil marks for her height could still be read in the family home when it was sold.

She didn't look up from the paper. 'A huge fire in the National Museum of Brazil,' she said. 'Over 90 per cent of the archives lost.'

Pete paused and sighed. Archives were a special interest of his. She knew he'd be keen to follow the story. It felt like an olive branch. 'Oh gosh,' he said. 'A fire?'

'Yes, you'd think sprinklers. They've lost vast treasures.'

'Hmm.' He was trying to work up some enthusiasm, but oddly he felt very little beyond mild annoyance. The archives of Brazil? Why didn't they take better precautions? It seemed very stupid. He put a piece of bread in the toaster. 'I'm walking Gus this morning.'

'Yes,' said Mary, not looking up from the paper. 'We have the appointment this afternoon.'

The appointment—that was lodged too, like a splinter. 'I remember.'

'It's not all that warm out. Wear your jacket.'

'It's that wind again.'

'Did you hear me—about the fire in the archives in Spain?'

'Brazil,' he said.

'Brazil.'

'Terrible,' he said. She was handing him the piece of paper to read about it. She smelled of soap and her face was still flushed from the shower. She seemed vaguely annoyed still. Her hair sat very flat, not yet properly dry.

'How did you sleep in the end?' he said.

'It was dreadful.'

'Your hair's still wet.'

'Is it?' She touched it with her fingers. 'I thought I . . . Oh, yes, the plug thing kept popping out.'

'The cut-off switch?'

'Yes, so I stopped. Didn't want to cause a fire or something.'

'Okay, I'll have a look at it.'

'You? With your vast experience in wiring?'

'It should just re-set and start again.'

'I'm saying that's what I tried, Peter.'

Peter. His toast had started to smoke and he hit the cancel button. 'It's not our morning for electrics, is it.'

'Mourning Becomes Electra,' said Mary.

'Ha!' said Pete.

'What does that mean anyway? Do you know?'

'It's a play.'

'Yes, we all know that but what does it mean? Don't worry, I'll look it up.'

The conversation made his head spin. 'Are you all right?' he said.

'Me? I'm all right. Are you?'

'I'm okay. Do you want to come to the beach with me and Gus?'

'No, no. I never come. That's for you. You go. Not my part of ship.'

After breakfast, Pete went across the road to collect Gus for his walk. It was good to get out of the house. Mary had another list of jobs to get through. He'd help when he came back.

Gus, an ancient black lab, belonged to Jan, who had a spinal condition and was now limited in her mobility. 'I'm sort of matching my dog,' she'd told Pete. 'Both of us limping into the sunset.'

'Describes us all,' said Pete.

He enjoyed the trundle of their beach walks, the dog's doleful body, the kindness Gus showed to whatever creature, animal or human, came into his slow orbit. Yep, he seemed to say, have a smell, have a stroke, this is me, I am here. For now. Hello. Greetings. And Pete liked Jan, even liking that their front-door conversations were mostly limited to the subject of the dog. It put them on the same wavelength as Gus. *Hello. I am here. Greetings, fellow sufferer.* Slowly Jan's scoliosis was taking over.

Today she called out to Pete from further inside the house. Her carer was there and she told him to just take Gus, he was ready. Pete could tie him up by his kennel and give him some water when they got back. She was so grateful to Pete for doing it.

The dog raised his head slowly and lifted his tail twice. Walks were not ecstatic moments for old Gus these days. He had miles on the clock, one careful and damaged lady owner.

Never having owned a dog, Pete was unsure about the etiquette. Did others talk as much to their dogs as he did with Gus? Did it worry the animal to have to listen to this strange old human? Was Gus always on alert for the sounds which really were important to him as a dog and which he might have to act on? And was all the other stuff kind of a drag? Anyway, they mooched along in the direction of the beach and Pete was updating Gus on events.

They had to stop and wait for a neighbour's car to back out of the driveway. It was Trent, the youngish man who'd inherited the house when both his parents died within a year of each other. Terrible. The house sat in an alarming hollow with a stream running behind it. Periodically the back yard would flood and the council would turn up to pump the water out.

Trent lived alone and kept to himself, avoiding eye contact. Once, he'd come over to ask if they'd seen his cat. They were unaware he had a cat. He spoke to them from about five yards away. Nah, he wouldn't come inside. The grass of his driveway grew up to the top of the tyres of his parents' old car, which maybe he was keeping as some sort of memorial. The whole place seemed like it was sinking, and him with it.

Gus knew all this.

Occasionally Trent did exercises in his back yard, moving his arms in small circles, twisting from side to side. Was it a kind of tai chi? He wore the same heavy black clothes no matter the temperature. Nothing was ever hung on his clothesline.

Trent appeared never to generate noise that wasn't contained in his headphones, which he wore everywhere. Very quiet, though always with the sense that there was some huge sound barrelling into his brain. At dusk, before he pulled the curtains, they could see him sitting at his computer.

Pete had the idea that one day they might be drawn into some saving act, some intervention. Trent hovered in their consciousness. He seemed to have no one else. No one visited him, as far as they knew. Had he inherited enough money to let him sit all day at the computer, unless this was also his job?

Had grief overtaken his life?

Of course, it was most likely that in Trent's mind Pete and Mary were interchangeable with any other old people. They could move out and probably he wouldn't even notice. They'd never much tried over the years to establish a connection, only hearing about his parents from another neighbour further down the street with whom Mary sometimes shared gardening tips. She told Pete once that she felt they'd let this strange young man down and that he was suffering. Could she deliver a meal? But he wasn't starving. Drop off some lemons from their tree? But how many lemons did a single man of thirty need? Pete thought Mary was putting them in the centre of a situation to which they were utterly peripheral. He also wished this neighbour would mow his lawns more often. And take off those headphones. Go for a run on the beach. His sporadic exercise regime looked half-hearted. Pete was flooded with strange reactions whenever Trent crossed his vision. Were these the kind of things a certain type of father might think? He felt a wave of tenderness for the young man who could live whatever kind of life he wanted to live without some old codgers wishing otherwise.

Trent in his reversing car was looking the other way over his shoulder and failed again to take in man and dog, waiting. They watched him drive off.

Gus's nostrils twitched.

'Car need an oil change?' said Pete. 'I agree, old man. I agree.'

The sea was greenish and choppy. Matted weeds swirled on the frothy tide. A wide strip of driftwood, shells, plastics, pumice, bones, sticks hemmed the beach from a week of southerlies. The stormwater outlets had carved new channels. Pete let Gus off his lead, not that it made any difference. The dog still walked by his side, nosing in the sand occasionally, checking ahead for anything of interest. Far off a woman was coming their way, tossing a ball to two small dogs. They barked and ran. Gus regarded them hardly at all. Seeing this frenetic activity, he was looking so far into his own past it must have made almost no sense to him. Are those . . . dogs?

Pete put the remains of a transistor radio in the rubbish bag he always brought on these walks. He also picked up bottle caps, two cans and a section of nylon rope. Gus watched, approving—or perhaps that considering look was just him working his bowel into a position of release. *Soon, old chap.* They always went to the same dune, the same overhang, to complete the business. Pete would step off and allow him his privacy, then move in for collection. Gus's turds were remarkably consistent, dropping as neat little logs and never those less manageable shapes Pete had seen, the ones which looked as though they'd been squeezed from an icing funnel, tapering to a creamy moist twirl. You'd need a shovel. Gus's stuff was almost odourless too. He was just so decent and accommodating.

'You know we're moving,' Pete said to Gus. 'Picking up sticks, shipping out. It's time eh.'

Poor Gus glanced to check if Pete had said something relevant. Stick? Nope.

'We're going to see the manager of the rest home today. Head honcho of the village. Her name's Maureen.' He started singing, 'Maureen, Maureen, oh where have you been? Maureen, Maureen, what have you seen? Oh Maureen, why are you so mean, Maureen? Yeah, it needs work. Sure. That's the blues, Gus. You and me, on the beach, with the Kāpiti blues again.'

The two little chasing yapping dogs were getting closer. They'd left their owner and her ball behind, having spotted Gus.

'Prepare yourself, old chap. Incoming.'

Gus, long-suffering, moved his head from Pete to the dogs once more.

When the two visitors arrived, they walked around an utterly still Gus respectfully, quietly. Was this—a statue of a dog? The sniffing was modest, disappointed. The little dogs looked back to their owner, who was now jogging towards them. Pete didn't recognise them from previous walks. He and Gus knew a lot of the regulars. People knew Gus's name but not Pete's, and that seemed fair.

'Hello!' the owner was calling out. 'I hope they're not being a nuisance.'

'Not at all,' said Pete, raising a hand in greeting.

The woman was wearing a puffer jacket and a beanie. Her long grey hair stuck out the sides of it. A bone carving hung around her neck. Her cheeks were red. 'What a grand fellow,' she said, pointing at Gus.

Pete did the introductions and then heard the names of the two little dogs, which he instantly forgot. They had wandered off to look at a clump of washed-up spinifex. This might have been the cue for the woman to move on, but she was looking at Pete closely.

'Sorry,' she said, 'but do I know you?'

He stared at her and tried to think. No. He shook his head.

She said, 'I know we've met.'

'Perhaps,' said Pete. Maybe from library days? It happened. You stood in more less the same place for decades and people recognised you. She was in her late fifties, he guessed, though with the beanie it was hard to tell.

'Where did you work?'

'Years ago I was at the central library.'

The woman shook her head, then she clapped her hands and pointed at him. 'I looked after your mother!'

'Oh, yes.' He failed to recognise her.

'At Ruth Godfrey, right?'

'Right. Mum was there.'

'I knew it. I'm Pauline.'

'Yes, of course, I'm Pete.'

'Hello again!' She was smiling, and her dogs had come back to her when she clapped. They stood beside her. Gus stared off to sea. 'You don't remember me, do you?'

'I'm sorry.'

'Don't be sorry. There's no reason why you would.'

'It was such a strange time.'

'I remember your mother. Very well. Margaret?'

'Yes.' That was impressive.

'I want to call her a sweet old lady.'

'But she wasn't,' said Pete.

'Not much. Not then. Sorry.'

They both laughed.

'No, I agree. It was difficult.'

'But she made an impression. She was quite something.'

'Were you one of the ones she hit with her stick?'

'I was far too quick for that. No, your mother was a star.'

He felt a flash of pride. 'Are you still involved in that sort of thing?'

'Oh no, left all that a long time ago.'

'What do you do now?'

'Real estate.'

'Quite a jump.'

'Yes and no,' she said. 'Still looking after people, I suppose. Big life changes. Helping them in their next goals.'

Goals? He couldn't think what his mother's goals had been in the dementia ward. Sometimes she wanted to kill another resident.

The two little dogs had seen another dog coming along

the beach and took off in that direction. 'We were all sorry when Margaret passed. We missed her.'

'Thank you.'

'It was a family at the home. We were a whānau, tried to be. I suppose the families hear that and say, yeah yeah. But it was a whānau. And it was always an important moment when we lost a member. Often we didn't get a chance to mark it. Clean the room please, that was all. The new person was coming. Turnover. Snip snap. Shampoo the carpet. The waiting list was there. It's much worse now of course. Much worse. They rot in hospital. Anyway, your mother, yes. Quite a lady.'

'That's very nice to hear.' He was trying to remember this Pauline, put her in one scene where she helped his mother, was kind to her, made a difference. There were plenty like that, but he couldn't remember Pauline. Most of the staff were from the Philippines or India. He thought of Juanita, who put aside afternoon-tea treats for his mother if she missed them on the first round, who combed her hair if she saw she was going on an outing and Pete hadn't noticed. *We can't have you going out like that, Margaret! What would people think?* When Juanita bent over to help her, the little cross she wore on a silver chain would fall forward and Margaret, like a child, would instinctively reach up and hold it.

'So I'm pleased to have run into you,' said Pauline. 'And to think of Margaret.'

'Yes.'

She looked up at the sky. 'Better get moving, eh. Those clouds. Nice to see you again.'

'Nice to see you again, Pauline.'

The awful time. He'd not thought about it properly in ages.

He and Gus turned for home via the spot where the dog could find relief.

In the first weeks at the hospital, where his mother was stranded, there'd been a torrent directed at his father, who tried at first to defend himself and then had simply listened, nodding and looking to leave as soon as he could.

'When we all lived in Germany,' his mother would say, 'if that priest—I forget his name—had not hidden us, we wouldn't have survived. The Jews were after us, you see.'

His mother had been a South Island schoolgirl in the war.

'Well,' his father said to her, 'we were never in Germany.'

'Never in Germany! Then how do you explain the fact that we speak German?'

'I can't speak German.'

'Because you had to pretend not to in order to evade the Jews!'

'I see.' He'd make a great show of looking at his watch. 'What's the time?'

She would turn to Pete. 'It's incredible what your father has forgotten, but I can't blame him. It was a brutal time.'

Looking out to sea while Gus manoeuvred himself into a crouch, Pete thought he himself could cope with memory loss, the gentle fumbling, the mild confusion—his own or Mary's. They had it now. Making cups of tea twice and finding the first one in the microwave. Forgetting passwords on the computer. Mary's driving. The fog would reach towards them, but they'd be together, comical, sweet. He longed not to have to listen to Mary tell him all the terrible mixed-up things. Would the material come from her time as a cop? There was a lid on all that. He feared her mind in some way. It was changing a bit. Most likely it was the stress of everything.

The thought wouldn't release him.

Maybe if things were going to end there, with one of them loopy and the other marooned in sense, the conversation could be channelled into simple things: the plum trees they'd planted, their search for a survivable spot for the lemon tree. Please god, he thought, no popes and Jews and twin uncles fucking on the farm just to stay warm in winter. 'So cold,' his mother said, 'the stuff from their—not to be indelicate—penises emerged and froze in mid-spurt.'

In the early weeks of her delirium, before the drugs found the spot, disinhibited, his very correct mother created an astonishing, free-flowing and delighting account of sexual deviancy among their as-far-as-he-knew respectable family of railway workers, domestics, sharemilkers, then teachers, stock agents and hoteliers. Irish mainly. When she'd been well, she had worked on that history, created a file on her computer. She had it all now at her fingertips, and she shredded it for salacious fictions. Uncles approached her with 'massive phalluses'. Rape was utterly normal in the family home. For several weeks most of her stories carried this edge, leaving her listeners worried they were about to receive news of past events they themselves were nastily caught up in as innocent children or babies. His mother's mind went obsessively to such figures and she frequently believed she was pregnant or whoever was visiting was pregnant and didn't know it. 'Look at you,' she once told Mary, then in her fifties. 'How many weeks? Boy or girl?' She accused Pete of keeping it from her. 'Do you think I'm easily fooled? Did you think you could hide it?'

She'd bring up Will frequently, never quite forgetting that

he was dead, though sometimes she placed him in an in-between space, asking Pete if he felt Will was with them. 'I feel he's here,' she would say, looking meaningfully around the room as if the boy was playing hide-and-seek and would pop out at any minute. This upset Pete at first. And then he thought, Well, she's keeping Will alive in a way. Failing to finally consign him to oblivion—this was okay really. 'Yes,' Pete would answer her, 'I feel he's here.'

'Do you?' she would say. 'That's interesting.' Things were always interesting. She liked to nod in an assessing way, as though she knew more than she was letting on.

It occurred to him that her mental collapse might be associated with her grandson's death. The back-to-frontness of it—a boy she loved gone before she was gone. Delirium could be connected with stress and emotional upset.

She begged the nurses to take her own baby from her womb, a child who she assured them would be born with 'a long Jewish beard'. They were not to be frightened by this, she told them. Pete, she said, had been born with just such a beard. Will too.

No one had any idea where the anti-Semitism came from. And for a period the identities would switch and his mother, and all her family, *became* Jewish and victims of persecution so vicious they had to change their names and even the shapes of their faces. Fake Irish, they became. This wasn't too hard to do because they'd all received medical training of the highest order in Munich—though, she explained, 'That wasn't what we called it. We called it München.' And here she would indeed sound German. 'München,' she would repeat. Cracking up, she added, 'München my sandwich by the seaside!'

She could laugh so much she'd cry and start coughing.

'Calm down,' he told her. 'Calm down, Mummy.'

Disappointingly for Pete, after an initial period of engagement, the doctors showed less and less interest in these details. Maybe they'd seen and heard it all before. Jews, babies, sex, morbidity—it would get tired quickly. It was their best guess that the sudden delirium would never resolve—unusual but not that unusual—and it was most likely now indistinguishable from dementia, and they'd proceed with a low dosage of the anti-psychotic and observe. The meetings were quickly depressing. None of his mother's creative powers—because her stories were imaginative—made an entrance, and Pete shared less and less of what he saw in her behaviour. What was the point? Soon he only told the staff about things they could see and fix—the rash on her legs, the bloodshot eye, the hearing-aid sagas, the various thefts of her possessions, some of which were true.

Stuck on a loop for weeks, his mother repeated a story or a memory to Pete of when she'd been a young girl and her father had come to her in the night and carried her to their bed. It was a horrible story to start hearing. Each time he thought she was about to reveal something awful. She told it with the curious and off-putting smile she'd now developed as a raconteur. Having never been much of a talker, she was now unstoppably a performer. Free of her husband's social dominance, she blossomed. It was remarkable. She was not doddery and unsure at all. She commanded the space. Pauline the former nurse had been right about this—his mother was memorable. When she finally made it into proper care, she stood out. *We haven't had anyone quite like your mother. To be honest, we're not really sure about the diagnosis.* Most of the other residents slumbered through their days or had episodes when they were suddenly loud, upset, and then fell back into their stunned poses, their quiet and puzzled requests. *Have you seen my purse? Can you lend me some money?* His mother asserted her superiority over them. They were all mad as snakes, she said. She skilfully imitated voices and moved readily into a simpering child's voice when needed. 'Daddy would lift me up and say, "Oh sweetie, won't you sleep better with us?" And I would say, "Yes, Daddy, I will" but I'd been fast asleep and quite happy in my own bed. Anyway, I thought it was very strange how he put me between Mummy and him. I always wondered about it.'

She would pause here and stare at Pete, checking he was paying attention. She hated if you weren't with her, hanging on her every word. If she was entranced, the least you could do was follow her there. He also noticed that when she told this story her accent grew more and more Irish. She had never done an accent in all her life, but here she was, whispering and confiding to him as if they were in a radio drama.

'Why do that?' she said, eyeing him. 'Were they worried about me? Why were they worried? But now I realise what it was. I do. They needed me to help them. If I was there, sleeping between them, they would be all right!'

'Okay,' he said.

'Do you see that?'

'I do,' he said, sounding a bit Irish himself. 'I do, Mummy.'

She sat back in her armchair, very pleased with herself. 'They needed me. Well. It was a marvellous day when I worked that one out.' Tears formed in her eyes and she really appeared to be back there with her ancient parents as a very young girl, loved and warm between them in some mythical or real bed.

This was exactly what he and Mary had done with Will at a certain point when the child was having nightmares.

Pete had told his mother about it years before. He recalled this because she'd asked if this was the best thing to do. Was her story now just a demented version of his? He cringed away from her vandalism, half convinced she meant to be malicious. Sure, a lot of parents, including her own, would have done similar things with their children. He tried to be understanding.

But then any story he brought in, she converted at once to her own ends. If he said they'd been to a concert, she said she had been a violinist who'd performed around the world, having one day found a broken violin in the street. 'Daddy fixed it for me!' she said. 'But he knew so little about violins he didn't know I needed a bow and so for the first year I plucked it with my fingers. Which turned out to be great training. Even now my fingers are extremely dexterous.' Here she twirled her fingers in his face.

She had a child's appetite for sweet things—ice cream, liquorice, cake. When she wet the bed, she explained to him that a woman had come in the middle of the night and poured a pot of water over her head. Someone else with a pair of scissors 'concealed on her person' was trying to cut off Margaret's ear.

Frequently he was bored listening. The fantasy seemed so wasteful of her and his time. After a while, he didn't bother much repeating to Mary or to anyone what his mother had come up with. A feeling of trespass was sneaking in. Equally, however, the self-consolation of her stories could stretch out and grab him. She had to work so hard to make sense of her new world. The sheer labour of it. He would often find himself having to pull the car over on the way home and sob. What did it cost him to sit with this person who he was responsible for?

*

He scooped up Gus's latest and knotted the bag while the dog took a few steps away from the whole business, wearily admitting he was the author and reminding Pete this was the deal for Gus listening to him and making social interaction with others possible.

They began to trek homewards. The cool wind had come up again.

He spoke to the dog: 'Nurse Pauline in real estate! Should I have mentioned the sale? But she would probably know the house and Gary, their agent. Should I have asked her opinion about the village? What do you think?'

A great feeling of betrayal came over Pete. The idea of his mother had, for years, been just a generalised feeling of unhappiness, a blurred sort of pain, and the vague consciousness of a danger pushed back.

He remembered a certain pressure from that time. His mother's madness belonged to him in a way. Not that he was mad or felt himself going mad. But he definitely shared in it. Her madness was not simply a terrible event to befall her and his father and him; it was their setting suddenly. It was their air. They all breathed it. He tasted it now, despite the sea and Gus's shit.

Being unwell, she couldn't be his mother.

It was so obvious. It hurt terribly. It didn't matter that he was a middle-aged person. His news meant nothing to her.

Sometimes she said, 'Hold my hand. Quickly now. Oh, Peter. Hold it properly. I can hardly feel it.' She would squeeze her eyes shut. 'Are you holding it?'

She knew it was him sitting there in front of her, and that they were mother and son. She never forgot who he was but she had lost all consideration of him.

People said it wasn't really her and that he shouldn't take any of it personally.

But it was her. These were her hands, her legs. She looked at him with her eyes. The way her front teeth slightly crossed—this was her mouth. Her skin.

She forgot his birthday, and when Mary on one of her visits reminded her, his mother said she thought he'd stopped having birthdays.

He could forgive her all of this. It wasn't her fault. People were right of course.

But it was her.

Believing it wasn't her allowed him to discount the person who carried her name and history. Even if he felt his neglect sharply, she would forget it, he thought. Nothing mattered. Sometimes he invented a reason he couldn't visit her. His father didn't even bother to invent, simply telling Pete that he was doing a great job and that he was sure Pete would let him know if anything happened. *How is she? That's good to hear.* It took his father a long time to come around to visiting her. He was in his late eighties, alone for the first time in decades. Now what was he supposed to do? Start all over? Remarkably, this is what he did. The two of them together—his strange parents—it had all seemed fixed and eternal. Suddenly it wasn't. His father's form of ruthlessness was still in place. This development was shattering to him— Pete saw it. And it was also a chance to set out again on a new course. He was okay. A woman came three times a week, and Pete once visited the house and found his father lying on the sofa with his feet in the woman's lap, getting his toenails cut. It was clear his father wanted Pete gone. To be discovered like this was too much. Father and son were frozen. Yet the woman, unaware, continued to work away, really grinding at his father's horny nails. It was like watching a smithy with an ancient horse.

Mary's parents had died comparatively young, her mother of a stroke and her father of a heart attack, both in their late seventies. Pete's and Mary's age now of course. It had been a powerful shock. Both gone just like that. He guessed it was why she watched him so closely now.

The suddenness was terrorising, he'd seen that. But it was better than any lingering—Mary said it herself. She meant for Margaret mainly. He also thought that sometimes she was tired of his mother, impatient with his own duties there, wishing it would end.

With his poor mother, Pete knew he himself had been disloyal even as he recognised he'd had to survive. He despised his own behaviour. She died after two years in the place, and Mary had encouraged him to see someone, though he never had. She'd not pressed all that hard. When her sister had died, had she seen anyone? When Will had died? No, you got on with things. Other people were always going through worse.

And it had got better for his mother, comparatively. She was much more affectionate than she'd ever been. She craved touch. He combed her hair. 'You can press harder,' she told him. He rubbed cream into her puffy feet. 'Don't worry that you're going to hurt me,' she said. 'Really work your fingers into the flesh.' They embraced deeply when they met. She always thanked him for coming. 'I've been expecting you! Great to see you.' Her complaints and her conspiracies ran alongside a sort of contentment, it felt to him. Occasionally she would say she was looking forward to a holiday. This seemed wistful rather than despairing. She would make jokes about his father and his new bachelor's life. 'I've heard he has a new woman. He'll be enjoying all that.'

Getting up the access path from the beach was hard on Gus, and no picnic for Pete either. His left hip pinged on any steep slope. He felt it worse coming down but even going up was undelightful. At the summit they paused, and both looked back at the beach as if surveying a great ascent. Also he needed to pee urgently. 'Stay,' he told Gus. The dog took this in—it was the first meaningful thing he'd heard. Pete ducked off the path, past the Do Not Walk on the Dunes sign, and into a little hollow guarded by a few lupin bushes. The dune crew would forgive him for this, surely. Adjusting for the wind direction, he peed a clear thin stream into the sand. As a kid, he'd carved his name. Today there wasn't enough for the E.

When they were back on the street, Pete started telling Gus about Gary from Coast Estate. On their first meeting, Pete had found himself receiving a ghost ball delivered by Gary. This was their listing producing what Gary called 'a result'. Pete's job was to catch it, and he obliged the first two times whereas Mary kept her arms at her sides. Gary said he appreciated her tough attitude. He would be working very hard to please her, he said. He liked being kept on his toes by his clients. When he completed the bowling action, his white shirt would come out of his black trousers and he'd have to tuck himself in in a way—Mary told Pete later—she found almost indecent.

'Back at the office,' she said to Pete, 'he probably calls me "that tough old bird".'

'Or worse,' said Pete.

'Or worse,' said Mary.

Gary liked it when he learned that Mary had been in the

force. He had a brother-in-law in Aussie who was a detective in the Northern Territories. Gary raised his eyebrows in some odd signal when he provided this detail. Pete quickly moved him off that topic. They didn't need to hear racist remarks from the man who was selling their beloved house. 'I say "home",' Gary had corrected them the first time. 'A house is just framing and a roof to keep the rain out. You guys are offering a home.'

'Please don't tell us we're selling a dream, Gary,' said Mary.

'Ha!' said Gary. 'Love it. Love it. We'll stick with home.'

Gus heard it all and seemed incredibly uninterested. He padded into his garage and waited by his bowl while Pete got the biscuits and some water. Then Pete listened to the dog eating and drinking, enjoying the slurping, the appetite— and willing him to keep on eating and drinking until the bowl was empty. It was his turn to listen to his companion. He wished Gus a long life, a longer life. Jan's prediction for the dog wasn't great. Here he was though, really tucking in. He couldn't leave Pete now. He couldn't. Pete would make trips back to walk Gus. He'd promised the dog this. He did so again, speaking aloud. 'Don't worry, mate, I'll be back.' The dog failed to hear, or it didn't matter to him in this moment of replenishment. Water from the bowl went everywhere. He was tremendously thirsty. Yes, thought Pete, that's the spirit! Then he had to turn away. He felt ashamed suddenly to be watching this. It reminded him of something: being in the dementia ward at lunchtime, seeing the residents with their meals. His mother looking into her plate. *What on earth is that?* But it was always wrong to watch someone else eat if you weren't eating. Watching an animal was no different. He left Gus to it.

Four

They sat in the manager's small office, looking at the brochures and information sheets. Maureen was in her sixties, white, with a mild South African accent. She wore a blue blazer and black trousers with blue trainers. She looked like a netball coach on game day. She'd been at the village for five years, having taken over from the previous and founding manager who'd had the position for fifteen years. There was a lot of continuity, she told them. Instantly the word made Mary think in the opposite direction, of turnover, of mortal coil. While management stayed, the residents exited. It was an impeccable business plan, if only folk wouldn't keep on living. Still, Mary appreciated that a stable head office probably meant good things for the residents, and Maureen seemed efficient and there was no hard sell. Her grey hair sprang from her head in a way which suggested she didn't especially care for the level of grooming usually expected. Mary didn't expect it either, so she wasn't bothered.

Maureen gave them a mini tour, showing them the empty dining area, the two large lounges where a few residents sat in chairs, some reading, others with their eyes closed, then on to the separate small library (empty) where Pete, as was his habit whenever he entered a room with bookshelves, stepped closer to the shelves to eye the books. Next was a games room where a group of four women were playing bridge and another woman worked at a large jigsaw puzzle of a steam engine pulling into a station. So much steam! They passed the various service rooms (hairdresser, pharmacy, mini market) and said hello to everyone they came across; Maureen knew everyone's name.

The 'it'll do' quality spread throughout the place. On Maureen's office wall hung a big, dispiriting painting in a gold frame of a beach at sunrise (not sunset). Perhaps this was a legacy from her predecessor. But decorating the alcove where a filing cabinet sat was a group of children's artworks: a handprint, a house with smoke coming from its chimney, an animal which might have been a cow or a horse, Mary couldn't be sure. The grandkids? It was a jolly and encouraging arrangement.

The village vibe overall was vaguely corporate without the overkill. There was no marble lobby with a fountain. No Greco-Roman pillars when you drove in. The reception area was a little cramped, with two sofas, a couple of over-size armchairs, a long coffee table and an ATM in the corner. No one was going to be mugged withdrawing money, Mary thought. Two vases of flowers flanked the front desk. It, too, was nice. Modest but not dowdy. As they'd waited to see Maureen, two residents in tracksuits and sneakers had come into the building carrying tennis racquets. The receptionist knew their names. They waved the racquets at the receptionist. 'Windy,' they said, laughing. It seemed almost staged and Mary had raised her eyebrows at Pete.

In talking about the various accommodation options, Maureen gave the impression that the set-up could speak for itself and that Mary and Pete would have ample means of checking on whatever they wanted to check on. This was accurate. They'd done their due diligence. The village was solidly reviewed online and mainly endorsed. Its chief virtue was the environs, especially access to the wetlands and estuary and the sea. One reviewer had written: 'Mum is so happy here. Such beautiful walks. The staff are excellent. The whole place is super friendly and clean. Her one complaint is that sometimes happy hour is only fifty minutes.'

When Maureen asked them if they had any initial questions, Pete said, 'How long is your happy hour?'

Circling back to one of the lounges, they went through a sliding door to an outside area with raised flower beds and planter boxes for vegetables. Residents could take charge of any part of the garden if they enjoyed that, said Maureen.

The phrase 'take charge' filled Mary with a sudden dread. It suggested they would not be taking charge of much else. Only the carrots and the rocket would you rule. Anyway, it was a relief to be outside. Mary had felt increasingly troubled by her glimpses into the rooms. A red throw on someone's armchair. A packet of mints beside someone's bed. A pair of slippers.

Of course, this residential wing was not where they were going. Maureen had showed them only to give a fuller sense of the village and its range of options. They were years away from the bedside mints and having their hearing aids stolen by others in the same condition.

Upstairs, where they didn't go, was the Special Care Unit. She thought then of Pete's mother.

Pete was inspecting the lettuces with exaggerated interest as Maureen talked about the microclimate. Mary recognised the signs of his disequilibrium. He was rubbing his chin and bending forward as you would with a sore stomach, though his face wasn't particularly troubled. He was leaving the scene at the exact moment he appeared most engaged. She wondered about his heart; she was always wondering about that now, and it tweaked a shot of resentment.

Suddenly he straightened and said to Maureen, 'Where are you keeping all the men?'

Maureen laughed, taken aback.

It was true. They'd seen just two men and one of them was a nurse.

'The numbers,' said Maureen, 'are rather in your favour.'

Pete had just read a futuristic novel about a society where all the men suddenly vanish from the planet and the women, after a brief period of missing them, get on with things. Here was the future already. He'd told Mary about it.

A starling landed on the top of a garden stake and the three of them watched it until it flew away.

They walked around the main building to an area with a putting green and a bowling green. Three golf balls waited by a hole but there was no one around. At the far end of the bowling green, a single figure was sweeping the bowls together with his feet. The path took them close to him. The man glanced at them, not really looking carefully, and raised his hand, greeting Maureen who'd said his name. He was squinting into the sun, which had just broken through the clouds. They were probably just silhouettes. Mary stared harder. Ross? She should have known him at once, from the broken nose, from the funny way of leaning into one hip. Yes. He wasn't as tall now, and he seemed a bit slower, though not by much. Old Rosco was in good shape. Ross Hayes, former Chief Inspector, whose time in the force had intersected with her own at various moments and who'd gone on to have a decorated career and who she hadn't seen in decades. For a moment, Mary considered moving on. Why bother Ross now, when he was enjoying this private time on the bowling green? It was interesting he was here. Maybe they'd bump into each other at some future date. But she'd not sought him out up to now, and he'd not made any move. Why should he have? She'd never attended the various reunions, the functions and commemorations. The invitations had come for years and she'd ignored them all. That part of her life was finished. Then the invitations stopped coming, and she was peeved for a while. Who made these decisions to drop people from such lists?

'Chief Inspector,' said Mary.

'Yes?' said Ross, peering at the speaker, not seeing her yet.

'Mary Brunton.'

'Mary?'

'Remember?'

Ross stepped forward, puzzled. He looked carefully into her face, and Mary thought for a second that Ross's mind might have seen better days. She suddenly didn't want to encounter this version of him. He'd been a good boss for the most part. Fair and straightforward. He'd given her responsibilities, saw her worth and advanced it. Plenty of others had operated in the opposite direction. But Ross was also tied up in the last, unhappy chapter of her time on the job when she'd felt unsupported, then utterly cut adrift. She'd blamed him in some way she couldn't now put together. Will, of course. Maybe Ross had just fallen back into that image she carried of her colleagues closing ranks. She'd thought he was separate, an ally and a friend, but in the end Ross Hayes was also the system, which had spat her out. Yes, he'd treated her shabbily and it was all ancient history. Was this why she didn't want to meet him in a reduced state—because she didn't feel she could extend him the required kindness and understanding?

'Mary! How lovely to see you.' He reached out and gripped

her hand. 'And Pete! Hello, hello. Gosh.' Ross was shaking Pete's hand and grinning.

He had his marbles.

Pete said, 'You're here then?'

'I am!' said Ross. He looked at Maureen. 'I see you've met the prison warden.'

Everyone laughed. They chatted for a while about when Ross had moved in (after his wife died) and where his apartment was (third floor, North Wing) and how he was trying to learn to play bowls but he didn't think he had the patience for it. 'You need a light touch,' he told them, 'and Mary knows I never had that.'

Mary thought that this didn't seem true. 'You're looking very well,' she said.

'You should see my pills drawer,' said Ross. He patted his ribs. 'I'm 80 per cent pharmaceuticals.'

'Tell me about it,' said Pete.

Ross studied him. 'You're too young for this lark, aren't you?'

'Parts wear out, Ross,' he said.

'And there's no warranty, you find!' laughed Ross.

Maureen was looking meaningfully at her watch. She announced they should probably crack on but that now the connection had been re-established the old friends could no doubt find each other again.

'I'm glad to see you both after all this time,' said Ross. He waved at them and turned back to his bowls.

There was a vacant unit they could inspect. This one was already taken, Maureen said, but it would give them an idea. At the entrance, she stopped them and said, 'Now, it is unfurnished, so take that into account. Imagine your own lovely things in here.'

Mary was hardly listening. She was thinking about Ross Hayes. A funny anxiety pressed on her. It meant something. It was familiar from a long time ago, from when she was in uniform, naturally. It was unpleasant and distracting. She blinked a few times and looked up at the hills whose tops were lost in grey cloud.

It was Ross who'd come into the station one night Mary was on the switchboard. That was nightshift for female officers back then. Night patrol was considered beyond them. He'd asked her how she was going, and Mary had told him she was bored out of her mind and that answering the phone wasn't what she signed up for. To her massive surprise, Ross said he agreed. The next night she was on the beat—a pioneer!

Anyway, here was their new house, or one very like it.

Oh, what were they doing?

She realised she was entering with no expectations and zero investment. Pete seemed the same. They were still ready to walk away.

In truth the place looked okay, the sort of property for which the word 'presentable' would be twisted into service. When Maureen closed the red front door behind them, it made a satisfying sound, like a vault shutting, and at once they were sealed in quietness. Their own house was porous by comparison and Mary didn't mind this new feeling. Cream walls, venetian blinds, grey carpet, tiled patches of floor. The two bedrooms were adequate, both with good built-in wardrobes. Mary remembered her sister always going on about storage, storage! Only the stupidest people bought a house with inadequate storage.

The bathroom was light and roomy, probably the best room in the house. *Shed your tears here.* They noted the handrails beside the toilet and in the shower. The open-plan living room connected to a smallish kitchen. If cooking wasn't quite a thing of the past, it was no longer a focus. Most of the eating could be done in the communal dining room in the main building, if that was what they preferred. There was a sample menu Maureen could send them later. 'To be honest,' she said, 'I'd eat here every night if I could. It's just so . . . easy.'

'We like easy,' said Mary. For years they'd shared the cooking and were both now happy with eating less, and less interestingly. Pouches of soup filled their fridge alongside the packs of hot cooked salmon. Their pantry had boil-in-the-bag rice, cans of tuna. Everything tasted vaguely of its packaging. If Colin came for dinner, they got a rotisserie chicken from the supermarket and a bag of coleslaw, and watched Colin drink most of the bottle of wine he brought and half of theirs.

Pete asked Maureen about the heating. She pointed to a large heat pump positioned high on the far wall of the living room. Odd he hadn't spotted it. He hated heat pumps. Whenever they stayed in motels or places with them, he wanted to shut them off as soon as he could.

Maureen was composing out of mid-air a poem about heat pumps to which no one, including Maureen herself, was listening.

Mary stood in front of the centrepiece of the room: a huge oil painting of a bull with curling horns and a shaggy fringe falling over its eyes.

'Previous owners haven't come back for that yet,' said Maureen. 'Apologies.'

The bull looked doleful, almost bashful, like an animal in a human wig.

'Imagine staring at that every night,' said Mary. The moment she spoke, she realised she wasn't sure if the painting was completely ghastly or rather good. Staring at it every night might actually be quite wonderful.

'The children of the owners are in a bit of a dispute about the painting,' said Maureen. 'One of those tussles that can happen when Mum and Dad are gone.'

'They all want it?' said Pete.

'I'm unsure of the details. Only that we're having trouble removing it.' She turned to him. 'Do you have children?'

Pete went to answer but a weird noise came out of his mouth. He'd been caught off guard.

It was a surprise to all three of them.

Dave Monk's stupid phone call flooded Mary's mind for a moment. And Ross Hayes—as if planted. Then she said, 'We had a son but he died a long time ago.'

'I am so sorry,' said Maureen.

'No,' said Mary. 'It means no one will cause any problems with our oversize artworks.'

The rest of the tour (laundry, patio, garden shed) took no time, and then they were standing in the neat and empty garage which smelled of drying clothes and oil. The dead child was still present, and Maureen now made sure to stick close to Mary and address everything to her. Pete was silent, though he walked over to the built-in bench and said something approving about it which neither of the women could properly hear.

Outside again they shook hands and agreed to be in touch very soon. It was unclear to all three of them at that moment whether this was meant sincerely.

On the drive home, however, a funny truce emerged and Mary and Pete found they shared a sense of satisfaction.

They'd both been prepared to hear the other's sarcastic take—on Maureen, on Chief Inspector 'Rosco' Hayes trying his hand at lawn bowls, on the venetian blinds, on the bull—but it didn't happen. Their prejudices wilted.

Wasn't it all, in fact, quite nice?

Mary mentioned the sensible overall design; Pete agreed. He spoke of the good natural light. She said she was expecting to feel hemmed in by the neighbouring units but it didn't really bother her. They'd done clever things with angles. Privacy. The view to the hills. The kitchen was small, she said, but not tiny. It was probably sufficient. Pete agreed again. He said he could imagine the garage working quite well. They'd be able to store a lot of their stuff there. Or, Mary suggested, they could just get rid of a lot of it. Sure, Pete said. A stocktake was overdue. The garden shed wasn't a bad option either.

They both felt a growing excitement, and because this was unexpected, the feeling was more intense.

One issue, Mary said, was wall space for bookshelves and where to put all his records. Pete nodded. But he said he'd been thinking it was probably time for a bit of a clean-out there too. Okay, said Mary. Good. That was good to hear. She told him she hadn't heard him use those words about the books and records before. Well, he said, was he really going to re-read them? And there were plenty of records he hadn't listened to in years. Which was an argument Mary said she'd used in the past. He clarified that he wasn't talking about dumping the lot. No, she said. Pete said he would oversee that process. Right, she said. Since, he said, sometimes you ended up regretting throwing out things. Mary said she wasn't sure about that but they could follow Pete's process and see where they ended up. It was a significant change they were making which would mean certain decisions, tough decisions, necessary ones. Pete was nodding. Mary felt that if he burst out crying it wouldn't have been a surprise. Yet he held himself. She was proud of him and of herself. They had passed this part of the test.

They felt there was a clarity finally, after the months of indecision and second thoughts. They were energised in a way they'd not felt for a long time.

'And Ross being there!' said Pete.

'I know,' said Mary.

'Not sure why but sort of makes it imaginable?'

'Hmm.'

They drove the rest of the way home without speaking, suddenly flattened and exhausted.

Mary was on the edge of asking Pete about the moment when he'd been unable to answer Maureen about having children. The time to ask seemed to have passed, or not arrived—one of those. And she didn't want to be put in a position where she might have to tell him about Dave Monk. She felt terrible about that. Still, didn't this show Pete wasn't ready?

That night Pete told Mary about meeting Pauline from the dementia unit on the beach. Mary remembered the name at once. Very competent, Mary said. She was so quick and certain, Pete heard himself agreeing. He didn't feel like admitting he'd totally forgotten her. But Mary's mind was trained. She had amazing recall of people.

'We're almost your mother's age when she went in,' said Mary.

'Mum was older,' he said.

'Not much.'

'I suppose that's true. We're in the ballpark.'
'I thought of her today.'
'Did you?'

Lying in bed, he had an image of sitting with his mother outside in the sunshine. There was a small courtyard with some bench seats. She'd been in a benign mood that day, taking delight in everything and everyone except a woman she was routinely convinced was trying to kill her and whom she requested Pete 'get to first'. There was a pair of scissors she could lay her hands on and a couple of old ducks who could help clean up the scene afterwards. 'The target,' his mother had whispered to him in a hardboiled American accent, 'ain't that popular.' His mother hated the group singalongs, and the leader of the singing was in her sights. *Pack up your travels in an old whatsit. I'd like to tell them where to pack up their troubles! Makes me want to vomit.* He remembered another visit when they'd been sitting in the lounge watching rugby on the giant TV (*You want to watch this, don't you.*) The singing came through to them. One of the staff put a plate in front of them, saying, 'It's happy hour! Enjoy.' On the plate were two small medallions of fried fish and two grey meatballs. They looked repulsive. It was 3pm. His mother had stared at the food, looked at Pete and burst out laughing. He'd laughed too. It was so ridiculous—the rugby, the singing, the happy hour morsels. 'Look,' said his mother, 'it's made us both happy!'

The day in the sunshine, looking out at the woody lavender bushes (*No one here knows a thing about gardening*), she spoke about how she'd become aware of how the world 'twerked'. It was a revelation, she said. Pete asked her what she meant. Did she mean 'worked'?

'You know,' she said. She made fluttering motions with

her fingers. 'Everything twerks, in a healthy way. If things are healthy.'

Just then a pair of sparrows flew around the lavender, and his mother laughed and waved her fingers. 'Ah, the twerkers are back!' A bee then flew near them, circling the air. She laughed again in utter delight. He was smiling too. 'Twerk away, good creatures!' she said.

'Twerkers are good then?' he asked.

'Oh, they protect me, yes. They warn me.'

His mother had always been a skilled gardener. She had made the surroundings of their family house, and then the house she and his father moved to when Pete left home, places of beauty and repose. The gardens she created weren't just pretty displays. The flowering plants lived alongside other plants chosen for shape, scent, relief, and their appeal to pollinators and birds. She understood relationships. When he was old enough to see it, Pete regarded all this with wonder. She was also at her most relaxed in the garden, describing whatever successes and failures were playing out in the soil. She'd never been demonstrative. She had to lose her mind to start initiating hugs. The garden was a canvas which talked back to her, coaxing other things from her. She softened. His father had little interest and so this was her realm. She seemed to expand.

When she was first admitted to the unit, Pete had had to fill in a questionnaire about his mother's professional life and her interests. The gardening loomed way larger than her working life. He had to struggle to put the career together. She'd done book-keeping for an uncle's marine supplies business and then fulfilled a similar role for an engineering firm before taking up another administrative position with a freight company. She seemed content enough in the back room. No one had sought her out for management. It looked like an ambition-free trek, with the solid role of homemaker behind it all. Pete remembered an old colleague of hers had come up to him at Margaret's funeral and used the word 'diligent' three times. This couldn't be her real life.

He had the sudden thought, sitting with her, that now was her real life. That her new-found capacity to articulate her inner life was vastly meaningful.

Wasn't it the case that she was sensitised to how she had lived her life up to this point? Many of her stories were about this in a way. She'd told Pete about a resident who could make a shocking noise if he was touched. 'It makes me physically ill. We all want to kill him,' she said calmly. Indeed, there was such a man; Pete had heard him on other visits. 'Now the reason he can make this sound, which is like a foghorn, is because he was a sea captain. So he makes a sound that is quite incredible. Now what I've done is this. I've used my choir skills to help him. I told him that instead of the awful blast of the horn, he should try to make a melodic sound that stretches right across the valley, spreads over the hills, in the treetops. A sound that stitches the choir together. That is what I used to do, stitch the choir together when I sang.'

She raised her arms and gestured to the surrounding hills, and for a moment it was lovely and persuasive. He felt her power. Yes! The hills are alive with the sound of music, he thought.

Still it came from him: 'You were in a choir?' Sometimes he felt he needed to intervene, and he wasn't sure why. His mother had never sung. His father was the one who'd been in choirs, who at birthday parties and other functions often sang. 'Old Man River'. 'Shortnin' Bread'. 'The Rose of Tralee'.

'Was I in a choir?' She gave him a funny look, as if to say, are you stupid? 'I was in the human choir.'

'Aha.'

'That was what we were called.'

'It's a good name. It's a good thing to be in the human choir, Mum.'

She studied him again, unsure if he was humouring her. 'Oh, I was known for my singing but only by the real experts. They knew what I was doing.'

'Right, okay.'

She sensed his scepticism. 'The reason I never stepped forward all my life and kept a low profile was to allow others to flourish. If I had announced my gifts, everyone would have said, "Oh bother, what's the use of trying when I can never attain her level of expertise." This applied to my piano skills, my singing and pretty much anything you can name. It was quite terrifying to add up all my talents. But I had to stay in the background. Now, when people are just beginning to understand the sheer range of my abilities, they're likely to go into denial. "No, you were never like that," they tell me. But of course they know it's the truth.'

The boastfulness was edged with a comedy she seemed aware of too. She giggled sometimes, as if she knew it was all unlikely and she was waiting for the act to collapse. A whistle would be blown and the game would be up. In the meantime she pressed on, enjoying it, in a sort of trance, able to talk seamlessly for ages. It wasn't that crazy, he thought, for his mother now to reflect on a lifetime's pattern of not stepping forward more and to come up with some reason for it. Looked at plainly, she had let others flourish—him, for instance, and his father. And Will.

From inside then came the sound of a woman screaming. They'd met this woman earlier and she'd shouted in their faces. She had long dirty yellow hair and acne across her chin and down the deep folds of her neck. Her bare feet were swollen, just like his mother's. It was not the woman his mother wanted to kill. In the garden his mother flinched at the sudden terrifying noise. But she focused again on the birds, who'd come back, landing on the grass close to their feet. 'Twerk!' said his mother, gripping her walking frame. 'Twerk, you fucking bastards.'

When he first thought about his mother's crack-up, he believed it had arrived without warning. That wasn't quite true. His mother had been in a bad mood for months. Very short with his father. Fed up, he thought. There was a long-running saga with the central heating. A progression of plumbers had come and given conflicting and unsatisfactory diagnoses. The house was cold for weeks in the middle of winter. He visited and found his parents sitting in their coats. Pete brought around portable heaters. He tracked down the first plumber, who said he hadn't been paid. He arranged the payment; the plumber returned with a new part for the boiler. This worked. Then it broke down again. His mother was exasperated about all that, with good reason. It's a joke, she told him. A complete joke. They put their coats back on and Pete chased up the plumber. When Pete came around, he found they hadn't turned the portable heaters on. They didn't want to waste money, his father said, on such inefficient machines. Behind his father, his mother made a face. Besides, his father said, it was warming up. Spring was around the corner. No matter the weather, he'd long insisted on sleeping with their bedroom window open a couple of inches. 'If I try to shut it, he tells me off,' his mother told Pete. 'In a northerly the rain can drive in and wet the curtains so now when that's the forecast he insists on leaving the curtains open. There's a streetlight which hits me right across the face.'

Then she needed a procedure in one of her eyes. The macular degeneration was advancing. It was recommended she have an injection into the right eye. It was done through Outpatients. She didn't tell anyone about it, not even his father. After she came home on the bus, she pulled the curtains and collapsed on to her bed. Apparently it had caused her a lot of pain. Walking out into the sunshine she was nearly blind. She'd tripped getting on to the bus, and someone helped her. She closed her eyes the whole way, she said. Which meant she missed her stop and had to walk back a mile. His father rang Pete that night and said she hadn't even cooked dinner. When Pete phoned the next day, his mother gave him an overlong description of the entire previous day—overlong for her especially; she didn't like to talk much about herself. *Tell me about you*, she would always say. *Tell me about Mary.* She enjoyed hearing about others. This time on the phone she was unstoppably detailed about the hospital, her route along the corridors, the unpleasant nurse, what was said, what was done, the bus. It was all about her, in slow motion. He put it down to the traumatic experience of having her eyeball poked with a needle.

After that she seemed to recover for a few days. She was running the house, mopping up around the toilet, paying the bills, cooking the meals. They'd rejected home help every time Pete suggested it and offered to pay for it.

One evening the following week she left a message on his phone asking what he thought about the obituaries in the paper. He got the paper and read the obituaries. The names didn't mean anything to him. He rang her and asked who she meant—was there someone she knew?

'Are you looking at today's paper?' she said.

'Yes,' said Pete.

'And you can't see it?'

'Can't see what?'

'Oh my godfathers. He can't see it!'

'Tell me the name.'

'Tell you the name? Tell you the name? When you're pretending not to see it.'

'What?' She sounded utterly contemptuous. It was very strange.

'Godfathers! It's quite incredible. Do I have to come around and show you?'

Pete understood something was wrong. The hostility was extraordinary. 'Maybe I do have yesterday's paper.'

'I thought so!'

'Tell me who died.'

He heard her emit an enormous sigh.

'All your cousins. All the family. The extended family. Something like forty of us. Forty-three, I think I counted. Completely devastating.'

'Okay,' said Pete.

'And clearly you knew nothing about it.'

'No.'

'Which confirms everything. But at least you're safe. For now.'

'I am safe. I'm fine, Mum.'

'And Mary, is she safe?'

'Mary is fine.'

'It's good to hear. However, I hold grave and ongoing fears for your safety and mine. Now I've got to ring some other people. I have a great many tasks.'

He asked her who she was going to ring, and she answered

with a list of names of family members who'd died many years before, including Will and Claire, Mary's sister.

His feet felt concrete heavy. 'Mum, is Dad there?'

'Why?'

She's suffered some kind of stroke, he told himself. It was temporary. 'Can I have quick word?'

'Have you been listening to anything I've said?'

'Yes, yes, it sounds very bad. But is Dad there?'

She was silent for a few moments. 'Your father is in utter denial. Just like you. Now I need the line.' She hung up.

He told Mary what had happened. He was calm. He felt he was describing something they were ready for. Mary agreed it was probably a temporary set-back. Margaret, she said, was so strong and healthy. He would drive to their house by himself. If they both went, it might be too alarming. Play it cool, they thought. Pete would assess the situation. Yes, Mary told him. She gave him a quick hug. Go now, she said.

When he'd arrived at their house, his mother had leapt up from the table, excited to see him. 'Good, you've come!' she told him.

Pete noticed his father was sitting quietly at the far end of the dining table, touching his spoon, his head down. He appeared to have removed himself from the scene. Perhaps he'd been listening to her all day and was now shattered. He hadn't called Pete, hoping—Pete supposed—that whatever had seized his wife was only temporary. If she would just go to bed, she would wake up normal again.

Meanwhile his mother had found the newspaper. She thrust it at Pete. 'Now,' she said vehemently, 'will you see with your own eyes! Will you just look.' She grabbed his forearm with force, pinching the skin and causing him pain. She'd never touched him with such violence.

'Okay, okay,' Pete said, 'calm down now, Mum.'

'Calm down? Me? When all of this is happening? That's what he's been saying too!' She jabbed the newspaper in the direction of his father. 'I'm trying to alert you all to something. I'm doing my best. But just read it, will you!'

Pete took the newspaper from her and looked. 'Sorry,' he said, 'can you point to where the names are? I'm afraid I don't recognise them as our family.'

'Oh for goodness sake! Are you serious? Are you in complete denial? Both of you?'

'Margaret, please,' said his father.

'Of course I thought you might have this response,' she said. 'They've got to you. It's all so frightening, the speed of things.'

Pete rested his hand on her arm. 'Mum,' he said, 'I think something might have happened.'

She recoiled at once, stepping away and shaking her head, angry. 'No, no, no.' She slapped the paper from his hands.

'I think something in your head might have been shaken up a bit. Just for the moment.'

'Keep away from me!'

'If perhaps we go to the hospital, just for a check. Not to stay. Just to check things out. I'm sure we can get to the bottom of it.'

She screwed her face into a mask of contempt. Her features had never appeared to him like this. 'You will not take me anywhere! You will not! If I go in there, I'll never come out.'

She went to the kitchen bench and yanked open the cutlery drawer. For a second he thought she might be searching for a knife to brandish. But she took out two spoons and carried two bowls of pudding to the table, placing one in front of his father and sitting down to eat the other. Pete moved towards the table and she turned away from him, hunching her shoulders and scowling. She might have even made a hissing sound. Then, in a way which suggested she was protecting her bowl from someone getting ready to snatch it from her, she began to shovel food into her mouth. She might have been a scared child in a boarding school. Someone in a prison. A condemned figure. She was already in the shape of an institutionalised person. He looked for a time and then had to look away. He was profoundly shocked. What had happened? Slowly his father was lifting his own spoon to his mouth.

The day after their village visit, Maureen the manager rang to say there'd been some movement on the waiting list. A place was available right away. A very cute spot, she said. It was theirs if they acted now.

Five

Dave Monk was solid and compact. His white shirt grabbed at him around the arms and at the neck. Behind the knot of his tie, Mary saw, his top button was undone. He was the updated version of any number of cops she'd worked with back in the day. The tight haircut, grey at the sides. A tenseness in the body. He moved as if he had a rugby ball tucked under one arm. The way he turned his head to the side to listen, as if he had one good ear.

They'd been talking about living up the coast. His in-laws had a place. The kids could run around, disappear for the day. Nice. 'Sort of old-fashioned,' he said. He glanced at her. 'No, that's not the right word. Relaxed? Easy? Anyway, nice.'

They were sitting in the far corner of the café across from the library. Dave had been there ahead of her even though she was a few minutes early. Maybe he'd wanted to secure a good spot, with maximum privacy and a good outlook on the room. The morning coffee crowd were mostly gone, the lunch one not in yet. Dave had a flat white in front of him, which he hadn't touched, and Mary had a short black. He'd paid despite her offer.

He'd put his briefcase on the floor between his feet, as if he was worried he might lose it, or was just not used to carrying one.

'It must be hard to have this all back again,' he said.

'It was a long time ago,' she said.

'Still, I'm aware there will be lots of different emotions.'

Mary took a sip of her coffee. How she hated the tremor in her hand and the way Dave would interpret it. The tremor was not connected to any emotions.

'Your husband . . .' said Dave, '. . . did he prefer not . . . ?'

'He had an appointment he couldn't break,' Mary lied. Did Dave believe this? Perhaps he even preferred that Pete hadn't come; that it was just two cops, no civilians to worry about.

He was reaching down for the briefcase. 'The file wasn't at Central of course, but then there was some fun and games tracking it down because the storage place was being refurbished and everything of a certain age had been temporarily moved from there to . . . Anyway, we got there.' He lifted out a faded green folder and placed it on the table, his hand flat on top of it.

Mary experienced a sudden jolt. Here it was. She felt a bit sick, and then it passed.

'As you know, we've got the various statements in here. The account of the events leading up to it. All the relevant information. And the coroner's findings.'

'Accidental death by drowning,' said Mary.

'Yeah, some recommendations about health and safety.'

'Health and safety, right.' The coronial report was in a box somewhere in the attic. Mary remembered skimming it very fast and putting it away. *This is not an inquiry into the circumstances around the death and it makes no findings in regard to culpability. My findings relate only to the manner of death.*

They both studied the unopened file now that Dave had removed his hand. There weren't many pages. Mary thought there should have been more. Was that it? Will deserved better than this thin, crappy file shunted around storage lockups. She remembered that the case had been handled by a DI from out of town—maybe Palmie? To avoid any conflict of interest with her own station. Pearson. Jim Pearson. He was near retirement. Very slow. Pleasant and slow. She'd heard that his wife had died from cancer a few years before and that he had great people skills from going through all that. She had a memory of being in the room with him while he typed with stabbing fingers. And the smell of the correction fluid he was constantly applying. In DI Pearson's little covering dabs Mary had felt her son's reality disappearing.

Dave looked at his coffee, puzzled about it—or about what to say next. Then he drank it all in one go and wiped his mouth with a serviette. He opened the file and read: 'Shaun Anderson.'

'The driver,' said Mary.

'The driver of the vehicle.'

'Toyota Hilux,' said Mary, '1977. The boys were in the back, open tray. Old-fashioned, I suppose.'

Dave Monk nodded. 'I'll hardly need to jog your memory.'

'Oh, I forget a lot these days. But not this.'

'In his statement, Anderson says he was taking the boys for a spot of night shooting. Possums. He wasn't employed by the school.'

'He did odd jobs around the holiday camp. Painting, fixed the loos, maintenance. Bit of a bushman.'

'Right. And little adventures for the campers.'

'The previous year, I think, he'd done some survival skills stuff. The teachers thought he was pretty good. Rough bloke but good.'

Dave read again from the file: '"Mr Anderson has established himself as a helpful and talented part of the camp experience and the school has been happy to avail itself of his skills to enhance the camps." That was the principal.'

'Reg Perry,' said Mary. 'He was terrified.'

'Of what?'

'Damage to the school's reputation. They made Shaun Anderson cut off his beard and wear city clothes for the appearances. He looked like an insurance salesman.'

'What did you think of him?'

'I tried not to.' This was successful. She couldn't believe such a person now and forever had decided something in all their lives. He was nothing. Back then she had no interest in his future. The idea of justice was completely unimportant. Jim Pearson's investigation seemed irrelevant. Pete could not say Shaun Anderson's name. At a certain point, when they saw where it was going, they disengaged, or attempted to.

Dave looked at the file again. 'There's a fair bit about the state of the bridge they went over.'

Mary shook her head. 'No seatbelts of course. They think Will was most likely knocked unconscious by the crash. They were all in the water. In the dark.'

'It would have been chaotic.'

'Shaun Anderson had a head wound. He was bashed up. So I guess he couldn't count to five.'

'Will was recovered downstream. The next morning.'

'The teachers and the parents who were there, they all set out with torches. But for whatever reason they didn't spot him. And they had four injured boys and Anderson. It's quite a remote place. No cell phones of course. A long drive to the nearest farm. Chaos, as you say. Yeah, we went there.'

'Just extremely sad. I'm sorry, Mary.'

To picture Will out there alone in the dark, on the edge of a river, waiting . . . She knew he would have been unconscious through it all. She knew. When they'd visited the camp it had been a beautiful day and the river looked completely innocuous. A kererū landed in a tree just above them and they were startled. It was like a sack of sticks had dropped from the sky.

She turned and saw that an old woman hunched over a walker was making her way carefully through the chairs and tables. She was with her daughter and granddaughter, Mary guessed. They were carrying a tray of food and drinks. The granddaughter was mimicking the slow and bent progress of the woman with the walker, really hamming it up.

'I can't think what this new development could be, Dave.'
'Shaun Anderson would like to speak to you.'
'Why?'
'He's dying.'
'Aren't we all. Ha ha.'
'His daughter contacted the police in Whanganui.'
'Whanganui?' She was mystified by these words: daughter, Whanganui. As if the man had claim to a real life. It was evident how deeply she'd suppressed Shaun Anderson, and now he was back. It was an outrage. And why get your kid to make the call?

The rat she'd seen that night in the garden—it wasn't Will of course. It was Anderson.

She pictured his moustache—he hadn't got rid of that for the proceedings. Cops back then had moustaches. Did they still?

'They live there. You know, you don't have to do this. You don't have to see him.'
'I know. I know very well.'
'We have made zero promises to the daughter.'
'I see.'

'We debated the value in passing it on. But on balance we felt it was important to at least contact you and let you decide. I wasn't even sure if . . .'

'We'd be alive.'

'Well,' said Dave, touching his tie to loosen it some more, 'I see you are. Very much so.'

'I need to tell my husband.'

'Of course.'

Did either of them believe this was a decisive consideration? Pete seemed almost imaginary at that moment. He thought Mary was at the supermarket.

Dave pushed over a separate sheet of paper. 'The Andersons,' he said. 'I can be there too, if you want. If you decide to meet.'

'No,' said Mary. 'No thank you. And it's not decided.'

'Right.'

She took the sheet of paper. 'We have a lot going on. We're moving, you know.'

'That's big.'

He'd been about to add 'at your age' but stopped himself. 'Yes,' she said. 'We're seeking an even quieter life.'

She saw that Dave didn't know whether to laugh or not; he ended up with a wince. He was leafing through the file again.

'You would have seen a lot in your day,' he said, meaning the force.

Had he been poking into her file too? 'Loved every minute of it,' said Mary. She hadn't intended to say this. It was something she'd heard other retired cops say, looking back. Every minute? Really? Well, no. Was this what Ross Hayes would say too? Maybe. She felt the quick stab of memory: crawling out a toilet window, having handed over the marked twenty-dollar notes to the woman who'd agreed to do the abortion, and two young constables, waiting in the alley to swoop in for the arrest, pointing at Mary and grinning, giving her the thumbs-up. She was undercover in Auckland. The abortionist was a nurse at the hospital. Perhaps not that minute, or plenty of others. Mary had visited the nurse in prison to apologise. The nurse had said she bore Mary no ill will. How?

Mary thought of Barry Must and closed it down immediately.

Anyway, Mary didn't feel like retracting the statement and Dave would know what she meant. He liked her for saying it, she could tell. And she liked being here with him, discussing things. They understood each other. The force was no doubt unrecognisable from her day; also it was the same as it'd always been.

Dave had pulled another sheet of paper from the file. He sighed, looking at it. 'Anderson had history.'

Mary said, 'Makes sense.'

'I don't know if you want to read this.'

'I'd have to find my glasses. Please.'

Dave started reading, 'Previous convictions, all driving. May 1972, driving causing injury. Fined $1000. February 1973, driving while disqualified, failing to ascertain whether any person was injured, failing to stop after an accident. Fined $2000. August 1975, driving with a blood alcohol level of 380 milligrams. Fined $1000.' He looked up at her.

'Okay,' said Mary.

'This one, October 1976, shook hands with a passenger in another car while travelling at speed—'

'Talented, wasn't he?'

'Dangerous driving causing injury, disorderly behaviour,

six months PD, one year disqualified. November 1978, tried to settle a dispute while driving, swerved in front of other car, blood alcohol content of 430 milligrams, disqualified one year, fined $4000.'

'Busy man.'

'He was on his way to someone dying.'

'At the camp, he was never tested for alcohol.'

'Would have been too late, I guess.'

'People said there'd been no drinking. I remember that bit.'

They were both watching the woman on the walker, who had now reached her destination. She waited for her daughter to bring the chair into position and then she sank back into it, dropping the last two inches with a jolt. The granddaughter wiped her brow in mock relief and then, copying her grandmother's actions, fell loudly into her own chair, giving the old woman a fright.

Dave shook his head.

'Shall we arrest that little shit?' said Mary.

Dave grinned in appreciation.

'Everyone drank and drove in those days,' she said.

'Not everyone,' said Dave.

'It was the dark ages,' said Mary. 'You know, when I joined, female officers weren't allowed to view dead bodies.'

'Really?'

She saw the way Dave had kept his response neutral, as if he was in an interview room, about to hear a confession. A dead body? Okay, that's interesting. Now don't scare the suspect. Act as if people always say such things.

It was changed suddenly between them.

Mary said, 'It was in the Constable's Manual.' This hardly explained why she'd made the first statement. Still, she had instant recall of the feel of that small black ring binder. In the early years she kept it close. Slowly the metal bits rusted. She remembered Pete helping her study the manual. They'd lie in bed at night and he'd ask her questions from the section she was swotting. Five things to do if you come across a suspected suicide. How to obtain a search warrant. Gathering evidence at a domestic burglary. Four things to prove when charging someone with drunkenness in a public place. It was intensely bureaucratic. Very dry, sometimes strange. There was a small drawing to illustrate how to get a ring off the finger of a corpse using a piece of string. The manual was dull work, disconnected from what you faced, but the memory of Pete quizzing her was a tender one. How they'd worked together to help her become something neither of them quite thought possible. It had been a mistake not to involve him this day. What was she playing at?

Perhaps she'd been about to tell Dave Monk something else about dead bodies but she'd lost her train of thought. He was saying something about the future and being in touch and thanking her. He was ready to leave now. The meeting was over. He had real stuff to do. She understood that she was now firmly back in the category of citizen and had been granted her former status only for as long as Dave required it. In holding her chair out when she stood up and keeping his arm in a guiding position, she saw that in some key respect she was, for him, hardly different from the old dear with the smart granddaughter.

Six

The illustrated For Sale sign had been attached to their fence. The photos glowed with red and yellow light; the rooms looked unending, shiny, not theirs—good, Pete thought. Now they were on this path, he felt committed. Couldn't wait to have it all settled. Mary was the same. Their attachment to their beautiful house had dissolved and with it their anxiety and doubt. They moved among the hired dress furniture as if they were staying in a hotel or a museum display of a hotel suite since they couldn't really touch things anymore. Only their bed remained of all their possessions. The other beds were inflatables which could be moved with a fingertip. The elegant side tables looked solid and were constructed of some kind of cardboard. Mary and Pete were instructed not to place a glass of water on them. The dress sofas and chairs were handsome and awful to sit on. The new dining table was too low. Outdoors, they watched the white furniture rearrange itself as if moved by magnets. Much of their life now happened in their bedroom, where they perched on their old bed, stable and expectant. They longed to leave this weightless kingdom and start the new life. The books and the LPs were all in storage, along with everything else. If they caught sight of the new, vague paintings—abstractions of the sea, the sky—they got a fright. How did that end up there?

Anyway, it made it easier to bear the idea of a crowd of

strangers, most of whom had no interest in buying their house, walking through it and judging how they lived. They'd done the same over the years at other people's open homes.

Through the windows, the great island seemed flimsy too, hovering on a bed of misty sea.

A few days before the first open home, Colin visited. He wanted to see if the oldies were preparing everything in the right way. Aside from a couple of rental properties, he'd bought and sold six houses. If your solo mother dies when you're in your teens, he liked to say, it really sets you up in life. There were also his two marriages and the accompanying liquidation of assets. He was therefore in a great position to advise them, just not on marriage, he added, ha ha.

In the kitchen, Colin opened cupboards, looked in drawers, turned on taps. 'People will be incredibly nosey,' he told them.

'Like you,' said Mary.

'They'll check the shower pressure.'

'We checked the shower pressure when we first came here to look,' said Pete.

'They'll take moisture readings with a gauge, or their building inspector will.'

Mary said, 'The house is dry.'

'Mostly,' said Pete.

'It's good you haven't slapped new paint everywhere.'

'We booked someone and they never showed up,' said Pete.

'Good job! Buyers are wary of new paint—what's it hiding?'

'Old paint,' said Mary.

'A multitude of sins, Auntie Mary.' Colin opened and closed the window by the kitchen sink.

'Can you stop doing that?' said Mary.

'Shame you fixed the chimney. Oh well. Nice for the new owners. Make sure the agent points it out. People love to think they're getting a bargain on some small thing.'

Overall, Colin seemed happy enough. For a house literally built on sand, it felt solid. And he liked the new look. He said it was just the right side of banal.

'Just don't sit down anywhere,' said Pete.

Pete took him down to the ancient garage to inspect things there. They'd done the minimum, as advised by Gary, the agent. It was cleared of paint tins, old tools, timber offcuts, various garden potions, pots, the bikes, the badminton set, the exercycle Pete had bought and hardly used. They'd kept the lawnmower, and a broom for the final tidy. Question marks hung over the crumbling insulation paper which drooped down in strips from the ceiling in the far corner and whether Gary had been right in telling them not to bother repairing either this or the cracked pane on the large back window. Pete's eye now always went to these flaws, but Gary had indicated the new owners would probably want to bowl the garage anyway when they concreted the driveway and put up a decent front fence. Gary's vision was something of an insult, of course, but when Pete repeated it to Colin, he simply nodded. Yeah yeah. He looked at the ceiling. 'You start pulling, you don't know where it'd stop.'

They had a cup of tea outside, under the shade of the olive tree. Speckles of light patterned Colin's pale face, and Mary produced a straw hat for him—one of the few things allowed to remain in the downstairs cupboard. Wearing the hat, Colin seemed less aggressive. The inspection complete and no great problems uncovered, a kind of melancholy settled. They talked for a while about the garden, the recent weather. The mood of their nephew's visit had grown strangely listless. He had something on his mind. Mary asked about his work. Usually there was an annoying patient to be indiscreet about. He'd taken over a well-established practice in a good part of town and now he too was well established. Quite a few of his patients, women mainly, just wanted to talk—and to be asked a question or two. How are you? was usually enough. When did you first notice this? Which, Colin had once said, would be the title of his memoirs. Today he seemed almost storyless. They prompted him with questions. At the surgery they were finally getting rid of the fish tank, Colin said. He'd never seen the point and the colleague whose idea it was had long moved on. Amazing how much time the receptionist and even the nurses spent fussing around with the blasted thing. 'When a fish dies, it's a black day and I have to remember to be sad.'

Pete started telling the story about a fish tank which one of the branch libraries had had for years and which had burst one day and a child had found a goldfish and put it inside a book about goldfish.

'I think Colin's heard this story before,' said Mary.

'Okay,' said Pete.

A slight breeze moved the leaves of the feijoa tree they'd planted a couple of years before. They'd never see the fruit!

The agent had told them to tidy up the vegetable patch. 'These,' Gary said, 'can we get rid of them?' It was Mary's spinach and no they couldn't. 'Get flowers!' he told them. 'Pots of flowers! But not too many. Men start to think it's not their sort of place.'

'I was doing a bit of my own cleaning up recently,' said

Colin. 'Going through some things of Mum's.'

'What sort of things?' said Mary.

'Just some ancient boxes I've had in a storage place. It was time to renew the fee and I thought I should check out what I was actually paying for. Turns out, a lot of junk. Decades old. Chucked a whole lot—off to the tip. Lamps and chairs and stuff. Rugs. Random tables. From the old place, mainly.'

'From your Mum's house?' said Mary.

'From our place, yes. Forgotten I had it, to be honest. It didn't look great. The storage place was basic. That didn't help. I should have paid more attention. There was some mould, and things had got damp, then dried out. Stains. Anyway, that's sorted.'

'That would have been hard to go through,' said Pete.

'Not really,' said Colin. 'I didn't recognise most of it.'

'I would have liked to see it,' said Mary.

'Why?'

'Because it would have been interesting.'

'Well, it wasn't, believe me. But I did pull out a box of papers. Mum's collection of postcards and letters mixed up with bank statements, insurance documents. I kept a few things.'

'That's important,' said Pete. 'You want to keep some of the personal items.'

Colin turned to Mary and said, 'Maybe you'd like to look. Her handwriting was terrible. I tried but I gave up. Tiny scrawls.'

'I would.'

'All right.' He looked around the garden and suddenly said, 'For me, this is not your house. Your house will always be 25 Princess Ave. That's where I see you.'

'We've lived here longer,' said Pete.

Mary knew Pete didn't want to talk about Will. And perhaps nor did Colin. In a funny way, he avoided mentioning his cousin. She'd noticed this over the years. Yet Will was always there. He was more present because he wasn't mentioned. He was the reason Colin came to see them. Colin had blundered close and both he and Pete were now backing off.

'Funny isn't it,' said Colin. 'You've lived here longer.'

'Just houses,' said Pete.

It was a laughable statement.

Colin quickly asked them again about the new place. They'd already given him the highlights. What's it like? he asked. How many bedrooms? Garden? North-facing? Pete engaged enthusiastically. Colin cut him off, asking, What kind of agreement did you have to sign? Ah, so they'd lose a bit but it was worth it, Colin told them. Definitely the move to make. He seemed to be convincing himself more than them, as if he'd suddenly had second thoughts. Mary tried to tell him the story of the painting of the bull, but Colin didn't appear to take it in and asked her if they really needed such a large painting because it might shrink the room. She put him right but he wasn't really following it.

'We met someone there, a resident, who used to work with Mary,' said Pete. He wanted to move them from the bull painting, perhaps remembering—Mary thought—how he'd choked up with Maureen's question about having kids.

Every subject seemed delicate recently. They were living on an edge.

'Good,' said Colin. 'You'll make new friends as well.'

'Steady on,' said Mary.

'It was someone from the police,' said Pete.

Colin stared at his aunt. She seemed to come into focus

for him for the first time this visit. 'I can hardly remember you as a copper,' he said.

'Same here,' said Mary.

'Whereas for me,' said Pete, 'it feels like yesterday.'

'Really?' said Colin.

'Really?' said Mary.

Pete smiled. 'You were a shit stirrer.'

'Were you, Auntie Mary?'

'Not really,' she said. 'Or in those days you didn't need to do much to get that reputation.'

'She did plenty,' said Pete. 'Tried to drag the force into the . . . whatever century they needed to be dragged into.'

'I can see it,' said Colin.

'A funny thing happened recently,' she began. Did she really want to start this? She felt ready suddenly, as if Pete's reminiscences had summoned the time again. 'I had a call from the Wellington CIB.' The two men looked and waited. 'It was about Will.'

'About Will?' The name carried a huge current. Colin instantly flushed red.

'The bloke who was driving the ute when they went off the bridge, he wants to meet.'

'What? He wants to meet you?' said Colin. 'After all this time?'

'He's not long for this world. Maybe he wants to be forgiven, I don't know.'

Pete dropped his head and stared at the ground, pushing his sandalled feet through the grass. They still needed to mow this bit. 'When did they call?' he said, not looking at her.

'The other day,' she said. It was too hard to explain the weeks' delay and she couldn't really.

'The other day,' said Pete.

'Are you going to meet him?' said Colin.

The long list of Shaun Anderson's previous convictions came to her mind. A real ratbag. Mary looked at Pete. 'Are we?'

He put both hands on his head as if to keep it in place.

'Must have been weighing on him all this time,' said Colin.

'The poor devil,' said Mary mockingly.

Pete raised his head again. 'Certainly we need to see him.' He seemed surprised to have said it. 'Certainly. Don't we?'

'Okay,' said Mary. 'Good.'

'Okay,' said Colin. 'Wow.'

'We owe it to Will,' said Pete.

The three of them were immediately trapped there, lost in considering what had happened all those years ago to make them three not four. Three not five if Claire was in the picture, and she was. In that brief period—hardly two years—their worlds had been ripped apart. If Mary saw a news report of a tornado, she thought that was what they'd been through—they'd been picked up and deposited elsewhere, here.

Finally, Mary started clearing away the tea things and the other two stood up, stretching and looking in the direction of the sea, which just showed on the horizon. Pete felt strongly Colin's desire to say something—but what was there to say? Standing together, he longed for the other man to remain silent. And this, for once, is what happened. Pete turned and hugged Colin. It was electric. The nephew's body had a charge, or was that Pete's own body? They pulled away and walked back inside the house to help Mary. She seemed to be dropping dishes from a height on to the bench. Pete had noticed this recently. Was it connected with her hearing?

She'd not told him immediately about the call. Why? He could tell she was feeling defensive about it, and guilty. She knew she'd made the wrong decision. Was it worth bringing up?

When he was leaving, Mary walked with Colin down to his car. On the path, a tiny sharp piece of stick pricked her foot through her sandal. She made a noise and bent down to remove it.

'Let's see,' said Colin.

'It's nothing,' she said.

He bent down and inspected the area. Just a scratch. 'Okay,' he said. 'No need for the hospital.' He looked for longer than he should have.

'Find anything down there?' she said.

'Your feet,' he said. 'They're like Mum's feet.'

'I suppose they are.'

He stood up. 'Remember that time she stepped on a needle?'

'I do.'

'You had to come around.'

'It was the middle of the night.'

'I was in bed. I only knew about it when I woke up and found Uncle Pete there, and Will asleep on the sofa. You'd had to bring him too. It was still the middle of the night but I must have sensed something was wrong. Pete tried to calm me. I was so worried. I thought something terrible had happened.'

'She didn't want to wake you up.'

'How on earth did she manage to get a needle in her foot?'

'She'd been sewing the previous day, I think. It went in very deep.'

'Crazy things were always happening to her.'

What did he mean? Perhaps he was right. 'That wasn't so crazy. But yes.'

'I guess you and Pete were the only people who could help her.'

'We lived close by.'

'She relied on you.'

The night of the needle came back to her. Claire's hushed voice on the phone. *I've done something stupid, can you come?* They'd had to wait for hours in the ED, Claire with her foot up on Mary's lap. Finally the doctor saw them. It was straightforward. In those hours, the sisters had spoken to each other in a quiet, relaxed way they hadn't been able to in years. Somehow, in the centre of all the coming and going of the ED, they created a calm spot. Mary couldn't remember what they spoke about, only the feeling. It was one of her favourite times with Claire.

Colin spoke to her through the open car window. 'It'll be a bit sad to leave here but it's going to be great at the new place.' He was still working hard. It was sweet.

'I know,' she said. 'I know.'

Seven

In week two of their new life, Mary found former Chief Inspector Ross Hayes snoozing with a newspaper open on his lap by one of the large windows which looked out on to the bowling green where they first met him. It was all artificial turf, that tinselly lime which made Mary think of the coverings they rolled over the edges of graves to tidy the broken earth. His glasses rested on the paper. Sunshine touched the top of his bald head, making a single bright shape like a slice of cake. Mary thought a neurosurgeon could have used this light to make her first incision.

She was feeling bleak.

She'd been walking back from a meeting in Maureen's office where she'd signed some remaining paperwork.

She had doubts. What had they done?

The tremor in her hand holding the pen had been embarrassing. Maureen, professionally, had not said a word about it. They had both waited for it to steady, as if the hand belonged to a third person in the room.

Ross opened his eyes when she spoke and was quickly alert. Yes, he was fine. Box of birds and how was she? Good, good. What a nice day. He'd been for a walk earlier. He rotated his feet a few times, as if reminding himself that this was what walking entailed. Mary had caught sight of him but had kept her distance. He always looked like he was on a mission. She knew he took part in the daily outdoor exercise class—one of the few men who did—and once she'd spied him carrying two small dumbbells. Unusually for this cohort, Ross often wore short-sleeved polo shirts, presenting forearms which still looked strong. Proving something, she guessed. He'd always taken pride in his physical stamina, and as he ascended the ranks, getting trapped behind a desk, he made sure to stay fit, stay connected to the front line as much as he could.

He asked how they were settling in. Adjusting, she said. Yes of course, he said, there's a period of that. It's a big change, he said. Then they started talking about the daphne bushes which had come into bloom around the village. It turned out Ross had been a keen gardener. A lot of cops, in Mary's experience, liked plants. They liked booze and plants, and probably deployed them in similar stress-releasing ways. She had an image of one particular DI, near retirement age when she'd just started, a known bully, who lovingly tended a large collection of cacti in his office. There was talk of pricks sticking together of course but Mary had overheard this grizzled figure speak sweetly about the plants. Word was he even spoke *to* them. Ross remembered him at once. Wallace. Stu 'Wally' Wallace. 'Had his good points, I suppose,' he said. 'Cacti.'

'And he would always hold open the door for a woman,' said Mary.

'There you go.'

'Ladies first. But when you walked through, he would make himself as large as possible. It was hard not to make physical contact.'

'Yeah, Wally.'

'We all worked that out fast.'

Ross nodded slowly, grimacing. He rubbed his calf muscle. Was he in discomfort from Mary's story or from the leg? 'You must have put up with a lot. I always admired how you got on with things, Mary.'

'Did you?'

'Yes. It feels like we lived in a different country then. So many changes. It's good.'

'Do you remember,' she said, 'when the long leather boots came in on the job for females?'

'Not really.'

'Maybe '74 or something. Keep our legs warm. Up to then, we didn't have much.'

Ross smiled. 'I might be having a flashback.'

Was he being lewd? She remembered him as one of the least problematic. What did they used to say? *A real gentleman.*

'Winter at Trentham,' she said. 'Boy. Or on the beat in a southerly. I think my flashback is different to yours.'

'It got cold. I remember that. We were always too cold or too hot. There's better materials these days.'

'Do you remember Rosemary Gibson?'

'Who? No.'

'And Robin Christian.'

'Maybe that name is . . .'

'First ever women photographers, appointed in 1979. I came across Robin that year on a case. The sexual assault and murder of Angie Cook. Aged thirteen. Really nasty. Terrible scene. In a woolshed out by Mākara. And Robin walks in. I could have cried. Probably doesn't make much sense to you. But it was important.'

'No, I get it.' He looked out the window where one of the gardeners walked past with a bucket of weeds. 'Progress is slow.'

'People used to ask her, lower-ranking officers asked her, did she do weddings too, did she do fashion shows.'

'They call it a learning curve.'

'I don't know if curve is the right word. Cliff maybe. Sheer rock face. Immovable mountain of sexist rubbish. What do you think, Ross?'

'Could be right, Mary. Could be right.'

Why was she telling Ross Hayes all of this? She was remembering what Pete had said in the garden that day about her being a shit-stirrer. Being with her ex-boss had shuffled this part of herself forward again. 'And if you had a kid, that was it. Career over. They looked at me very hard. Some people were very unhappy about me coming back, like I was a terrible mother.'

'Different times.'

'Jesus, it was not that long ago.'

'Now we've got the Taliban.'

'What?'

'The Taliban, you know. Girls can't go to school.'

'Leaping sideways, Rosco. But okay. Sometimes I think the Taliban exists everywhere.' Mary didn't really know what she was saying. She was just annoyed—at him, at this place, at herself. She gestured around the lounge, with its collection of mostly female residents snoozing or turning the pages of magazines or staring at the giant mute TV on the wall. A pair of male carers in face masks and see-through surgical gloves were slowly assisting a bent woman from the room. She was sobbing her apologies. 'Even here.'

Ross raised his eyebrows and scanned the environment. He looked at his watch and made a motion as if he needed to get going. Where? 'I always enjoyed talking to you, Mary. Working with you. It was a big loss. Always had a sharp mind. I think the Taliban would take you out of the picture quite early on.'

The gardener was now on his knees, poking in a flower bed near the little pagoda where bowls players could sit watching in the shade.

She said, 'Remember that night you had to give me a lift back to the station on the back of your motorbike? I don't know why exactly we were in that position. We were always figuring things out on the fly, weren't we? Making it up on the spot.'

'Sounds about right, but I don't remember that one in particular, sorry.'

'The only reason I do is that it was the days before tights. They weren't around. Hard to believe. We had to wear stockings, with suspender belts.'

'Okay.'

'And this night, a car pulls up alongside us at the lights, and suddenly there's all this hooting and carry-on and I look across and these young blokes are all pointing at me. I realise my coat has been whipped back and my skirt has ridden up my leg. They're getting a really nice eyeful!'

'That's funny. Would have made their night.'

They looked out the window again. Then Mary said, 'Why didn't you push harder with Shaun Anderson?'

'With who?'

'Shaun Anderson. He was the driver when Will was killed at that camp in 1982.'

Ross rubbed his cheeks with one hand. Mary heard the stubble reacting. She could see him stiffen. He resented that she'd brought it up, that she'd ambushed him. The dynamic was familiar from long ago, when she'd bring him something about a case he didn't care to consider at that moment but which they both knew was significant. Even decent and obliging DI Hayes had his limits.

He said, 'I might need more . . .'

'Details?'

'I can hardly remember what I had for dinner yesterday.'

'Potato gratin and chicken in a yellow sauce which might have been mustard.' She and Pete had joined the dinner room. They'd eaten with a woman who used to run a large drapery shop until it was undercut by cheap imports. Mary kept thinking of some pun about it being curtains for the business.

Ross said, 'Mustard, you say? Colonel Mustard in the rest home with the golf club.' He leaned forward in his chair, preparing to lever himself up. The sharpness of his knees pressed through his trackpants. 'Sorry, Mary. I'm an oaf. It was such a terrible time. Unimaginable for you. For a mother.'

'Shaun Anderson was charged with manslaughter but then the charges were dropped.'

'Downgraded, I think. It's going back a way.'

'To dangerous driving causing death. Then he got off with more PD. Mitigating factors.'

'Was that it? Yes. Gosh. It was a tough moment. For all of us.'

'Tell me again how it all worked.'

'Oh Mary. Such long time ago for this struggling brain.'

'Anderson was a complete cowboy—is that how you remember it?'

'Sounds right,' he said. 'I wasn't in charge of course, as you know.'

'But you were on the team.'

Ross nodded and rubbed his face again. 'From memory, we had very few options.'

Mary said, 'Right. Manslaughter was never going to fly. The other boys who were in the back and got tossed out, they were all okay. Cuts and bruises.'

'You know all this, Mary, and it must be upsetting to bring it back.'

'Don't worry about me,' said Mary. 'So Will was just incredibly unlucky. To be knocked unconscious and to end up in a deeper part of the river where the current was. Whereas Anderson's lawyer got incredibly lucky. The bridge, you remember?'

Ross nodded.

They'd found that the bridge had been scheduled to be decommissioned, demolished. It was a known hazard. Just not known by the camp people. The council engineer's name was Derek Lonnard. These old names! No one was called Derek anymore. Were there any more Marys being made? He wore a jersey in court. Her sister Claire went for them, and she reported back, not that they asked for it. She gave them handwritten notes. Pete would walk out at this point, leaving the sisters to it. A hideous homespun jersey, Claire told her. He rubbed his glasses on the jersey. She always reported on his clothes, his gestures.

How she'd loved her sister for taking this on.

'It's coming back to me, sadly,' said Ross, finally taking it from her. 'It all got very messy. The lawyer suggesting that maybe the council should have been prosecuted, not Anderson. The bridge was an accident waiting to happen. How Anderson was just in the wrong spot at the wrong time. Our side . . . seeing how the cards were lining up . . . If it was me, Mary, in your shoes, I'd have felt the same way. No question. No question. If it was me.'

'No,' said Mary. 'The thing is, at the time, I couldn't have cared less. Nor could Pete. It wasn't . . . important. It wasn't the important thing.'

'I see.'

'We couldn't . . .' The lunch crew were wheeling in the covered metal vessels, bringing a sweetish smell of boiled vegetables. 'Because everything was . . . At the time, that was how we both felt, me and Pete. We let Will down. But now . . .'

'I don't think you let him down.'

'Well.'

'I don't think there are rules for any of this, Mary.'

'He's reached out,' she said.

'Who?'

'Shaun Anderson. He wants to meet. Some deathbed thing. Guilty conscience, I don't know.'

'Christ,' he said. 'What do you feel about that? Will you meet?'

It was decided. They would meet him. Yet Ross's question scored a hit. She didn't know what she felt. Until Pete had said they must certainly meet, she was undecided. She hadn't even really decided whether to tell him—then she'd come out with it, when Colin was there too. And of course she should never have withheld it from Pete for as long as she did. She saw how that had confused him, hurt him. She was not the sole keeper of the flame. It was good that Colin knew too. It was good that Ross knew. Everyone should know.

They waited a few moments in silence. Then another resident had appeared and was asking Ross something in a very quiet voice and pointing at the paper. If he was finished with it, could she possibly borrow it? For the crossword?

'Sorry, love,' said Ross, 'it's done. I always do it first thing.'

'Bother,' said the woman and walked off. She was really annoyed.

'These people, why don't they buy their own fucking paper?' Ross was on his feet. He was taking the opportunity to get away, and Mary didn't blame him. He put a hand on the arm of the chair to steady himself. This was a surprise. She hadn't seen him with a walking stick, but it magically appeared. 'Anyway,' he said, 'good luck. Good luck, Mary.'

Almost immediately they were miserable in the village, in their fine new home. Mary had not been able to say this to Ross Hayes or anyone. Give it time, they told themselves. It felt unlikely. Pete seemed depressed. She asked him if he was feeling okay, with his heart and so on. He waved her off. He missed his books. He hadn't unpacked his LPs. Their furniture and possessions looked odd in the new setting—worse than the air-filled stuff of the open homes. Shabby. Unsympathetic. *Old*. As though they were camping in a hotel. They felt ashamed somehow. But that wasn't the worst of it. They disliked being on the flat, though of course it was easier to get around. But get around what? The pretend streets, the crawling cars, the pretend letterboxes (black with gold lettering for the word POST). The word weighed on her. Post was what they'd become, Mary thought. Post-living. The painfully trimmed grass edges of the paved walking paths. The constant buzz and whine of mowers and weeders. The fanatically weeded flower beds. The insane prettiness of the shrubs and conforming trees. They felt drugged in the scented and circling routes. The tinted windows and ranch sliders flickering with shadows—sometimes the white nose of a small dog would shine through the tint. Naturally Mary and Pete escaped to the estuary and further to the beach, where they felt loosened, exposed, winded by the wind. Yet they still had to go back and sit under the heat pump.

They went to one session of the village choir. Pete had sung a bit. He still hummed. A nice woman called Penny stood in front of them with an acoustic guitar. They did rounds of 'Sloop John B'. It sounded fine. Mary listened to Pete join in. She'd not heard him sing in so long. Maybe he was softening towards their new life, and maybe she could do the same. Hello, their fellow residents said to them. Welcome! We always love new people. Lots of smiling, lots of encouragement. See you next week. *Around Nassau town we did roam.* Afterwards, Pete said to her, 'All these old people singing about getting into a fight and staying up all night. I can't go back.'

Maybe they were simply in denial. This phase would pass. The people they met were very pleasant. The shared meals in the large dining room were pleasant. Sure, it was good to stand up and walk out, leaving the dishes and the clean-up for others. These others, though, seemed to loom large. You were aware not of being served but of being looked after. She and Pete were becoming children again. The woman next to her looked at her stew and said, 'Oh goodie!' Mary watched an elderly gent tuck some bread rolls into his trouser pocket. Their eyes had met and he gave her an encouraging wink. *Go on, help yourself.* Balloons often hung from the ceilings. Wherever they walked, balloons. Someone explained these were blown up by residents as therapy for respiratory conditions.

There was an oversupply of bunting and fairy lights.

They saw their neighbours walking to a concert in the main building wearing paper party hats. Mary and Pete ducked down sometimes to avoid being spotted. Meanwhile they did nothing about contacting the daughter of Shaun Anderson—was this the true toxin? Once they sorted that out, perhaps they could settle into their new life. Then they could really get into happy hour.

Eight

Some months after Will was killed, Mary was on a job in the Hutt. There'd been a series of break-ins on High Street. Three restaurants had lost kitchen equipment, including some seriously large and expensive items. The thieves had done their research and come with the right tools, getting away with industrial-size dishwashers, a new stove, freezer units and anything else that was lying around: knives, cutlery, dinnerware, glasses, even tablecloths and napkins. They had blow torches, trolleys, sufficient muscle to move it all, and a van or truck. It looked like they were stealing to order, or to set up their own place. The case was out of the normal range—big news—but the Hutt cops would still have handled it, only they were down on numbers following sickness and retirements. Hence Mary was re-deployed. She felt the push at her back. *You go, Mary, and sort it out eh.* I'd prefer not to, she said. She couldn't imagine starting anew, making connections, establishing herself again, being looked at, even for a short time. But it was an order.

The restaurants, it turned out, were just the beginning. Presumably the same crew, or someone inspired by their daring and success (always keep an open mind), had then hit a jewellery shop, an electronics place and a sports store. They usually struck very early in the morning, and always dodged the beefed-up patrols which were now in place. People were worried and upset. Some owners had taken to sleeping in their shops. The paper carried stories about a crime wave and the general incompetence of the police. A letter to the editor alleged the fridge in the Lower Hutt Police Station had been stolen. Two men had walked out with it in broad daylight. This was untrue. The men were from the hardware store, taking it in for repair.

A vigilante group had formed. There was talk of a round-the-clock roster, with men sitting in cars, ready with softball bats and crow bars. One of the group's organisers was ex-police and a former colleague of the DI in charge of the op. Rumour was the two men had come to blows in the garden bar of the Bellevue. This was true. The cops were being made fools of. Morale was low.

That was the atmosphere Mary entered. She didn't care. If other officers tried to get her onside or explain their situation, the various pressures they were under, she gave them nothing. Yeah, she told them. Yep. Tell me about it. She didn't linger in the tearoom or hang out in the staff bar, saying with dark overtones that she wasn't doing all that again. People understood something had happened with Mary. There were rumours. She let them circulate. One day she overheard a constable using the words 'cold bitch'. Okay. Fair call. Most days in the car she didn't have a partner. Relief all round.

She knew she was being sent out to the Hutt because they didn't know what to do about her now she had a dead kid. Having a live kid was bad enough. She'd walked out on the counselling sessions, having completed just two hours of the allotted ten. Ten hours with the police psychologist—they had to be kidding. It was for the psychologist and not for her, those ten hours. So he could learn something, or just clock it on his timesheet. He wore sandals. The tops of his toes were covered in curly black hair. She felt mean and petty to judge him on his feet but there they were, right under her nose, and she was supposed to avoid them how? Wouldn't a good psychologist know that psychologically he should meet his patient/client wearing shoes?

His name was Philip. He was a bit younger than her. He had a very minor stammer, usually on words beginning with 'f', and he would blush if it got him. His own name was a problem. In the two sessions they had, she developed a terrible fascination with drawing him into vocabulary which might trip him up. Something was *farmed* out. She'd been to a *film* recently. A *famous* person said something. There were *fringe* benefits. It was *freezing* outside. The game was cruel, and he was nimble and practised in avoidance. Did he know she was doing it? For a psychologist the better question was why she was doing it. Because she was unhappy and vengeful, she guessed.

Drawing a blank with her feelings, he aimed for strategies.

'I don't know what a strategy is,' she told Philip.

'It's a "what if this, then let's try this". Faced with a situation which might be difficult, we can be organised to respond. Pre-planning, I suppose.'

'Okay,' she said. 'What situation?'

'Anything. Just whatever happens to you on a daily basis. And there's a response in you.'

'What sort of response?'

He smiled. 'I can't tell you what sort of response. That's internal to you.'

'So I don't need to tell you my response? It's private.'

'Of course, Mary. Though sometimes articulating our responses can—'

'Worry people.'

Philip looked at her, checking. 'Do you think people are worried by some of your responses?'

'Can I control how other people respond? Is that a fair expectation?'

'It's not a question of f-f-f-fairness.'

No matter how hard he tried, the little stammer cut into his thinking and, disappointed in himself, he would often set off on a different tack. Mary knew she was a nightmare for him, though that might have been making a larger claim than she warranted. It was likely that counselling a bunch of cops who didn't think they needed it was routinely tough and thankless. She was in a long line, surely. Still, it was pretty punishing the way she immediately converted his well-intentioned efforts at conversation into a quasi-legal interrogation. She couldn't stop trying to catch him out. It was as if they were being taped for evidential reasons and neither of them could afford to concede anything on the grounds that it would be used against them. It was nuts. Philip must have seen this too. The last half hour of what turned out to be their second and final session, he was almost silent, matching her. This felt to Mary like a reason to abandon the whole thing, though Philip probably believed his withdrawal was just another step along the way. Whatever, the counselling lapsed and her boss didn't make a move to insist on its resumption.

Pete knew nothing about this. He had his own suffering to deal with, and they had no way of talking about what had happened. She noticed he'd stopped reading. She saw how she'd relied on Pete having an interior life unconnected to her. She liked it. His nose in a book—good! She enjoyed his resourcefulness. It wasn't all down to her or to their relationship to provide. Were books where he put his feelings?

Without a book in his hands, Pete seemed in great need, and she had nothing to give him.

One cold winter's night on car patrol, with absolutely nothing happening the length of High Street, Mary decided to drive around some side streets. Quickly she was in a residential area near the Hutt Recreation Ground, where she thought she saw a figure crouching by a car. It was too dark to see properly, so she drove closer. Someone was definitely there. She pulled over, wound down the window and shone her torch. The person shielded their eyes. They were on all fours on the driver's side of the car.

Mary called out, 'Stand up please.' The figure made a noise and continued to move about on their hands and knees, as if they were looking for something. Mary pulled over and got out of the squad car. She pointed her torch at the ground as she approached. 'Can I help you?' It was a woman in her eighties, Mary guessed. 'Ma'am?'

'If you could shine your torch down in this area,' said the woman. 'I dropped my keys. They must have bounced away. They might be under my car but I can't see.'

Mary crouched down. It was disappointing not to be engaging with the crime wave, but policing took many forms. The keys were in behind the rear wheel; Mary scooped them out and gave them to the woman.

'Oh, you're my life-saver.'

She saw that the woman's walking stick was resting against the side of the car. She handed it to her. 'You off somewhere?'

'I was but now I think I'll give up on that plan. I went back inside but could I find a torch that worked? I've been scrabbling around here for ages. I was supposed to be going down to High Street, but by the time I find a park and wobble there, I'll be too late for the service. I don't like to walk in late.'

Mary watched her start to move off on the walking stick. 'Thank you again.'

'Wait,' said Mary. 'I can give you a lift if you like. I'm going back that way.'

The woman turned around. 'No, no, I don't want to cause you any more trouble.'

'No trouble at all. Would you be able to get home okay?'

The woman considered this for a moment. 'I could get a taxi, do you think?'

'Come on then.'

In the car, Mary said, 'How fast do you need to get there? Do we need to put the siren on?'

'Can you do that?'

'No.'

Her name was Alice. Widowed. A teacher her whole life.

'I've never been in a police car. I'm eighty-three.'

'You've led a spotless life, Alice.'

'Let's not go too far. Is there a gun in the car?'

'No.'

'I smell a gun.'

'Really?'

'My father had guns, on the farm. He had a cabinet. I got a whiff of the cabinet. Funny.'

Alice was going to church. Not a church which people like her parents or even her siblings might recognise, she said. 'Full of joy.'

A burst from the car radio covered whatever grunting sound came from Mary.

'I found it late,' said Alice. 'Religion feels better at night.'

'I'll take your word for it,' said Mary.

'My children are worried I'll leave the church all my money. Do you have children?'

Mary didn't miss a beat. 'Yes, a son.'

'He must be so proud of his mother. How old is he?'

'Eleven. But he's . . . no longer with us.' No longer with us? As if she were a preacher. Dearly departed.

'Dear, I am so sorry.'

'That's okay.'

They drove on in silence.

'I can't imagine it. Losing a child.'

'Nor can I,' said Mary. They were almost outside the place—a large warehouse, just across from the river's stopbank, surrounded by car yards. Neon letters were fixed above the entrance: City Church. Mary thought of a casino. She pulled into the loading area. 'This do?'

'Perfect,' said Alice.

'That'll be five dollars.'

'Sorry?'

'I'm having you on, Alice.'

'Oh, right.' She was trying to release her seatbelt but couldn't work it. Mary turned on the car's inside light and leaned over to help. The belt was obscured by Alice's coat and Mary had to get even closer to find the button. Her head was almost in front of Alice's stomach. Then she felt a pressure on her head. She waited there underneath it. Alice had rested her hand gently on Mary's hair. It felt wonderful. It felt silly. Mary closed her eyes. 'Dear,' said Alice softly. She stroked. 'My dear.'

They remained like this for a while before Mary straightened again and Alice was free.

Alice said, 'Will you come in?'

'Where?' said Mary. 'Oh no, no. Got to get moving, you know.'

'You're at work.'

'Crime never sleeps.'

'But it rests,' said Alice. 'I just worked it out—you thought I was breaking into a car!'

'It looked suspicious.'

'If I'd been a great hulking man, you still would have approached. How brave.'

Mary was now out of the car and helping Alice towards the entrance. Behind the automatic sliding doors she could see a brightly lit space, with a curving bank of seats and a central aisle leading to the stage which was covered in flowers. The doors opened and live music could be heard, drums and guitars. Mary stopped and let go of Alice's elbow. 'Have a great night,' she said.

'Will you help me to my seat, dear? It's just in there.'

The church was almost full. Five or six hundred people. Unbelievable. On a Wednesday night in winter. Mary felt like laughing out loud. She remembered the first time she'd visited a jail when she was a recruit. A similar shock. Look at all these people! Where are they from and how did they come to be here?

She took off her police cap. It was as if she'd removed a piece of her skull.

The people in the back row moved along to allow Alice a seat, smiling at the newcomers, and suddenly there were two seats and Mary had also taken her place. Alice touched Mary's knee and smiled.

'Not really my thing,' Mary whispered.

Alice nodded, not hearing, or ignoring her. She'd passed through into a different realm.

The band was quite loud. A man in a white shirt and jeans had walked on to the stage carrying a microphone. He raised his arms to the ceiling and, as one, the whole crowd rose to its feet. 'Brothers and sisters!' the man called out. 'Brothers and sisters!' Beside her, Alice lifted her walking stick a few feet in the air. She was grinning broadly. People had their hands up, their heads thrown back, their eyes closed. Five or six hundred people on a winter's night in a converted warehouse. They didn't know or care about her son. Alice had forgotten him already. It was astonishing how this happened. She—Mary—would have to care about him. She saw it for the first time. She would have to find ways of caring which didn't eject her from society. How? She had to find ways of being with Pete again. They had to find ways of being in the house without their son. The band was coming to a climax. Mary slipped from the room before the final cymbal crash. With a sizzle, it chased her from the doors.

In the squad car she drove to an empty, unlit street, pulled over and wept and wept. It was the first time she had cried since losing Will. It was what the psychologist had assumed she'd already done. You've had the tears, he said when they first met and he was explaining the process. Why assume such a thing? She'd taken against him even more. There was a box of tissues on the table between them and she was staunch.

Approximately six hours after fleeing the City Church, and more from luck than anything, she was part of the team which stopped a truck in Petone and discovered welding equipment, overalls, balaclavas and nearly six thousand dollars in cash. The four men in the truck lacked a credible explanation for these items. Working from the vehicle registration and the men's driver's licences, they raided a number of properties that same morning and located enough stolen property to fill the Hutt station's lock-up. It was a triumph. They'd arrange the loot for the newspaper photographer. Front page.

At the debrief the next day, the DI called Mary their lucky charm. Now she did burst out laughing. Hearing those two words. Lucky. Charm. A real explosion. Snot came out her mouth. The other cops might have thought of this as a sign of modesty or something—oh no, please don't single me out when it was a team effort. But the snot? The barking? She saw that a few of them were taken aback, as she was. She hadn't meant to make the extraordinary noise. Who was this weirdo? 'We hope you go well back in town,' the DI added quickly. And they all applauded that. It was something to get on board with—the end of Mary's placement, thank Christ. She herself was clapping herself. Well done me! There was a celebratory morning tea, but the catering had turned up an hour earlier and been demolished by people eating at their desks, turning away and snuffling up the muffins like ferrets.

A long time after this all happened, when Mary was finally telling Pete about what she'd done in the Hutt—when they were both ready to listen to each other—he said, 'Do you think this woman Alice and the visit to the church had something to do with stopping that truck and arresting the thieves?' Mary was shocked. She laughed and asked what he meant. He said he didn't know what he meant. He was just adding two and two and coming up with five. 'The way you told it,' he said, 'I thought you were making a connection.'

'No,' she said. 'God abandoned Lower Hutt a long time ago.'

Nine

After Will died, many of Pete's work colleagues at the library had book suggestions. Of course they did. They believed this was the answer; or, if not the answer, then in the books were the right questions for him—he supposed—to ponder. They saw him as full of pondering time, wise now and a bit beyond them. Remote, adrift, until he came slowly back to them. They'd have no doubt about his return. The old Pete, with his gentle ironic manner, his kindness, his vast institutional knowledge, would one day be among them again. They were nice people, floundering. In their position he would have been the same. Here were their thoughtful ideas about how to help. Books about grief. Novels about grieving parents. They photocopied poems and put them in his tray. They were very kind and hopeless. He didn't tell them he couldn't read. Not just the books or the poems. He couldn't read anything. Even if he'd wanted to read all these things about and by people who'd gone through the same thing as he and Mary were going through—and for now, he didn't—he found it impossible. Cognitively.

He'd taken the week's bereavement leave, spent it clearing up under the house, trying to tire himself out so he might sleep. It didn't work. He avoided print for the week, hoping he might come back to it renewed and able. Didn't happen. The words moved around. People's names danced about: who was who? It was like Russian to him, a Russian novel set in New Zealand. With the newspaper, he studied the photos and worked back from there. He didn't confess anything to Mary. He was terrified and curious. Where would it end? Nouns and adjectives—they were in strange combinations. He looked at a sentence and the verb walked from the middle to the end to the beginning and back again. Extreme sudden-onset dyslexia, he wondered. Was this in the literature? Well, he couldn't research it since, on looking, the available texts were no longer glued in place but floating and wholly unavailable to his brain. It was quite funny and stupid. Work documents were blurry blocks of language. He was careful to ask anyone who came to him with paper to sit down and have a chat about it. 'I'd like to hear it in your own words,' he said. Listening to speech was not without its problems but it was much better than reading. He could write, but slowly, as if learning to write. His slowness with everything was fully tolerated. People understood. He'd not been speedy to begin with. He was always conscientious and considered. They all thought he was now even more like himself.

When the problem first occurred, he wondered if he'd had a stroke. At home he took off his clothes and stood in front of the long bathroom mirror. He was more or less symmetrical. Nothing drooped that hadn't been in that condition before. He lifted each arm in turn. He looked tired. Yes, in his face. More than that, individual parts of himself looked tired. The skin on the undersides of his arms. His toneless thighs and legs. Someone had sculpted an odd falling angle starting just below his navel to his genitals, almost as if he had a hernia. He explored his torso with his fingers and small spots began to stand out. Splotches of rash. Ugly tufts of hair sprouted from his upper arms—this was new and unwelcome. The hair on his head was thin and a bit too long. Mary had not come near him with the scissors for months. Who could blame her? Even when he paid attention and tried to self-groom, the unkempt bits of him showed through. He was ugly. Disgusted, he quickly dressed again. He wasn't only disgusted by his body. He was disgusted he was thinking about his body. No one cared and he didn't either. To wish himself dead was also the wrong thing to wish. It again placed his actions in the centre.

Wasn't he dead?

He carried on. He got by, burying the problem. He felt a little like those people who wear all their clothes on the plane to save weight in their luggage—why, though? Because there was too much of something around him or that he bore on his person. Working in a library was now a sort of cosmic joke for a man unable to read.

One day he went to work and it was nearly lunchtime before he realised he was wearing two different shoes—one brown and one black. Of all the things happening to him, for some reason this was peculiarly horrifying. The shoes! He avoided walking around. At lunchtime he almost ran to the nearest shoe shop and bought a new pair. He entered the shop and quickly sat down, taking off the odd pair, putting them in his bag and walking around the place in his socks. That evening, Mary said, without interest, 'New shoes.'

Then one weekend, when Mary was out, he looked in on Will's bedroom. They'd not changed anything. There was no hurry, though he understood Mary wanted to act in some way. She'd mentioned Will's clothes and how they might eventually go to another child. Some of the other possessions too, she said. The games. It would be nice to think of them in circulation. He'd not managed much in reply to this. She was just planting the idea, he knew. She saw him as requiring tact. It was infuriating in a way.

Pete scanned the walls: the *Raiders of the Lost Ark* poster; the Extinct Species poster. On the floor by the window, the chess set, their game in progress. Will didn't care at all about winning—anything. He was curious about patterns. The crammed bookshelf—so many bookmarks! Will was always reading three or four books at the same time without a strong need to finish any of them. His notebooks recording the feeding schedules of his animals. Yes, the faint whiff of animals still—like hay or damp fur. The cardboard box with window holes cut in its side. The Stanley knife and the bottles of glue. Rolls of masking tape and packing tape. The pair of sneakers under the bed. Old cut-up shoeboxes there too. The pillow! Pete remembered the day he'd entered the room and seen the pillow had been moved. Mary had puffed up the pillow. He was staggered by this. The dent of their son's head was gone. He couldn't speak to her about it, which was silly. What did he expect? That the room would be preserved forever? He'd pulled back the duvet and seen that the sheets were missing! She'd washed the sheets and not re-made the bed. The cruelty. Was she trying to wipe Will out? Treat him as no more than a house guest who'd moved on?

Other aspects were changing as time passed. The smell was different today. The unused objects were slowly losing their scents. No one being in the room was obviously the crucial factor. Regularly Pete sat on the bed for ten or fifteen minutes, just to activate the air. He knew he was being foolish and morbid. Sitting with the dead child's things. Feeling important and connected, unlike other people who moved on. Feeling special. Rejecting all the advice. Suffering more and knowing better. He knew nothing.

He went downstairs and poured himself a glass of water. It went to his head like alcohol. It was the most extraordinary drink of his life. His teeth ached. His throat burned. He felt things clearing.

Part of him felt the loss of this loss. Wasn't it too soon?

The newspaper was on the kitchen table. He picked it up and read perfectly the headline and the story underneath. Muldoon's wage and price freeze. He turned some pages and understood whatever he read. So this part was over.

Shortly after he'd regained his ability to read, Mary's mother, Patricia, came for afternoon tea. She had made a lemon cake for them, with a separate container of lemon drizzle, only the container had leaked and most of it had ended up on the floor of her car. She was talking about this when she came into the house. She was really annoyed. 'Such a sticky mess,' she said. 'I don't know what I'm going to do about it.' And Pete had to go out to her car with a soapy bowl of water and a cloth to clean it up, even though Patricia had told him she would do it. Mary had told her not to worry, they would clean it up. All three of them ended up outside, dealing to the spill. It was a crazily windy day and Mary had to hold the car door open while Pete bent inside and her mother gave unnecessary instructions. The lemon drizzle had gone under the passenger seat as well as on the foot mat.

It struck him that Mary's mother had this habit of drawing people into her crises, whether big or small. His own mother was the exact opposite. If she'd lost a pottle of lemon drizzle on the floor of her car, she wouldn't have mentioned it. She'd have pretended there was never any lemon drizzle. And she would have criticised her own cake for being dry.

Cleaning the car, with the wind almost taking the door

off its hinges so that both women had to grip it, Pete thought, This is how normal people behave. Mary and her mother were shrieking and laughing as they battled the gusts and called for Pete to hurry up. It was the first time he'd heard Mary laugh since Will had died.

Patricia was impulsive, he supposed. Things happened to her and she reacted. She said what she thought and felt. People liked being around her. Whereas his mother gave off the feeling that she didn't need others.

He saw these things now.

Mary's mother had somehow broken through. They saw more of her than before. Mary needed her. They were always on the phone too. And she was there for them. Slowly, he felt their world resuming, or at least beginning to take its new shape, minus Will.

It was odd then that some days he resented Patricia and her encouraging lightness, and he longed for his mother's heavier nature to enter and hold everything at arm's length, hold it down.

After Will was killed, it turned out his mother had a variety of views on what was likely to happen. She didn't push these views on to Pete and Mary. They came out almost by chance, it seemed. When they were discussing something about the house, Margaret said, 'Well, eventually, you will have to sell it.' She also assumed that Mary would now quit her job. Again, it wasn't advice; Margaret had somehow concluded this was what would happen. When she said this, Mary asked why.

'Oh, it's nothing to do with me,' said his mother. 'But after all this, I would have thought it'd be hard to carry on in that environment.'

He and Mary had discussed her job and not reached a

conclusion. Avoid acting in haste was one of the slogans they'd received.

'We'll see,' said Pete.

His mother never suggested that he should leave the library. Presumably being around books and book borrowers was fine for the bereaved.

'I'd like to carry on,' said Mary.

Margaret briefly narrowed her eyes. 'It's your decision.'

'The thing is,' said Mary, 'the environment—I like it.'

'Good colleagues,' said Margaret.

'Hmm.'

After Margaret left, Mary said to Pete, 'When I said that thing to your mother, I meant something else.'

'What did you mean?'

'I like being with criminals.'

'What?'

'Not as in, I am secretly twisted. A fireman who lights fires. I mean, I'm alive in their company.'

'The adrenaline, you mean. Catching them. It's exciting.'

'No. I mean something else. I can't explain it.'

'You like it.'

'I feel they're there, you know.'

He almost screamed. 'No, sorry.'

'It's difficult to put into words.'

'You think they're "there". As opposed to everyone else who's not there?'

'I think a lot of police feel it.'

'You're two sides of the same coin?'

She shook her head. 'Not really. Maybe. I don't know.'

He tried not to respond. He was exhausted. He couldn't cope with what Mary was saying. She was being deliberately perverse, talking to rile him up, talking against his mother—

she'd always had a funny relationship with Margaret. He should have walked out of the room. 'Come on, Mary, a lot of it is just sad. Tragic. A waste. What are you saying about liking being with the people you have to arrest? All those victims too, whose lives are turned upside down. You think about them all the time. I know you do.'

'Yes, that's true too.'

'And you complained about it. You've talked about leaving.'

She nodded.

She was infuriating. He should have dropped it. He knew they were moving towards something awful. He felt ill. He said, 'How can you say you like being with criminals? It makes no sense.'

'I didn't say it did.'

'And would you like to spend time with someone like Shaun Anderson?'

'What?'

'With him, with Shaun Anderson, a person like that?'

She was still and unblinking, just staring at him as if he was a monster.

'Is that what you're saying, Mary?' His heart was pummelling him. The blood was pulsing—he felt it knocking in the back of his head. 'You'd like to be in his company because he's there?'

'Don't be cruel,' she murmured.

'Am I the cruel one?'

'Pete, don't.'

He felt demented, as if his arms would fly off. He held them at his sides with great effort and turned away from her. When he turned back, Mary had put her head in her hands and her body shook. He should have approached her. Go to her, he told himself. Yet he didn't have the right suddenly. It would have made as much sense as hugging someone on the street who was crying. She was so separate, like a post or a chair.

It was the first time they'd spoken the name between them. He felt ashamed. He'd long imagined breaking through somehow, and now he was sick with regret. 'I'm sorry,' he said stiffly. He didn't move. 'I'm sorry, Mary.' Even using her name felt sarcastic.

There was a Citizens Advice Bureau in the same building as the branch library where Pete worked then. Over the years Pete had come to know a few of the staff who worked there. They'd bump into each other at the café across the road. Sometimes they sat together at one of the tables. There was always gossip to share about the library building and its various inhabitants. In one of the other rented spaces there was a business consultancy run by a couple who'd ended up in prison for fraud. That had been exciting. He was shifty and she was rude—it all made sense.

'How disappointing,' someone had said. This was Helen.

Helen was around Pete's age. She'd trained as a lawyer but had married just after graduating and only properly started her law career once the kids were in school. She'd worked at a Community Law office and had joined CAB two years ago. Her marriage had ended, and he had the kids most of the time. The arrangement was at Helen's request. This was fairly scandalous, though it seemed to suit everyone. Another slightly incongruous fact: Helen was an accomplished skier. Somehow Pete associated skiing with other markers: affluence, social confidence, robustness. Helen was thin, fragile-looking, indoorsy. Money probably wasn't a huge problem but nor was Helen noticeably well off; she dressed plainly. Apparently, she was always going up to the mountain alone. She didn't add up.

Pete had learned most of this from Helen's co-workers in their casual talk about families, holidays, careers. Helen herself didn't say much. She was, he thought, a private person. When she leaned forward to drink her coffee, her long black hair fell across her shoulders, obscuring her face. Then she would sit up suddenly, pin her hair back behind her ears and look around, as though surfacing from some deep moment, vaguely affronted. He supposed she was seen as 'odd' by her colleagues. They certainly had a special tone for her. There was a 'Helen' who they liked to gently and experimentally tease, conjuring a person Pete didn't quite believe in, someone who might appear to be critical and constantly unimpressed but who was really only joking. She wasn't joking though.

'What do you mean, Helen?' one of them asked.

'Fraudsters,' said Helen, with a kind of shrug, 'shouldn't they be less obvious?'

There followed a conversation about fraudsters they had known and whether it was advantageous or not to appear dodgy. Helen had zoned out, he saw. Soon she stood up and, without a word, walked back in the direction of the CAB office. Classic Helen. She was one of those adults who, like children, never said hello or goodbye—what was the point? People saw you were there and they saw you leave.

There was a way in which she was like Will. It struck him now, this connection. The single-mindedness, the bluntness that was without malice.

Possibly in the same way the others had projected their versions of Helen, ages ago Pete too had made her into a figure with whom he'd formed a kind of relationship. At least he thought there was an understanding between them. It was all based on nothing, of course. A look or two. Some small exchange by which he'd separated himself from her colleagues and from the other library staff. From time to time you had these figures who moved through your life and fantasies developed and dissolved. One time he'd been invited to talk to the CAB staff about how the library's resources might contribute to their work and the needs of their clients. Helen had turned up at the session late, not asked a single question, yet he had the impression she alone was fully engaged—or rather, that for those periods when she did seem to focus on what he was telling them, she was extracting the core. He had the strange feeling of being a teacher in front of the school's most brilliant pupil, a person who could demolish the teacher if she wished. No doubt he was over-thinking all of this. The others all busily wrote things down and put up their hands. He seemed to have covered their questions already in his talk. Helen knew it. She thought they were all very boring.

In the first weeks of his return to work after Will's death, Pete avoided the café and most social interaction. He took his lunch to a nearby park. He found it awkward and overwhelming to deal with people's sympathy. More than that, he dreaded the idea that very soon he would slip back into the old life, as if what had happened was not much really and there were all these other subjects ready to flood the emptiness, obscuring the great chasm. He didn't want to talk to anyone about it and he wanted to talk about only this. He was stuck. As a sort of solution, he found some tasks for himself in the small stack room, where he could stay busy and solitary. The low lighting, the smell of glue, the unwanted titles—it was comforting. Quickly people understood his situation—which didn't help either. How could they truly understand? The ragged sense of pride he felt gnawed at him.

He couldn't remember seeing Helen in the library until one afternoon she was there. He was pushing a trolley of books to the sorting area. The issues desk was unattended. He stepped forward. 'Hello there, can I help?'

She was hesitating. He'd never seen Helen hesitate before, though he immediately sensed the cause. When she began to speak, it was, surprisingly, some version of speeches he'd heard from any number of well-meaning people. Condolences, mumbled words, low-energy expressions. *Your son. Devastating. Mumble. Help.* She was especially unskilled at it.

Without thinking, he said, 'Disappointing.'

'Sorry?' she said.

Instantly they were both flummoxed. She was not being herself and he was not being himself.

'Thank you, I mean,' he said. He was affected by her incompetence; it bred his own.

She peered at him. Finally, he broke the look. 'Quiet day?' he said.

'Pretty quiet,' she said. 'What about you?'

He had no idea what they were talking about.

A few days after that they were at the park together, eating their lunches. It was the first time this had happened. Helen had followed him, or she'd come out of the building just behind him, and he'd turned and nodded at her, and somehow that had meant they were now together on the same park bench with a space between them where someone else could easily have sat.

She ate with total self-absorption, head down. The lunch,

in her plastic container, seemed mostly lettuce. There was a hardboiled egg, which she put in her mouth whole, as if she were in a movie and she had to get rid of some incriminating evidence. Eating was separate to talking. He liked this. Again, he thought of his son.

What to talk about? It wasn't clear this was even required. Certainly, the idea of talking about their children, his dead one and her separated ones, was not on the agenda.

When they'd finished eating, he mentioned the skiing and her trips to the mountain, but this didn't seem to interest her much once she learned he didn't ski. He guessed she felt he was humouring her. His inquiries about her work were also misses. That world was somehow irrelevant once she left it. Really he didn't know what to say to Helen. He saw how funny it was that he was trying to engage with this person who'd sought him out. The bereaved parent! The star of the show. He Who Was Suffering. She seemed to be making him work for it. Except she wasn't. She didn't seem to care.

They sat in silence and then he began speaking, without thinking or planning. He told her about the man he'd seen the other day when he was driving up Adelaide Road. The man had seemed to collapse on the footpath, and Pete had slowed down, looked back. If it was a collapse, it was controlled. He drove on slowly. There were pedestrians about and they would help the man if he needed help. Pete saw that a woman further along the footpath was looking back in the direction of the man. An hour later when Pete was driving back the other way, he passed the man again; he was now a few hundred metres along the road. He hadn't got very far. This time Pete pulled over. The woman he'd seen was standing facing the man, a gap of about a hundred metres between them. The man was prostrating himself on the footpath every few metres, raising his hands to the air and then sinking to his knees before lying on the concrete. He stayed face down for a while, then he stood up and looked at the woman, who took a large stride backwards. This was the man's cue to take a large step forward. Was he a monk? Some kind of acolyte undergoing a test or a ritual? He was dressed ordinarily. The man and the woman, he thought, looked Thai, perhaps. It was a striking thing to see on Adelaide Road, Pete told Helen.

Helen looked at him. 'Are you that man?'
'What?'
'Is this a story about you?'
'No, this is something I saw. I was driving.'
'Am I supposed to be the woman?'
He laughed. 'No, Helen, this really happened!'
'I see.'

The weather had changed and the wind had come up, taking the temperature down. They walked back towards the library in silence. Pete was thinking about how he hadn't told the story of the monk to Mary. Why not? Because he would have thought of himself as the monk. It was true! He understood it now. When he saw the man lying face down on the footpath, he'd imagined himself. Could he do that? Lie on the footpath in broad daylight, crawl along for hours, exposed. Should he do that? Yes! Why not? It was how his grief felt. It would have been in accord with his grief had he been asked to perform it. Quickly he'd suppressed the thought. Helen was right about him. He thought Helen was some kind of witch, with her dark hair and her ability to see through things. Not fully, however. When he'd seen the woman positioned ahead of the man, facing him and acting as a kind of magnet or a force commanding his slow and painful progress—getting up, moving, going down, getting up—and all in the undiluted heat of a cloudless afternoon, it wasn't Helen he'd thought of. Did he imagine Mary? Being with Helen had made him miss Mary. For a moment he might have had the idea that there was something between him and Helen, something reckless. Christ. He'd not thought of anyone else in all the years he'd been with Mary. This was what happened after a Big Life Event, was it? You went off the rails. Nothing mattered anymore. You were a librarian and now you were a vampire.

At the library, he said to Helen, 'Thank you for a nice lunch.'

It wasn't clear if she'd heard him. He felt grateful to her nonetheless. It was over. He'd survived. He would finish his duties in the stack room and step back into his life. Was that the meaning of the man or monk lying on the footpath, then getting up?

On one visit to the Special Care Unit, his mother had asked him where he thought people went. She didn't say 'die'. He'd noticed she almost never spoke of dying. 'Killing' was quite often in her vocabulary.

She said, 'We say, "Oh there's a heavenly place, even though we know there isn't." We say, "Oh he had such a great life!" We mustn't say otherwise. It's important not to say, "But where is he? Where has he gone?"'

They were sitting in the main lounge area, the large TV showing a cooking programme on mute. Some of the residents were watching it; some watched Pete, as if he were a show. There was a man in the armchair next to Pete. His arms hung down, his fingertips swinging rhythmically across the carpet. His head was on his chest, though he wasn't resting. His body seemed rigid in concentration.

'Now I've been watching people here and it's very interesting,' said his mother. 'I think people slowly edge towards something. Gradually they start to fade out. They know it too. It's all agreed.' His mother had begun to laugh, aware of how strange she sounded to herself but also intoxicated. 'They move sideways.' She looked at Pete, satisfied that this problem had a solution. 'What do you think?'

Pete said he thought that was probably a good way to think of it. 'A kind of sideways shuffle maybe.'

'Yes!' she told him, very happy to have his agreement. 'There are two women here in exactly this position. One of them carries a small bag, as if she's always going somewhere. The other one sort of tags along. She's not really as capable as the one with the bag, though we have to pretend this isn't the case. I used to be quite irritated by them. I mean, where were they going? But now I've changed my thinking. Now I think they're preparing to leave. Although "leave" isn't quite right. Fade out. Very gradually, they'll disappear. You won't be able to say when it happened. It's subtle. Almost unnoticeable. Has to be. No one remarks on it because that would mean it hasn't achieved the objective. I've only been able to work out the process by some very careful observation.'

The man beside them had then begun to move his chair in small jumps by gripping it underneath and hopping forward a few centimetres at a time. It took some effort, and Pete was surprised at the man's strength.

His mother touched Pete's arm. 'See this. Soon someone will come and tell him to stop. They'll let him get so far and then they'll arrive. It's unbelievable cruelty. Imagine working so hard to advance like that and then someone comes and tells you, "No! Back!" Really unbelievable. But this is how they operate.'

They watched as the man, after a rest, resumed his hopping. The others who'd been watching the TV now watched the man. He'd moved a couple of metres into the middle of the room. Everyone seemed focused on his journey, willing its success. He was suddenly a great heroic figure. He carried their hopes. From the kitchen area, Pete heard one of the carers say the man's name.

His mother said, 'We all know that people now don't really get sick. Not anymore. Everyone lives on and on. Look at us! It's just not possible to kill us all. That's why this process of gradual disappearance works so well.'

Ten

Before Claire came home to die, she spent several weeks in a large room at the far end of the neuro ward. Further operations had been ruled out and an external shunt ran from her head to a plastic pouch on the floor. Once the pressure was relieved, the shunt could come out and Claire could be transferred to another ward, to a better environment. None of this was certain. Several crises came and went, yet she held on.

She was unable to walk or move her limbs much. She had to be fed by a small plastic spoon. The tumour had taken away almost everything, including nearly all her speech. She had a single word left: 'Home'. She would repeat this word through the night. It came from her raw throat, sounding deep and ragged. 'Home,' she growled. 'Home!'

Colin, aged seventeen, couldn't bear it. 'Can you please persuade her to stop saying it, Auntie Mary?'

'I don't know if I can, darling,' she said.

'You're her sister. She listens to you.'

Which wasn't true.

Mary set up a roster of family and friends so that Claire was never alone at night, and they would listen to this word for hours. First-timers on the roster were devastated that this was the word and that it never stopped. 'Home.' 'Home.' 'Home!' They slept on the hard chair or on the floor, and then in week three a La-Z-Boy arrived from somewhere—

and they settled back into this massive chair, listening to the machines and to Claire's plea. Every hour a nurse would come in and check on the machines. Sometimes the nurses would touch Claire's arm. 'How are doing, my lovely?' And Claire would stare hard at them, as if trying to bring them into focus. Her lips curled. 'Home!' Her face had set in a mask of pain. Her head was shaved. She was ageless, sexless. The nurse would say, 'Oh, I know, I know, hon. Won't it be nice?'

Even though one of the surgeons suggested that it might be helpful to think of Claire as no longer the person she was—no longer really Claire—the persistence of this word and all its emotional power suggested that the old Claire was still there, even more there than normal since she was down to the essence of herself, Mary thought. She wanted this one thing: to go home. It was simple. She wanted to be with her son. She didn't want to be in this terrible room with a tube coming from her head and people sleeping on the floor or dozing in the big chair listening to her growling. These spectators! Who could walk out of the room any time they liked, return to their lives. Why wasn't anyone taking her home?

When Claire eventually left the neuro ward, Mary heard that the nurses had also found the single word 'Home' echoing down the corridor to be a tough listen. They'd been upset by it. Learning this fact had a huge impact on Mary. She'd thought the nurses would somehow be immune. She was proud of her sister for breaking through.

In the dark hospital room, at 2 or 3am, Mary, unable to sleep, would talk to her sister. She tried to keep the subjects run-of-the-mill: what was happening at work, what Pete was up to, how their parents had finally sold their ancient car, what their cat was doing. She aimed to keep the future out of it, but she quickly realised that most of her stories were aligned with the future and that she was talking about a time Claire would not see. The idea of what would happen to Colin lodged starkly in the room. She reverted then to the past, to their childhood, their days at school, people they had known, funny or strange or dramatic things that had happened. Claire was five years older than Mary. She was in her final year at high school when Mary was just starting. It was a big gap then and, in looking for shared history, it seemed large again. Mary was aware she was getting things wrong when she tried to dredge up stories of Claire as teenager, and that normally her sister would be cutting her off, correcting her, being impatient. Claire hated inaccuracies. Mary remembered how rude her sister had been when she had declared she was entering police training. Mary was always little Mary, though by age fourteen she'd grown taller than Claire, sturdier too.

For long periods, while Mary spoke and watched the small pinkish bubbles travel down her sister's shunt, Claire was quiet. Quietly fuming, probably.

'Remember the Reggie incident?' said Mary. Reggie was their puppy, and more or less Mary's pet. Their parents had gone away on holiday for a week, leaving Claire, aged seventeen, in charge. The silly dog had pooed in the corner of the kitchen and the sisters had had a row about who should clean it up. Claire told Mary it was her dog. Mary thought that it was Claire's fault since she'd moved the puppy's litter tray from the back porch to behind the garden shed and confused Reggie. When Mary came back to the house that afternoon, she found the poo deposited outside her bedroom door. 'I was staggered that you would have taken the trouble to scoop it up, carry it through the house and leave it by my door,' Mary said. 'Maybe I should have been grateful you didn't plonk it on my bed!' One of the machines Claire was hooked up to bleeped three times, as if it were transmitting her sister's thoughts. The dog's poo had remained there all week. The smell peaked on day three, when Claire screamed at her to get it out of the house. Mary refused. They weren't speaking. The house filled with a sour odour. Fur grew on the shit.

On the day their parents were due back, Claire cleaned it up. 'Fuck you, Mary!' she shouted. 'Fuck your stinking little arse!'

In the hospital, Mary said, 'Did you admire me just a little bit for holding out?'

They sat in the dark, lit by the small lights of the machines. A sucking noise came from somewhere and then it stopped. Footsteps in the corridor came and went. Far-off voices.

'Home,' said Claire, more softly this time.

'I'd take you if I could, darling,' said Mary.

'Home!' Louder again.

'You're sick of me, are you?'

'Home.'

One day Mary was contacted by their cousin, Louise, who lived in Australia and was back for a few days. She asked if she could visit Claire. It was a big surprise to hear from her. Louise and Claire had fallen out badly a few years before, though they'd been extremely close since they were girls. Right through their twenties, their thirties and now their late forties, they'd had this special connection. Somehow it had crashed. Mary had never really got to the bottom of the breakup, though she knew it had been bitter and final. Someone had said something and someone had said something back and it was all irretrievable. Claire had refused to discuss it. She said she had tried a couple of times to make peace but Louise had rebuffed her. Mary didn't know if this was true or not. Her sister could be a tricky person, capable of holding grudges and often unwilling to concede when she was in the wrong. In addition to the Reggie thing, she and Mary had had times as adults when they hadn't spoken to each other for months because of some slight or an argument where Claire felt Mary had overstepped. And maybe Mary had overstepped—she was capable of that, easily. But so was her sister. And so was their cousin. Mary had felt that the loss of Louise's friendship was more than a passing blow for her sister. If news ever came up of Louise's family, Claire would stiffen and act strangely. Obviously, she was still upset.

Mary met Louise in a café near the hospital. They hugged, and immediately Louise burst into tears.

'I'm getting it all out before,' said Louise.

'Good luck with that,' said Mary.

Her cousin was, as usual, dressed expensively and beautifully. In the good old days, this was what Claire and Mary talked about when they talked about Louise: her clothes and her love life. She'd had a couple of wealthy long-term boyfriends and she'd worked in London and New York in finance. She had bluffed her way into her first finance job and hadn't looked back. She maintained she had no real skills. Life was confidence. In the café, Louise wore a grey tailored jacket over a creamy white blouse and a long skirt subtly patterned in a lightly shimmering paisley—the kind of thing Claire would have instantly reached out and stroked. Her famous hair was a black cloud with a pair of sunglasses stuck in the front.

For a moment Mary hated her and regretted agreeing to the visit. Why put Claire through this now? And why give Louise the opportunity to make up when the other party lacked the ability to consent. The other party, god.

'I was afraid to call,' said Louise. 'But she's okay to see me?'

'To be honest, Louise, Claire can't really express her opinions.'

'Okay.' She nodded and her tears fell against the table. She showed no interest in wiping them.

Mary had never heard tears make a noise against an object before. 'I've told her you were coming to see her. She didn't raise a fist or make a face.'

'Thank you, Mary,' said Louise. She blinked and lifted her eyes to the ceiling. Her face cleared a little. 'And how are you all? How are you coping? I can't imagine. How is poor Colin? How are your parents?'

'They're doing okay, you know. It's hard.'

Colin appeared to be coping by treating this as an opportunity to learn everything there was to learn about non-Hodgkin's lymphoma and brain tumours. He announced he would study medicine. People who heard this thought it was very sweet and didn't believe it.

Their father had told Mary last time he'd visited the hospital that when he and their mother died, Colin would receive Claire's share of the estate. 'The sale of the house will be half his,' he said. Right, said Mary. She thought, yes, that would be standard. But her father was trying to say something else, she thought. He was trying to say that the natural order had been violated and they, as the parents, needed to die ahead of their children. He was reminding her that they planned to die, and soon. It was the least they could do. At no time during this period of Claire being diagnosed and then dying, which took six months, did her parents talk about the fact that Mary had outlived her child and that they were now in the same boat. This, she considered, was the opposite of thoughtlessness. It was impossible to bring up Will. Everyone felt it. He had died barely a year before Claire's diagnosis.

Their mother was bereft. When she walked, she moved lower to the ground. The hunch irritated Mary for some reason. Stand up! she wanted to say. Stand up! Her parents had aged drastically in a matter of days. They shuffled along, bent. They were always forgetting what floor Claire was on, and how to work the lifts. They spoke with great politeness, even to Mary, as though she were a stranger.

In the café, Louise said, 'Mum and Dad send their love. "Send their love"! Oh, Mary, is this the hardest thing?'

So cousin Louise too had placed Mary's own loss of her son into some separate compartment. It made Mary harden, not towards her cousin, who was tormented by her own estrangement from the dying person she'd once loved and perhaps still loved, but towards this next part of the morning, which she'd been dreading. 'We should go,' Mary said, standing up from the table.

Louise looked panicked. 'Is it time?'

When they arrived at the room, a nurse was just completing her checks.

'All good?' said Mary. She sounded like a nurse herself.

'All good,' said the nurse.

'Her bp?'

'Fine.'

Mary said, 'Her left eye was quite weepy last night. I think it was bothering her. Can we get some more of the wipes, the gentler ones? I think we've run out.'

'I'll get you a box.'

'Thank you.'

The nurse left.

Elegant, scared, guilty, remorseful Louise hovered at the doorway.

'Come in, come in,' said Mary. She touched Claire's arm. Claire opened her eyes and turned her head slightly.

Louise had caught sight of the shunt. She was pale and smiling weakly, still a few feet away from the bed.

'Come closer,' said Mary. All her hours in this room produced what must have looked like terrifying expertise to her cousin, the newbie. As girls, Mary had always regarded Louise with admiration and fear. That five-year gap again. And her aloofness and certainty. Now Mary was the boss. She felt her emotions retreat magisterially. She felt nothing. She was here to broker the reunion. She spoke to her sister. 'I have someone here. Look who's come to see you. It's been a long time.' She gestured for Louise to move around the opposite side of the bed. 'Can you believe it, eh?'

Slowly Claire shifted her head to study her cousin.

'Hello sweetie,' said Louise.

Claire turned back to stare at Mary—she hadn't shifted anything with such speed in weeks. Was she averting her gaze? Was this the great rejection? If it was, then Mary was proud of her again for holding out. Then her sister looked back at Louise, who had rested her hand on Claire's hand. The moment held. Then Claire opened her mouth. At first nothing came out, and Louise looked quickly at Mary for reassurance.

I am not helping you now.

'Ahhh,' said Claire. But it was not the gravelly, choked

voice of her cry for home. It was a little girl's piping soprano. 'Yeeee,' she said to Louise. It was as high as a falsetto in a song. Mary had never heard her sister make such a sound, even as a girl. 'Heeeee.' It was funny to listen to. 'Seee.' Claire was going pink making the strangled noise. She looked distressed.

'Hey,' said Mary. 'Hey, you, come on. What's that? What happened to your big girl's voice?'

Claire coughed and the next sound was back in her register. 'Hooo,' she said. 'Haaaa.'

'There we go. I think we got a bit excited. A bit overcome.'

Louise was smiling, her eyes sparkled with tears. 'Okay, okay. Yes, honey. Claire-bear. It's great to see you. So great.'

'Raaaaa,' said Claire.

Louise ran her hand over the thin ribbed blanket covering her cousin's chest. Then she was patting the blue cashmere throw they'd brought from Claire's bed at home. She didn't know the protocol around touching the patient's body. 'Oh.' She seemed about to lapse again into silence—what was there to say?

Mary encouraged her. 'I think Claire would be interested to hear how you arrived and, you know, details of the flight.' She spoke again to her sister. 'Louise has flown from Sydney.'

'I have!'

'Baaaaaaa.'

'Haven't been back in ages.' She looked around, and Mary thought she'd run aground again, but then Louise spoke more naturally. 'I like this room. So . . . spacious. And very state-of-the-art.' She pointed at the machines. 'Though I bet none of these makes coffee.'

Claire, with great effort, shook her head. 'Faaaaaa.'

'It's hard to get everything right.'

Mary stepped away from the bed. 'I'm going to let you two catch up.'

'Really?' said Louise, worried again.

'I'll just be out there. I want to track down that box of wipes. They promise stuff and it never shows up.'

Later, when they were walking out of the hospital, Mary told Louise that it was the most responsive and communicative her sister had been in a long time. It was quite baffling. 'She was really trying to talk to you. How did it go after I left?'

Louise said, 'I think we forgave each other.'

'I'm glad.'

'Either that or when I said I was sorry she told me to fuck off. One or the other, and I'm choosing to believe that your sister and I are now back on good terms.'

'You should visit again. Soon.'

'Oh, I want to.'

How painful to hear the lack of conviction in her cousin's voice. 'I know she'd like that.' Would she? It was so easy to make things up about someone confined to a hospital bed. Besides, dear Louise would be running a mile.

'I need to fly back home but I'll stay in touch.' She clasped Mary's hand. 'How sorry I was about your son, about Will.'

'Thank you.' Mary remembered the card Louise had sent. No phone call. An anonymous-looking condolence card. She remembered too that Claire had shaken her head when she heard about it. Unfuckingbelievable, she said. A card!

'Just devastating,' said Louise. 'You must think you're being punished or something.'

They kissed each other on the cheek when they said goodbye, and Louise held on to Mary for a long time. 'I'll come back,' said Louise. *I can't ever return.*

No. To believe you were being punished, Mary thought, watching Louise get into the taxi, you had to put yourself in the centre of it all. Whereas Mary felt she was at the very edges, being spun off.

Finally, Claire got to come home. Mary took leave from her new office job at the security firm and moved in too, which made it not at all the home Claire had lived in before she went into hospital. Occasionally, looks passed across Claire's face which Mary took to mean, *What are you doing here?* But then there was the other look she gave her, when Mary had said she needed to go away for the weekend on a course, which meant, *How can you leave me now? How can you be so selfish?* Somewhere between these two poles, they managed. And Colin needed someone as well. His father, divorced from Claire for a number of years, was unsure of his place. Little Mary stepped in. Every morning she drew herself up and created an image of herself as someone who could cope. It reminded her starkly of pulling on her police uniform. She adopted a manner. She did not stride around or give orders. But she looked as though she might. The carers who came into the house knew that she was in charge. They assumed also that she'd had medical training, but this was all just from the language she'd picked up over the past months in hospital. With Colin, too, they felt intimidated. He spoke like a doctor. They couldn't guess his age. He became astonishingly matter-of-fact.

Moving Claire in and out of bed was seen as desirable for the time being. It broke up her day and she could look out the window or see into the kitchen if there was action there. This was done via a sling operated by a little hydraulic device. With her now tiny legs folded up against her body as the sling raised and lowered her, she looked like a delicate animal, a foal perhaps, being weighed. She might have had four legs tucked up underneath her.

All of these were humiliations Claire would have said she'd never suffer. Never in a million years would her son and her sister be controlling a hoist with her as useless as a baby inside it. And here they were.

They only used the sling for the first ten days. After that Claire was confined to bed, where she slept most of the time. She had stopped making any noise through her mouth. The carers would change her catheter, wash her and, with Mary's help, move her on to a different side to avoid bed sores. They slipped into a routine. After the hospital, it was peaceful. No machines required. No hope left. Mary almost believed they could go on like this for a long time. She sat in Claire's bedroom and looked out the window at the high brick wall of ivy, home to a hundred sparrows when night fell. Claire had waged a war against the birds and had sent Colin, when he was younger, to bash the ivy at dusk with a broom and shout so they wouldn't settle in the leaves. But they always came back, and finally Claire gave up. 'They make such a racket,' she'd told Mary.

'But you've made your peace,' said Mary.

'We certainly have not!' said Claire.

Among the many things that happened, Mary always remembered two in particular.

The first was their favourite carer, Anna, a very tough no-nonsense Polish woman, crying on the last day of her shift. Mary had been surprised by this at first. Then she figured it out. Anna wasn't rostered on for another three weeks with Claire. She knew Claire wouldn't last that long. Anna was a fully qualified doctor who couldn't practise because of a visa problem. Her adult daughter was stuck in Poland. When Mary came into the living room and found her weeping, Anna spoke to her in Polish for an extended time. She finished her speech and wiped her eyes. She never attempted to translate what she had just said and perhaps she had no idea that Mary didn't understand. Anyway, Mary thought she understood.

The second thing: Mary found Colin pacing up and down in front of the open pantry door, looking in and shaking his head. 'What's the matter?' she said.

'We've bought far too many of these drinks,' he said. 'These Fortisips, look at them all!'

The little bottles came in packs of a dozen and they were stacked on the bottom shelf. There were probably fifty left. Claire had been going through three a day and now she struggled to finish one.

'Hey, that's all right, Col,' Mary said. 'No worries eh.'

He slapped the wall beside the fridge. 'Fuck! What were we thinking?'

She put her arm around him, but he stepped away and pointed again at the pile of drinks. 'What's the solution?'

'I'll drink them,' said Mary.

Colin looked at her. 'You?'

'Sure, I like strawberry. I like raspberry.'

Colin squatted down and studied the cartons. 'Who will drink the lime ones? There are twelve limes. Fucking lime.'

'Pete will.'

'Does Uncle Pete like lime?'

'He does.'

Colin stood up. 'I can't stand them. Mum can't either. She's right off them.'

'Yeah,' said Mary, 'that's why good old H_2O is the thing now. She likes that.'

Colin nodded and closed the pantry door. 'Sorted that.' He glanced quickly at Mary. He wasn't very good at eye contact. 'It's costing a lot.'

'No, the drinks aren't expensive,' she said.

'Not the Fortisip. The carers.'

This was true. 'Don't worry about that, Colin. There's no problem with paying for it.'

Actually, Claire's finances weren't in great shape. This was another stressful discovery. Her mortgage was bigger than Mary expected; she'd bought out her ex. And her income as a contracting interior designer was lumpy. Claire had always liked holidays and splurges. Mary's new access to her sister's accounts and to her wardrobe showed up a pattern of spending which meant Mary and Pete were now the guarantors to the nursing agency's contract. The bright light—and it didn't figure as that to anyone—was Claire's large life insurance policy. Dying was solvency, and a good nest egg for Colin. In the meantime, all these shoes and beautiful coats. Sunglasses and handbags Mary had never seen before. Jesus, Claire!

Colin said, 'She'll be thinking it's a waste of money.'

'No she won't,' said Mary. 'Believe me.'

'Sometimes I catch a look in her eye.'

He wasn't wrong here either. Her sister could summon a range of expressions through just the faintest pressure shift in her eyes. Disapproval seemed readable. So did relief—at least Mary hoped that's what came over her sister from time to time. The cream rubbed gently on her hands and feet. Being resettled in her bed after a wash.

*

In the last days a new carer arrived. Claire had stopped eating and was barely awake for any length of time. The agency said that this carer, whose name was Rina, had special expertise in the final stages.

'How will we know?' Mary asked Rina.

Rina had been sitting with Claire for the afternoon. Colin was out.

'It can help to think of it like this. Your sister is on a train journey.' Rina spoke slowly and looked slightly off to one side. She paused.

Mary instantly bristled at the idea of the train journey.

Rina was a heavy middle-aged Māori woman, not especially well-looking. She looks a bit like me, Mary thought. Under her eyes were dark rings. Her skin was puffy. She always took her shoes off at the door, despite Mary saying it wasn't necessary. There was something of the fortune-teller about her. In her stockinged feet she quickly made Mary feel as though she, Mary, was the visitor. Just as quickly, she accepted it. Now she was taking off her shoes, and she saw Colin was doing the same.

At one point, before all this was set in motion by Claire walking into the after-hours medical centre feeling strange, Rina's presence in her bedroom would have seemed bizarre. Now, Mary knew, Rina belonged here more than she did. She was the right person.

'I say it's like a train journey because it helps some people see there are stations to pass through and, down the line, a destination.'

'I see,' said Mary.

'If Claire has set off from Wellington on her way to Auckland, she's now in Palmerston North.'

'She went to university there!'

Rina smiled.

Mary saw the train now. Claire sitting up in her seat, looking out the window expectantly. 'So this is Wellington to Auckland.'

Rina nodded.

'And how fast is the train going?' asked Mary. 'I mean, is it real time? Twelve hours or whatever?'

'No, Mary,' said Rina in her measured voice. 'Claire will let us know how fast or slow the train is going.'

'I hope it doesn't stop in Hamilton. Her ex was from there.'

The joke didn't land with Rina. She was beyond jokes. Was Claire? Mary hoped somehow this wasn't the case.

They sat in silence, both looking at Claire, who was turned away from them, the blankets barely rising and falling with her breathing, which was slowing down over the hours. The train was travelling but it was also winding down. When it was very near the destination, it would be at a crawl. The single passenger would be looking out the window, wondering, Are we there yet? Are we there yet?

'I can see that Claire is surrounded by love,' said Rina. 'This will help her.'

Mary felt herself trembling. 'Do you think so?' She was uncertain if her question meant, was her sister surrounded by love, or would it help her.

'Yes, Mary, I do.'

'Thank you.' Whatever this exchange meant, Mary felt an overwhelming rush of gratitude.

They both listened to Claire breathing. Suddenly she let out a great sigh. There was a gap and then she was breathing again. Light puffs. Mary became aware of Rina's breathing then. The rhythms seemed to be connected. It was as though this total stranger was absorbing her sister's suffering.

That night Mary started explaining the train journey to Colin, but he stopped her. 'She's told me about that already,' he said. 'Rina told me.' Mary half expected Colin to be scornful of the image and of Rina. He was, however, utterly convinced. 'It'll be good when she gets to Auckland,' he said.

'It will,' said Mary. 'She's done so well and now it's time.'

'Rina says Mum knows what she's doing.'

'Yes, Rina has a lot of knowledge about these things.'

'Will I have to say anything?'

'When?'

'At the funeral. Will I have to speak?'

He was completely serious. 'Oh Colin, we don't have to think about that now.'

'I am though. I am thinking about it.' The struggle was in his voice.

'Well, no, not if you don't want to. You don't have to do anything you don't want to.'

'Do you think Mum would be disappointed if I don't?'

'I think she's amazed at all you've done so far. We're all amazed, Col, dear.'

'Where will I live?'

The question stunned Mary. Somehow, in all this time, she'd never thought about where Colin would live. 'With us. You could stay with us.'

He gave her a look, as if he knew she was making this up on the spot. 'Or with Dad.'

'Sure, with your father. There are options. You'll have options.'

'You don't want me,' he said.

'Colin! Why do you say that? Of course we want you. Of course.'

'In Will's room? Would I stay in his room?'

She felt the spirit of her sister in his twisting questions. 'Sure. It's empty. It's there whenever you need a room. You're seventeen. Legally, you can decide where you'd like to live. But obviously talk to your dad. He'll have advice.'

'He won't want me. I just remind him of Mum. He always says, Just like your mother, and, Did your mother tell you to say that?'

'He's still your father.' This sounded weak.

Mary was aware that their voices had grown louder than they had for ages. Claire's bedroom door was open. If hearing was the last thing to go, she might have heard all of this. Quietly she said, 'I need to go to bed, Colin, and you probably do too. It's been a long day.'

They didn't move. From the bedroom came a creaking sound—most likely Rina moving around.

'I wonder where the train is now,' said Colin.

Lying in bed in Claire's spare room, Mary found it hard to get to sleep. In her mind she was still in her sister's room with Rina, listening to the puffing. Sometimes she imagined she could hear Claire. She was aware of straining to make out the sound. Thank god the spell was broken by the noise of Colin coughing. His room was through the wall.

When Colin was nine or ten, Claire had asked Mary if she thought Colin was strange.

'Strange in what way?' said Mary.

'Just, you know, odd.'

'I think he's always been himself.'

'What does that mean?'

'He's Colin.'

Claire snorted. 'Have you ever thought of setting yourself up as a psychologist?'

'Claire, I feel I might be walking into a trap here. Has something happened?'

'No, nothing's happened. He doesn't make friends easily. He gets worked up about things. You know. He's pretty intense.'

'Yes.'

Claire sighed. 'I hope I haven't raised a weirdo.'

'But you're a weirdo too, Claire.'

'That's true.' She stared at Mary. 'In what way?'

'You're Claire.'

'Jesus, back to that.'

They both laughed.

Claire said, 'Will is a weirdo, right?'

'Definitely.'

'But Will is happy,' said Claire. 'I don't know if Colin is happy.'

'They're happy together,' said Mary.

'I know! Isn't that remarkable? I love Will.'

'I love Colin.' It was all true.

'Oh, Mare. Don't make me cry.'

Eleven

Pete met the dune crew on a blustery, clear day at the council plant depot—a shed by the boat club. Mary had a cold and decided to give it a miss. It was also the reason she wouldn't ring Shaun Anderson's daughter this weekend. She told Pete she wasn't up to it. 'Shall I ring?' he asked. She'd shaken her head at this idea. 'Let's wait,' she said. 'It's been so long, what difference does another few days matter?' It matters, Pete thought, because Anderson is dying, but he wasn't going to press it.

He'd gone into their new garage to retrieve his dune gear. Very little of their stuff was unpacked. Boxes and piles lined the walls. He found his boots and a wind jacket. Their packs were hanging on hooks. It took him longer to find the gloves he wore—they'd been buried under a kneeling mat and some garden tools. He'd had plans to get on to this job, but somehow he always turned away from it. Mary had stopped asking him when he was going to do it. They were both in a strange holding pattern.

He needed to reconnect with his old life. It was never the plan to cut himself off.

Quite a few of the dune regulars were absent because of various ailments and appointments. Gill, project team leader, did the karakia, briefed them on the morning's plan and then they set off in pairs. Pete was with Ken today, retired from the rural bank, a vigorous bloke who always wore shorts no matter the weather, and who regarded an hour behind a desk as completely wasted. The idea that a man might have worked his whole life in a library was mystifying to Ken. A library was a place for children, mothers, winos. In this outdoor setting, Pete almost made sense to him. They'd grown to like each other. Pete remembered that weekend a couple of years ago when spontaneously they'd hugged. The pingao they'd planted on the fore-dunes at the northern end of the beach was a raging success. The marram they'd removed was not coming back. Ken had stepped out the spinifex stolons and called out the measurement to Pete: 'Eight bloody metres!'

A great day!

Ken had started years before at the Petone Dune Restoration Project. Storms and tides together with human encroachment had denuded the environment. He'd seen what was possible if you put in the work. They'd planted natives. Ten thousand plants over the years, he reckoned. Ken was now known as the seed man. He'd collected seeds from the beach and got them propagated at coastal nurseries. The pīngao and muehlenbeckia plants with that sort of heritage had a much better chance of survival.

Gill always cautioned their crew, 'Dunes don't stop erosion. They're a buffer. And they need to move. Move and self-repair. The dunes are much cleverer than us. We're just reinstating the conditions which will let them do what they're meant to do. From now on, if you see a bulldozer down here, it's doing the same thing we're doing. Clearing the exotic species, releasing the sand. Allowing habitats to come back. So please don't organise you and your mates to chain yourself to the bulldozer. Don't lie down in front of it. Unless you want to become one with the dune. The dune will have you, I guess. The insects will enjoy you. All the critters. But just don't. We're on the same side.'

Gill was tangata whenua. Pete remembered his speech from a few years ago. 'I don't care if you're Pākehā or whatever. I'm only interested in one question: what are you doing to care for this whenua? You're here, so that tells me something.'

As well as planting, Pete and Ken had worked on fencing and maintenance of the accessways. Pete felt proud that people used the tracks he'd helped build. It was as though he'd written a song which people remembered and sang, forgetting who'd written it. Today was the basics: weeding and rubbish collection, with a bit of survey work thrown in. Gill wanted to know if there were any dramatic changes in the newly planted areas. They carried packs lined with large rubbish bags.

Ken had started off with Pete as a reluctant talker. Over time, however, words added up. Facts were squeezed out. Ken was a widower, originally from the South Island. He lived by himself in the township. He grew tomatoes. He sold limes for a dollar a bag at his front gate. Pete knew he had a daughter who was a chef on superyachts in somewhere like the Caribbean. She sent him video messages of these incredible boats. Ken had promised to show Pete one, though he never had. Pete had the impression that Ken just wanted her home, that the yachts were so over the top it wasn't a real life. 'She used to call her mother every few days,' Ken said. 'Months go by and then she'll call in a hurry. Not that I blame her. What would we talk about?' He played golf twice a week, though his arthritis meant he couldn't grip the club properly. He relied on his playing partners to tell him where his ball went. One time he told Pete that he wasn't really a beach person. He didn't enjoy summer and lying around, getting hot. He preferred mud, gumboots, an open fire. He liked winter. His wife had knitted him jerseys which would outlive him. A swim was something that needed to be short and swift, like a boxing match. He felt a bit sad that kids couldn't throw themselves off the top of dunes anymore. He remembered enjoying that all those years ago. Sure, the dunes needed to be protected but, as Gill always said, they were self-repairing, so what did it matter that some kids had fun for a while? He had a cat with eye problems which cost the earth. He listened to talkback radio to get to sleep. He liked people who smoked, even though his wife had died from lung cancer. He continued to miss smoking and sometimes had a cigar while looking at the stars. He owned a decent pair of binoculars and he'd once accidentally seen a neighbour dancing topless while she did the cooking. 'Hot nips,' he'd said to Pete.

The men weren't close at all, but it did seem to Pete that he'd learned a fair bit about Ken. Certainly he preferred working with him than with some of the other regulars, who treated the dune work with offputting solemnity. Mary was only an occasional helper for the same reason. There were a couple of women, wet cases, Mary said, who drove her best instincts for habitat renewal deep underground. When she'd turned up once with a plastic bag, it was like she'd brought along a dead kiwi.

Ken always walked fast over the dunes. Pete's hip slowed him down a bit. And he sometimes had to call Ken back to see something—a ridge of marram sneaking back in, or a flowering plant he couldn't identify. Ken would stomp back and offer an opinion. When he was in a good mood, he liked to call Pete 'Prof', presumably because of the library. Over time Pete had become much more knowledgeable about the dunes, but Ken still easily trumped him and usually expressed surprise that the Prof needed such help. 'Do you not know that one? Huh.'

They walked for ten or so minutes, picking up the odd bit of rubbish, testing the sturdiness of the signs they came across. The wind gusted, inflating Ken's loose bush shirt and whipping his silver hair straight up. When they were on the beach they took in the fore-dunes, seeing how the shapes were holding up after the recent large fronts which had moved through.

'Shit, Ken,' said Pete, 'look at that!'

'What?'

'That! The sea! Was that there the last time we looked?'

'Ha ha.'

'I'll make a note for Gill. He'll want to know.'

'Ha bloody ha. You had me for a second. Thought you'd found a dead body.'

They pushed on. Pete considered taking a few photos but he didn't want to get sand in his phone.

The others were now just blurry shapes far down the beach. The sand swirled up into Pete's face and he got some in his mouth. He spat it out.

'You had a hard night or something?' said Ken.

'Yeah, those happy hours at the village.'

'What's that?'

'We moved to the retirement village. One of the self-contained units. Good little place.'

Ken wiped at his face. Conditions were now quite unpleasant. They moved back off the beach and found a sheltered spot in a hollow and crouched down.

Pete pulled his water bottle out of the side pocket of his pack. He offered some to Ken, who shook his head. Ken never brought water (*Just makes me want to go*).

'You're with the creeping dead now, are you?'

'Ken, there's a putting lawn. You'd be right at home.'

'They're carrying me out in a box.'

'You know they don't use boxes. They use bags.'

Ken pulled lightly on some spinifex, testing the roots. 'The wife wanted to, did she?'

'The wife and the husband.'

'Well, good luck to you. It suits some.'

The vegetation on the side of the dune was pressed flat by a gust and then sprang back. Pete watched a sandhopper skitter past his boot, circling one way, then the other. 'We hate it.'

'Eh?'

'Mary and I hate it. We've made a terrible mistake.' It felt great to say it. He'd not come out and said it to Mary, nor she to him. But they knew.

'Nah,' said Ken.

'Ken, we really have. It was so stupid. What were we thinking?'

'Probably that you didn't need the hassle of a house, all the jobs, all that.'

'Exactly. But we miss the house. It was a great house.'

'Did it have steps?'

'Yes.'

'Then you made that call. I'm on the flat.'

'We're not totally crippled.'

'You're not Peter Snell either.' Ken cracked his knuckles. It was his thing. They really popped. 'It's just early days. You're getting used to it. Makes sense.'

'I thought it was the place of the creeping dead?'

'Well.'

'Carry me out in a box.'

'Or a bag.'

'Ken, we really stuffed up.'

'You're just facing up to a change. People don't like change.'

'Like you?'

'I'm not going anywhere.'

'And nor should we have.'

Ken looked around, shielding his eyes from the sand. 'Jesus, Pete. What a situation. Plus they have you over a barrel in those places with the re-sale.'

'I know, I know. We're sitting there like a couple of fools. Like a pair of bloody sandhoppers, not knowing which way to go. From our front door to the cemetery is three hundred metres.'

'Sends a signal.'

Trudging back, they battled the wind head-on. Conversation was impossible. The island didn't move but everything else did. The breakers went sideways into one another, and spray was whipped up, swirling along the top of the water and disappearing before reappearing in a different spot. Grey clouds sped by. Several of the baches had flags which were being thrashed. Pete hoped the poles as well would be ripped out and broken by the wind. He disliked flags. What were they claiming here? After a while Ken tapped Pete on the shoulder and pointed in the direction of two fellow volunteers working near the carpark. It was less exposed up there, protected by a group of Norfolk pines.

The two newbies were digging out a row of agapanthus. They'd drawn the short straw. Ken and Pete took a turn with the spades. Ken showed them that they needed to go deeper, make sure they had all the roots. They would put some kānuka and māhoe on this rear part of the dune, then taupata and harakeke in the middle region. Ken explained all this to them in a voice loud enough to carry. He was a good educator, Pete reflected. The men listened closely, grinning and nodding. With his windblown silver hair standing on end and his brown weathered knees, Ken looked like a dune creature himself, as if he'd crawled from some burrow, drawn himself up to full height and was now in command of the habitat. Pete laughed. The newbies turned to him. 'Isn't this good?' he shouted. 'Isn't it good?' They nodded, happy, standing among the slaughtered agapanthus like proud soldiers.

They dumped their rubbish back in the bins outside the depot. Inside the boat club there was a trestle table with afternoon tea. Someone had made scones with jam and cream. Ken took one and finished it in a mouthful, then put another one on his plate. A woman came out of the serving area with a plate of hot sausage rolls, and Pete took one. Ken grabbed one too, and they went over to sit at a table with some of the other dune crew. Overhead they could hear the footsteps of the boaties on the wooden floor. There was a bar up there. Generally the two groups didn't mix. There'd been a couple of ugly moments a while ago about vehicles on the beach.

Everyone was tired, and glad to be out of the wind. They talked about their patches. At the southern end, there'd been some fairly significant erosion in the fore-dunes. Also, the temporary ropes they'd strung up by the nearest houses had fallen down. Perhaps the stakes had been deliberately removed. There was evidence that people had been using the paths which were roped off. A better system was needed, or more education.

'I had to shout at some kids the other week,' one of the men said.

Ken mumbled, 'That must have made you feel good.'

'What's that, Ken?'

Ken didn't reply. He concentrated on his eating. There was cream on his face and his lap had collected pastry flakes. When he was finished, he took out his handkerchief and wiped his mouth. 'People are pigs,' he said. It wasn't clear who he was referring to and whether he was actually including himself and all of them in this classification. 'Which is probably hard on pigs, who are, by and large, a decent animal.' He stood up. 'Anyway, I'm off.'

'Me too,' said Pete.

In the carpark they met Gill, who'd been helping someone hitch a trailer to their ute. 'Good day out there?' he said.

'The cobwebs are gone anyway,' said Pete.

'This one,' Ken said, pointing his thumb at Pete, 'has moved to the retirement village.'

'Okay,' said Gill. 'You'll be the sprightliest bloke there, I imagine.'

Ken made a noise like a laugh.

Pete hadn't told anyone in the dune crew about his tachycardia. 'It's mostly women,' he said.

'Sounds all right,' said Gill.

Ken said to him, 'Would you go there?'

'Where?'

'When you retire.'

'Retire? We don't retire,' said Gill. 'We die early. Pay all these taxes and then don't get to kick back. We subsidise you fellas, playing bowls till you're a hundred and having your arse wiped by a Filipino nurse.' He slapped Ken on the back and turned towards the boat club. 'Any of those cream scones left, or did you polish them all off?'

*

Pete took a detour and, against the arrangement he and Mary had with each other, drove past their old place. The sold sign was gone. The new owners were coming from overseas and obviously hadn't turned up yet. It was remarkable and strange that their neighbour Trent, man of mystery, had been central to the purchase, that he had delivered the winning tender and signed the papers on behalf of his sister, currently living in London. She was going to live in their house! It felt, Mary said, as though they'd been hoodwinked in some way. This was nonsense, of course. Trent's sister won the tender by a good margin over the next best offer. And Trent's role? He'd alerted his sister to the sale. That happened. Plenty of people got tip-offs from family members or friends. Hey, check this out. That Trent had been paying even this much attention was interesting. Clearly, they'd underestimated him. Had he been secretively engaged with their house for some time, waiting for them to get old? Had there been a plan all along? Perhaps the sister had told him ages ago to keep an eye out and finally it had happened. Gary, the real-estate agent, had no other intel. He thought the price paid was good and he hoped Mary and Pete agreed—and they did. They shook hands. They were all happy. And on day two of their move to the village, a courier pack arrived from Gary. Inside was a giant chopping board with a brass plaque bearing Gary's name and his company's name screwed into one edge. Mary and Pete laughed. It weighed a ton and they didn't have a place for it.

Mary had turned it over in her hands. 'Murder weapon,' she said.

'Yeah, could be,' said Pete.

'No, I mean it was. One a bit like it. This poor old bloke was bludgeoned to death with his own chopping board. Three kids broke into his house—this was in Strathmore, way up on the hill. Amazing views. I remember everyone who went into the house said the same thing, "Amazing views." It was a 360-degree view. Planes landing at the airport, the Hutt Valley, whatever. The board had broken in two with the force of the blows. And these kids, they were giggling in court. They'd eaten his ice cream from the freezer. I worked the case with Ross.'

'What a lovely story, Mary,' said Pete. He took Gary's board from her. 'I'll put it in the garage unless you want to take it to show it to Ross. "Remember when?"'

'No, I don't want to take it to Ross.'

'I was joking.'

'Okay.'

In the car, after the dune work, Pete felt his hip stiffen painfully. Looking up at their old house, he saw the trees which needed pruning, the garage which needed bowling. He saw how the lean on the letterbox was even more pronounced. No one had done the berm. Trent was hardly going to get out there and prep the place. Twigs and leaves littered the footpath. The winds had made a mess. He thought he might quickly scoop up the larger stuff. He had his gloves and rubbish sack. The car radio was talking about the planned vigils for Grace Millane, murdered, her last moments caught on CCTV. Those poor parents across the other side of the world. He thought of Ken and his daughter. He turned it off. He'd never told Ken about Will. Why? Because there'd never been a moment? Surely there had. Because his story would trump Ken's story about the daughter who didn't call? Yet it wasn't a competition. They were both old men, fathers. And Pete was stupid and proud. It was astonishing that he had continued to grip the fact of his son's death so close.

For the first time—for the first time!—he felt Will loosen this grip. Somehow it worked like that. His son was shaking free. It was an act from the boy himself, and Pete sensed his presence, just as he'd felt the wind on the beach and the dunes rearranging themselves under its force. When he saw Ken next, he would tell him. He would have no choice. His son would be with him, just as his mother was with him.

A tūī landed on the fence and looked at him.

When they'd walked out of the house for the last time a few weeks before, it was not wrong to say they'd had a spring in their step. They were pleased with themselves. The baton, they felt, was passed. They'd acted as custodians and it was someone else's turn. It was a good way to think about leaving. Privately, however, a shadow passed over this moment. In truth, he knew custodian was being generous. Interloper maybe? Beneficiary? Thief? The land wasn't theirs, was it. The research had been done and the facts established. The whole coastline was acquired illegally, the iwi dispossessed. They'd dumped the shopping centre on top of land which had been cultivated for generations. They'd re-routed streams which were birthing places, built roads through burial sites. The breaches were so numerous as to overwhelm him. You couldn't shake this knowledge. You shouldn't, Pete felt. Mary agreed with him. The past was full of despicable acts, she said. She didn't read the Tribunal report, however. He'd printed it out. She said she accepted the facts.

The details of how it was done had gripped him, disturbed him through the time he'd read the report. Hundreds of pages. It was like finding out your father was a murderer, he told Mary. But that analogy was wrong, because you'd always known about the murder. It wasn't like the Strathmore house with the chopping board.

At a certain point she grew exasperated. What do you propose then, she'd said. That we give it back? Hand over the house keys to the next Māori person we see in the street? He wasn't sure what he was proposing. Her question made him even more unhappy. He understood his conscience was easily and routinely evaded. Mary was right to throw it back at him.

Anyway, he saw that the place was abandoned and in need of care. No one else had an interest in this care. Certainly not Trent. Pete realised this was the reason they'd agreed not to drive past the house. It would be distressing. The tūī lifted off the fence and zipped up through the trees; it had a spot in the back yard, on a branch overlooking Trent's place. Yes, the tūī was an old mate. Unhappily, Pete stretched his leg a couple of times and drove in the direction of the village.

He was thinking of the time he'd taken his mother on an outing from the dementia ward in the car. It occurred to him that he might have driven anywhere, even around the same block a hundred times, and it wouldn't have made a difference to her. That's what he thought, anyway. Of course, he had no way of knowing if it was true. She could still surprise him with moments of lucidity. She might not know which way to turn on the paths they walked every week around the home but she could point out a garden gnome which had fallen and rightly say that it was a new development. If we set him on his feet again, we'll be in their good books.

The three espaliered apple trees growing on the wall of the shed which housed the recycling bins was a regular stop on these walks, and here she grew back into the expert gardener, with accurate memories of her own attempts with such trees. The shaping of the branches, the sweetness of the fruit. Occasionally, if he made her stop her walker in front of the trees, she'd ask him why he was obsessed with them and hadn't they exhausted their conversation about the espalier apples last time or the time before? Or perhaps, she said once, you think I'm a dog you're taking for a walk and I should lift my leg against the tree? She wasn't bitter when she said these things. She enjoyed speaking like this and grinned at him. In the way she confided in him, joked with him, insulted him, teased him, he felt they were involved in a sort of romance, as if they were on a date.

In the car, his mother stared out the window, lost in her own thoughts. On previous car trips, she might keep up a running commentary on things they passed: houses, people, hedges, other cars. Once she told him a long story about how she'd recently passed her driving test and how she'd driven so fast the tester had had to grip his seatbelt in fright. She'd laughed at this. But the tester was never in danger because her driving was so expert. She could really travel at whatever speed she liked without compromising anyone's safety, she said. The tester was pale and shaking afterwards, she said, but he'd known he'd had nothing to worry about and he granted her the licence without a problem. When Pete listened to this story it was easy to recognise his mother as the terrified tester and his father as the dangerous driver. She was often scared travelling with him and he refused to see that there was any issue. Now she'd flipped their roles, recasting herself as the person with power. Pete marvelled again at the canniness of this. How clever the brain was, how it moved against itself and then for itself in dizzying patterns, making others feel dizzy. He was often disorientated in her company, stimulated and fearful, astonished and proud.

Today she was silent, and he wondered if she might have been falling in and out of sleep. When he spoke, she asked him to repeat it. He'd been saying something about the dark clouds coming from the south. Did it mean rain? The forecast hadn't been for rain. Saying it aloud made it sound vastly inane. Inane rain, he said. Sorry Mum. Oh well, she said finally, you're not supposed to be an entertainer. That's the loony's job.

He followed the road for a while, not knowing where to go. They'd stop at a local café and have a coffee but it was a little soon for that. Without meaning to, they ended up not too far from the house she'd lived in and where his father was still living. She'd never expressed any desire to go back there. It just wasn't a subject, and this was a relief for Pete. Whatever the trials of the dementia ward and however much she found to dislike about living there—all very reasonable feelings, as far as he was concerned—she didn't say she wanted to leave. The head nurse had told them exactly this when his mother had first moved there; that the residents might enjoy a morning out or an afternoon but that they were usually very keen to come back. Pete had been annoyed by this somehow. He felt it would reflect poorly on his mother if she just 'gave in' and accepted her lot: a single room, a single bed, a chest of drawers, one armchair, a sliding door to the bathroom, a window which opened an inch, and a locked ward. At the same time, this was what he wanted for her—peace, safety, care, others to take over.

She seemed to wake up fully beside him. 'Look,' she said, 'here we are!'

'Yes,' he said, 'your old neighbourhood.'

'I haven't been here for years,' she said.

'It's been a while for sure.'

He noticed that her face was suddenly more alive. The car turned into her street.

'The trick,' she said, 'is finding a park.'

'Would you like to stop?' he said.

'Would I?' Now she sounded worried. 'Would I usually stop?'

'We could, yes,' he said. 'We could stop outside your old place.' He didn't know if this was a good idea. Would it trigger something for her? This was the house where she went crazy. And his father would be there. He wasn't expecting them. Pete was at a loss to explain to himself why he'd come here.

They were almost alongside the house, creeping very slowly. His mother was staring at it.

'Stop,' she said. 'Pull in here.'

He pulled into the kerb. 'Would you like to get out?'

She was peering closely through the car window. 'No,' she said. 'I can see everything from here. It's really the garden I wanted to see, and things aren't too terrible, are they?'

'No,' said Pete. 'It's looking quite nice.'

'It is, it is.' She studied things carefully. By this stage she only had vision out of one eye. Was she pretending to see? 'Oh well,' she said.

'You don't want to get out, Mum?'

'There are too many pots. But what can you do?'

There were a lot of pots. 'We could change that. I could talk to Dad.'

'I doubt that your father would have any experience in that area, though he'd probably claim some.'

'True.'

She stared at the plants. 'You know one thing I've always known is that Māori knowledge is highly significant and vastly overlooked.'

'Okay, yes.' His mother had never expressed any such

opinion in the past. He wasn't aware of a single interaction she'd had with te ao Māori.

She said, 'We can learn a lot from them.'

'I'm sure that's true.'

'I mean all my life I've been learning from them.'

'I see.'

'When I gave birth, I did it in the traditional way.'

'Did it help?'

'Oh tremendously! It was quite marvellous. You see, when you give birth, you're really giving birth to yourself, a new version of yourself. That's why it's so painful. All these people are surrounding you, saying, "Oh look, she's crowning! She's crowning!" And you think, I know, I know. Tell me something I don't know. Because it's *you*. It's actually you coming out again. Except no one recognises you. How could they? You're in this new shape.'

He remembered she'd quickly fallen asleep as he started to drive back. Her head fell forward on her chest, and he listened to her slightly impeded breathing. He was grateful for the break. It was as if she'd been put to sleep or her mechanism had closed down in an act of self-care. Was it the story of giving birth to herself that did it? Or the sight of the plants in pots around the front porch of her house? Whatever, it had been a blow which only unconsciousness could repair. He too had had to fight drowsiness on the return drive. It was as if they were travelling through fog, the road in front of the car showing itself only in increments of twenty or thirty metres even though he knew visibility was fine. He turned on his lights and gripped the steering wheel while his mother slept. It took all his concentration not to join her.

Twelve

Will had not been keen on the school camp. He didn't grasp the concept. He would be separated from everything in his world and forced into proximity with things he'd chosen to avoid, namely most other kids and most of their interests—also the teachers. The only aspect of the school camp which seemed promising was the idea he might be able to explore the bush. There'd be wētā and skinks probably. Mary and Pete emphasised this. They had no idea if what they were suggesting was actually possible. Why did they want him to go so badly? It was a question they were to replay endlessly.

Why, when Mary found Will crying in his room the night before he was due to catch the bus, did she not simply phone the school and tell them their son would not be going to the camp?

Because they wanted him to be a normal kid? Or they were happy that Will was Will but they believed somewhere deep down that his quirks needed straightening, if only just a little? And that being forced to take part in group games and eat at long trestle tables and get up to hijinks and sleep in a dorm and listen to other boys tell whatever things they felt they had to tell in the dark was a good way towards achieving this slightly augmented version of their son, a boy who had shown absolutely no interest in any of this, and who was puzzled his parents thought it beneficial and was probably terrified by it.

Pete said that he felt sick whenever he thought of how they'd gone along with the camp idea. There was no school camp when he was a boy. Maybe he would have enjoyed it. In fact, this is what he told Will. *I wish I'd had the chance.* And Mary had said similar things. *How lucky you are.*

It was incredible that they'd applied such pressure.

'Here,' said Mary, organising Will's pack, the night before the camp, 'you can take your magnifying glass and your specimen jars.'

Will's teary eyes filled with dread. 'I can't take those things!'

'Why not?'

'They'd kill me.'

She was shocked that he had these instincts. Had she not always believed he was safe in his innocence? They thought he lived in his own world. But of course he crossed from world to world and of course he saw the dangers of this crossing.

In her worst moments afterwards, Mary believed her son had been killed not because he'd been thrown in an accident from the back of a ute but because of who he was. Would there not have been some force to get him into the ute in the first place? Then she imagined an ongoing struggle, the vehicle in motion, the other boys pushing and pulling. Not only had she and Pete failed to protect him, they'd actively urged him in the direction of this terrible event. *How lucky you are. I wish I'd had the chance.*

'When will I be able to contact you?' he'd asked them on the morning of leaving for the camp. They'd gone over this already.

'Someone will be able to drive to a place and phone from there,' said Pete. 'In an emergency or something.'

'What sort of emergency?'

'There won't be an emergency,' said Mary quickly.

'No,' said Pete. 'They've been doing these camps for years.'

They'd bought him a new sleeping bag. Will held it by the drawstring and let it twist around and around. When it stopped, he spun it again. His head was bowed, watching the turning green bag. He dropped it suddenly and rushed out the back door. He had to say goodbye to the rabbits one last time.

They drove him to the bus but he asked that they drop him off down the street and he'd walk the rest of the way.

'You sure?' said Pete.

He nodded.

They waited in the car with the engine running, watching him walk off. He turned around and made a shooing gesture with his hands. *Off! Off you go!*

That was an image which had burned into their brains. Go away, their son had told them. Clearly you want to be rid of me for the week, so make yourselves scarce. Enjoy your freedom. Dream of a new boy returning to you. Take a last look, because the next time you see me I'll be different, having realised you were right all along.

How had he been persuaded to get into the back of the ute and go out and shoot animals?

They'd not enjoyed the days Will was at the camp. Not really. Although they told each other encouraging things about what he might be experiencing, they knew this was all for show. It was finally too hard to imagine him there. In some way, they didn't even really believe the bus had arrived and the children had all disembarked and had read their names on the lists posted outside each cabin and had scrambled for the best bunks to be with their friends. On the first night, Mary and Pete stayed up much later than usual.

If they didn't go to bed, it meant Will would not have to go to bed, would not have to elbow space over the basin to wash his teeth, go to the toilet with boys peeing on either side of him, find his bunk, use his new sleeping bag for the first time, feel the light completely extinguished—he always slept with a night light—and be plunged into the darkness of the bush and the voices of the other boys plotting.

That next morning, Pete remembered, they'd both woken very early. It was still dark.

'Wake him,' said Mary beside him.

'What's the time?' said Pete.

'It's time. He needs to get ready.'

'Let him sleep a little longer.'

After a few moments, Pete sat up in bed. 'He's gone! He left yesterday.'

'Yes,' said Mary. 'How stupid we are.'

'It'll be all right, you know,' Pete said to the ceiling.

When eventually they had to make that trip to the camp after the police came to their door three mornings later, it was all just as Pete had imagined it: the layout of the buildings, the positioning of the ablution block, the long windows of the dining area, the veranda covered with stained mossy plastic roofing, the blue-painted doors of the cabins and their sharp door handles with the chrome peeling. He'd already seen it in his mind. Walking up the path made of small white pebbles and weeds, he thought, Yes, here is the path.

The lists of names taped to each door.

Sandra

David

Joanne

Astrid

Brent
Tracey
Michael
Devon
Chris

Other people's children. He knew a few of them. Yes, they were on this camp. He'd chatted to some of their parents. Everyone was excited.

Will.

It was only when he saw his son's name on the list that he suffered that fantastic jolt. He'd seen it all apart from this. It was as if he hadn't known until this second that Will had actually arrived and taken up residence. But there was his name. Pete staggered and steadied himself against a veranda post, and one of the policemen caught him under the arm. That was probably unnecessary. Next he was being handed tea in an enamel cup. It was horribly sweet. He thought he was drinking someone else's tea and offered it back but no, he was told to drink it. Like a kid. Everything was new from this point on. Everything was being discovered. Here is the bridge. Here is the river. Here is the vehicle.

And where were the children? He asked this aloud in a panic. 'Where are all the children?'

They were on a tramp for the day, they said. It would help take their minds off everything. In the afternoon, their parents were coming to pick them up. A few would catch the bus back to school and be collected from there. The injured boys had been taken to hospital.

'Good,' he said. 'Good.'

Then he heard Mary's voice, 'Where is our son? Where is Will?'

*

She'd been in police mode from the moment the two officers—one female, one male—had come to their door. He'd noticed her voice immediately dropped. She was speaking in a lower register, little bursts of police talk which it was hard to understand but which the officers could follow and respond to also in this shared deep manner. Suddenly it was as if three cops had come to their door, and he was alone. Mary was far off, with her kind. It continued through the night they had to spend at home. They'd be picked up in the morning by a squad car and driven to the camp. She moved around the house, tidying things, avoiding him. He lay in the dark on top of the blankets and must have fallen asleep. When he woke up in the middle of the night, he found Mary had put a rug over him, like a child or an invalid. She was downstairs, dozing in a chair, a sports bag at her feet.

'What's in that?' he said.

'Some of his clothes,' she said. 'Would you like a cup of tea or something?' She was already on her feet, moving to the kitchen.

'Did you come to bed?'

She shook her head.

'You won't wear your uniform, will you?'

'I'm off duty.'

He followed her into the kitchen. She was trying not to come into contact with him. 'Oh Mary, what will we do?'

She bent down to get the milk out of the fridge. 'They'll be here at eight.'

He said, 'I don't know if I can do it.'

She didn't look at him. She was pouring the milk. 'You can do it.'

He drank the tea. She put some toast in front of him. She was packing things in a plastic container. 'What's that? he said.

'Eggs and other stuff for when we get hungry. We'll get hungry.'

'Have you eaten?'

'I had a bit before.'

'Sit down.'

'There'll be plenty of sitting down today.'

'But sit down with me now, Mary, before they come.'

She looked at the chair as if it would break. She put her hands on the back of it.

'How could it have happened?' said Pete.

'We'll find out.'

'How, though?'

'No one knows yet.'

'He never wanted to go.'

'Don't start.'

'We made him go.'

She moved away then, back into the kitchen, to resume preparations.

Just before 8am a car sounded its horn. Mary said, 'They're here.'

Pete said, 'They tooted?'

'Yes, that's the squad car.'

'Jesus Christ, they're picking up the parents of a dead child and they fucking toot?'

'Calm down. Calm down, won't you. Why are you making this harder than it has to be?'

'I want to drive our own car. Why can't we take our own car? Three hours with these guys?'

'We talked about this. We can't take our car. We're in no fit state to drive.' She had picked up the two bags—one for them and one for him.

'We need to tell people. When will we tell people? Your

parents, my parents. Claire. Colin.'

'They know.' She opened the front door.

'How?' It occurred to him then that she had done the phoning when he was lying on the bed upstairs. She had proceeded with immense professionalism. He had lain in the dark and she had taken on this task. She would have had to start from the beginning each time. *I'm ringing with some terrible news, I'm afraid. Mum, it's me. I sorry to call this late.* She had spoken to her sister, to his mother. He'd heard her voice on the phone but had blocked it out. Telling it meant it was now true and circulating as fact. She'd carried this, using all her training and experience. He felt repulsion, awe. Who was she that she could do the things she'd done?

'Come on,' she said. 'You're all right. We're together.'

He didn't feel this was the right word. He felt she knew this too.

On the journey no one talked much. Some comments on the weather, the odd observation on another motorist's poor driving. In the back, they were sunk far into the corners of the car. Pete was bothered by a feeling that Mary had missed someone in her phoning. He kept going through the people again and again. Silently, he counted them off. Finally it came to him. She hadn't told Will. Their son was still unaware he was dead.

His mother had always collected ceramic birds. She placed them in her garden and in the porch of their house. A few lived on the window ledges inside, some in the kitchen, some in the bathroom. A reliable present for his mother was another bird for her collection. She was never displeased, though she did say, 'I've too many already!'

'Agreed,' said his father.

Will as a very young boy was fascinated by these birds. When they visited he would spend a long time looking at them. And while looking he would make peculiar movements with his mouth as if he was rolling an object around with his lips. Was he trying to communicate with the birds? Some adult—possibly Mary—had told him early on that he was not to touch Nana's birds. He could look but they were very precious and fragile. Neither of these things was particularly true. Pete had tripped over a duck in the garden once and it was made of concrete. Others in the collection had come from op shops. There were cheap things in with the pricier fine items. His mother didn't make distinctions. His father said that a lot of it was tat.

On one visit, Will came into the living room where they were all sitting, walked up to his grandmother and opened his fist. He held out one of the smallest birds to her.

'Hello,' she said. 'Look who we have here.'

Pete moved to take the bird from him, but his mother held up her hand. 'He's okay,' she said. 'He's right.'

From then on, Will was allowed to touch the birds and play with them. He lay on his stomach, down at their level. He moved them carefully into different groupings. All the blues together, all the reds, all the yellows. Or he made families, two large ones and a few smaller ones following them in a line. He took them on adventures through the garden. Soon he was gathering them into groups organised by type. All the hens together, all the geese, all the swans. He was four or five when he started. In a year or so, other groupings emerged which weren't so obvious. Pete's mother would ring Pete and tell him that she'd found a set of birds arranged by their tiny flaws—a crack somewhere, a chip, some missing paintwork. 'He's very clever,' she said. She said it as if she fully approved. Others were less certain when offering things like this. Another group consisted of birds without eyes. She was puzzled by one collection so various she couldn't think why Will had brought them together. So she asked him. The boy told her that all of these birds were very happy. The sad ones were with each other too, he said. How can you tell? she asked him. On the phone, Pete's mother said, 'He just stared at me as if I wasn't very bright or as if he'd never considered someone might not be able to tell the difference.' She laughed. 'I've never met anyone who keeps me on my toes like your Will. Your father is afraid to talk to him!'

In the dementia unit someone had pinned a nature calendar to the wall beside his mother's bed. On one visit, she pointed at the photograph of a bird and said, 'He hasn't left his perch all day. I check on him regularly. I think he's fine, you know. Just watching.'

Pete went up to the calendar and read the description. 'He's a St Lucia warbler, Mum.'

'Yes, I know. I like warblers. I have a few. Quite a nice song. Three segments with different pitches and then ending with a sound which they say is a bit like "Which you". If we wait long enough, he'll sing it.'

He remembered she used to do this with Will. Pete had found an LP of bird song at the library, and his mother would play it while Will moved her ceramic birds around the floor.

They both stared at the little bird, blueish grey on its wings and upper body, a bright yellow below that. Dark bands on its head, like raised eyebrows, and bands under its eyes.

'Do you think he looks tired?' asked his mother then, as if reading his mind.

'I do,' said Pete. 'Look at the rings under his eyes.'

'Oh, it's all so tiring.'

'I know, Mum. Are you tired?'

'I'm fine. Which you?' She made the call of the warbler. 'Which you are you?'

Pete said, 'Do you want to go for a walk?'

'I do,' she said. 'Which you are you?'

She didn't move from where she was sitting on the edge of her bed. They'd been trying to get her shoes on, but her feet had swollen up again and she couldn't make an arch to manoeuvre her toes.

She turned to the window. On the sill were what remained of her collection, four or five small ceramic birds. 'Do you think you could open the window?'

'That's as far as it goes, Mum,' he said. It was open a few inches. She was on the third floor. Sometimes she pushed a handkerchief or a sock through the gap.

'It makes it very difficult for them to come and go.'

'Yes, but they're clever enough.'

'Oh, they're clever enough. Cleverer than you!'

'For sure.'

She looked down again at her feet. 'Will would know what to do,' she said. 'When is he coming?'

'Will used to feed the birds on his window ledge, remember?'

'Of course I remember. Do you think I'm stupid?'

Even when Will was older, a visit to Nana's always included some moment with the birds—Nana showing him the new member of the flock, or the two of them discussing what the living version of the ceramic bird was really like, behaviour-wise, habitat-wise. Pete's mother had that knowledge too, and passed it on to her grandson, who soaked it up. He now had his bird books. Pete bought them for him and of course they also used the library. They installed a bird bath in the front garden at home. Will now had binoculars. Colin would come around and the pair would observe the birds from Will's bedroom window upstairs. Will had made friends with a few of them. They came to his window ledge to eat the seeds he'd scattered there. Then they came even without the promise of food. They sat on his shoulder and investigated his hair. The boys found injured birds and brought them home to care for. From birds, Will got to insects. From there, he went to mammals. Fish, shellfish, sea-life. He couldn't believe how much life there was!

When Will was eight or nine, they went to the rockpools on the south coast with his cousin Colin. Mary and Claire went off to a nearby café, leaving Pete with the two boys. The women had Things to Discuss and they didn't need Pete. Colin had started high school. He was a furious child then. His father had left home finally, after a long period of squabbles and bitterness. Claire was exhausted, free, with little left for her son. He reminded her of her husband, she said—not physically but just in the sense that he was male. She relied a lot on her sister during this time. Pete felt sorry for Colin, but this was the wrong thing to feel since the boy was highly sensitive to condescension. Recently he'd smashed a window at the apartment and denied it to his mother, even though she was nearby at the time and had found the rock he'd thrown and he was the only person around. It had come from over the fence, Colin said. 'He's testing you,' Mary told her sister. 'After all that's happened.'

'I'll test him pretty soon,' said Claire. 'Throw something

at him and say, Oh it came from over the fence. There are a lot of things that might have just come over the fence.'

At first Colin didn't show much interest in the rockpools. He sat a few yards away from Pete on the beach, scowling, while Will pottered around near the sea's edge. This was unusual. Colin's bad moods tended to disappear when he was with his cousin. Pete had a book and was lying back on the sand. It was a warm day, with a light breeze, just enough to turn a page once he released it. He felt the sun on the backs of his hands.

'Take your sneakers and socks off, if you like,' said Pete.

'Don't want to get my feet cut on the rocks,' said Colin.

'Are you going to have a look?'

'Dunno. Maybe in a bit.'

Pete called out to Will, 'Hey, your cousin's coming over soon!'

Will waved back. He carried a small bucket and a stick. Crabs were an interest.

Pete put his book down on his chest and raised his head. 'See that?'

'What?' said Colin.

'Diver.'

'Where?'

'Oh, he's gone now. Ducked under.' He'd seen a head against the dark blue of the water.

Colin put his hand up to his eyes to shelter them from the glare and looked hard where Pete had pointed. 'Can't see a thing.'

'Dived under, I think,' Pete said again.

Colin stood up for a better view. 'Maybe it was a seal.'

'Maybe,' said Pete. He lay back down and started reading again.

Colin said, 'Fur seals can swim at about thirty miles an hour.'

'That right?'

'The hind flippers rotate forwards so they can do pretty well on the sand. They're different from other seals.'

'Wow. I don't think Will knows that.'

'Really? I think he would.'

'I'm not sure.'

'Huh.' Colin started taking off his shoes and socks. Slowly he wandered down to where Will was exploring the pools.

When Pete raised his head again, time had moved on. He'd dozed off. His book had fallen beside him. The boys were talking to a diver, presumably the one he'd seen earlier. They were looking into his dive bag. Colin was holding the diver's speargun and had slipped his feet into the diver's discarded flippers. Pete stood up. He raised his hand in greeting and called out. He began walking towards them. Colin spun around and aimed the speargun at him. The diver quickly reached out and deflected the gun down. There was no spear loaded—Pete saw this as he came up to them.

'Careful now, Col,' he said.

'What?' snarled Colin.

Pete spoke to the diver. 'Thought you were a seal out there in the water.'

'I didn't,' said Colin. He threw the speargun on to the sand and tried to stomp off, forgetting he was wearing the flippers. He fell over, swore and kicked them away. Then he ran up the beach.

'Sorry about that,' said Pete.

'No worries mate,' said the diver. He was in his late twenties, with a bleached mop of hair. On his ankle was a tattoo of an anchor.

Pete looked back in the direction Colin had run off. He hoped he wouldn't have to chase him. The boy was surprisingly quick and not all that small now. His limbs were like pieces of Meccano. All the joints were on show. Will looked even younger beside him. Pete had an image of some nasty-looking tackle he'd have to make, with fellow beach users horrified and intervening. Colin, however, threw himself down again a hundred yards away and was motionless, his shiny white hair lying like some gleaming piece of coral on the grey sand.

'He's going through some stuff,' said Pete.

Will said, 'Dad, check these out.'

The dive bag contained some pāua and a large orange fish.

'Goatfish, aka red mullet,' said the diver.

'Nice,' said Pete. He glanced back towards Colin. The hair hadn't moved. 'We should get going, eh Will.'

'See ya around,' said the diver, picking up his flippers and speargun and walking up the beach.

In the car driving home, Mary asked, 'How was all that?'

Will said, 'Colin tried to shoot Dad.'

'Okay.' Mary laughed.

'But he was shooting the wrong dad.'

Mary said, 'I'm not following this.'

Pete explained about the speargun.

Will said, 'He told me he wants to kill his dad.'

'Not really,' said Pete. 'He's just angry and upset. His mum and dad haven't been getting on. It happens. And it's very hard for everyone. Poor Colin.'

Will was looking out the window at the sea. He'd lost interest in the conversation. It was common. Leaping from branch to branch. Sometimes they dragged him back, asking him to pay attention. Often they let it go. 'Mum,' he said, 'have you seen a goatfish before?'

'I have not.'

'Aka a red mullet.'

'Nope.'

'Almost orange in colour, I'd say,' said Pete. 'Rather than red, don't you think?'

Will said, 'Colin knows quite a lot about seals.'

'He sure does,' said Pete.

'When can we go back there?'

'Soon, love. Soon.'

'Tomorrow?'

'Not tomorrow.'

They drove in silence for a while. 'If,' said Will, 'a child kills his father, would he be arrested?'

'Nothing like that is happening,' said Mary.

Will considered this for a while, then he said, 'I think they'd send a lady policeman to arrest him. It would be nice if you arrested him, Mum.'

That night Pete had a dream in which he was diving. The water was murky. He wore a head torch but it kept cutting out. There were no fish and he couldn't make out the seabed. He kicked hard but made little progress. He looked down at his body and saw he was wearing ordinary clothes rather than a wetsuit. This accounted for why he was feeling so cold. His feet were heavy. He had shoes on. They were waterlogged of course. His speargun wandered about in front of him, pushed by currents. He was not in control of it no matter how tightly he gripped it. Ahead of him a shape came into view. It was hard to tell if the shape was coming towards him or moving away. He waited, trying to line up his speargun with the shape. Treading water, he saw one of his shoes fall off and drift down into the dark. It felt as though his foot had fallen off. Then his head torch flicked on again and caught the glow of white wavy hair, like some gleaming jellyfish. Colin swam towards him, his speargun aimed at his heart.

Pete woke, sweating. He got up, went to the toilet, washed his face and then stood in the kitchen drinking a glass of water. The moon made a clear wedge of light on the floor by his bare feet, which still felt cold, almost wet with the feeling.

On the way back to bed, he looked in on Will. He was sleeping in his usual posture, his neck twisted and his face pressed almost flat against the headboard. Someone had told them this is how he'd probably been positioned in the womb. It looked uncomfortable. When he was a baby, they would reposition him in the cot, but over the course of his sleep he'd always move back into this arched pose. They'd given up. It was remarkable how many things they'd learned to adjust to with their son. The pattern would go on like this, and one day Pete would be lying on the beach and a young man would walk out of the sea towards him, carrying a dive bag and saying, Dad, not a bad haul today. Not bad at all.

They were led into the kitchen area by someone, a detective, Pete presumed. He was wearing a sports coat. At some point they must have been introduced—maybe when Pete was having his foul cup of sugar tea—though Pete couldn't remember it. A blue plastic glove poked from one of the pockets of the detective's sports coat. Again, the detective was addressing his murmurings to Mary. He was pointing to the back room. This was where they needed to go next. The detective had then become aware of the glove and shoved it further into the pocket. The glove meant he had been touching something, Pete knew.

The shadows from that next room fell into the morning light of the place they were standing, staining the concrete floor.

For a second Pete wondered if it was just Mary who was being asked to do it, whatever it was—perhaps there was paperwork. There would inevitably be paperwork. The detective knew she was the best bet for this. Good old Mare. Who'd been tested in the fire and who'd come through. Scalded, damaged, changed, but intact. His astonishing wife. He'd witnessed her over the years become this person. He'd had a grandstand seat—though at a distance always. Just as in a grandstand, removed from the action, following it but always with that gap. Seen her perform, as she was performing now. Watched this remarkable person. Whom he loved. Without whom he was—what? Then Mary turned to Pete and motioned for him to step forward. He was rigid for a second. Fixed in place. They were both required. Ah well, Pete knew it, had known it all along. Here it was. Did he really think he could avoid it, delegate it, run from it, collapse in advance of it and be absent from the furnace of it? He stepped forward.

The back room was cold. Much colder than where they'd been. A door closed behind them. It was some kind of cool store part of the camp. Where they kept the perishables. The single louvre window was very close to a dirt bank and scrubby branches were almost touching the green streaked glass. There was a fluorescent tube in the ceiling, but they'd silently agreed not to turn it on. A long concrete bench punctuated by sinks ran along the far wall. Around the room was a gutter, ending in a drain by the back door. In winter, hunters would use the place. There was a hose hanging on a reel. You could wash everything down in minutes.

The dank earth smell of concrete about to spall.

Mary was moving towards an alcove, even dimmer than the rest of the room. Pete followed. The area emitted a humming. He saw the edge of a freezer unit and had the terrifying thought that this was where they had put him. Like the carcass of an animal. Something a hunter had brought back from the bush. Or like some large fish plucked from the river and now stiffened into a shape of its last living denying struggling moment.

'Here you are,' said Mary. 'Here you are, my love.'

She was with him, their dear boy. Speaking as if he was there, still there. And he was.

'Oh,' she said. 'Oh Will. We're here.' She turned to Pete and held out her hand, and he took it, drawing close. 'We're both here. It took us a while. Sorry about that. But we're here now.'

'We are,' said Pete. 'Here we all are.'

He thought at once, I'm glad. What did that mean? Warmth flowed through him.

Their son was in his wet clothes. It was the strangeness of that. Mary had packed fresh clothes. She'd imagined this. Pete had not. Two steps ahead. A thousand.

Will was lying on his back, very still. Highly unusual, totally unlike Will. Where was his normal sleeping posture, the head pushed back?

Mary was resting her hand on Will's arm, on his damp jersey. 'It looks uncomfortable for you,' she said.

Pete now registered the arrangement. Will was lying on a wooden table which had wheels and brakes. He imagined large platters of food, huge soup tureens, being wheeled around tables at dinnertime.

He touched his son's damp hair and ran his fingers over his brow. The skin not skin anymore, the hair not hair exactly.

Technically he knew they were being asked to recognise him, to identify him. They did not recognise him. They would not identify him. It was not him. Their child would never behave like this.

The smoothness of the eyelids!

'So pale,' said Pete. His voice sounded interested to him, as if they were discussing some kind of manifestation, a new occurrence, a find on the beach. *Look at this! Hey.*

They were both staring and staring at their son. He'd always bamboozled them. They'd never become used to him. Each day he'd returned to them. Each night he'd slept in the same house as them. He seemed to love them. Their love for him was like some great claw, clenching at them.

Mary bent towards Will and carefully removed something from his white ear. A small black stone from the river. She placed the stone, with a tiny clicking sound, on the wooden table, where it continued to pulse.

Thirteen

Anderson's daughter was not home when Mary called. Anderson's daughter's daughter answered the phone. No, Mary wouldn't leave a message. She'd try later, thanks.

It was such a letdown. She'd prepared herself for the conversation, and now she walked around the house uncertain how to fill the time until she could try again. The other option was not to try again. Hadn't she given it a shot? The good thing about being old was that no one could feel let down by you. You could say no, declining all kinds of offers and invitations, and people couldn't feel put out—or if they did, they experienced the irritation with regret. It would be like getting angry at a tree. The old were no longer obliged. We're like babies, Mary thought, returned to our natures, surviving, weight monitoring, unsteady on our feet, as if that needed to be learned again. How complicated it would eventually become to get in and out of a car, like a problem in geometry, as if you were moving a sofa through a doorway and not your own body.

The daughter on the phone sounded nice. Polite and helpful. Well brought up, her mother would have said. No one said that anymore.

She looked into a box of framed photos. What to put out? She wasn't sure about photos here. No one in the photos, aside from her and Pete, had come to this house or knew it at all. What would they think to be plonked down in the new surroundings? Besides, there didn't seem to be many places to put them.

Pete was in the garage, mucking around. There was still a lot of unpacking to do there. He was fine not to be part of the call. Mary could come and grab him if necessary. She felt a sudden physical longing for him. It was still strange. You walked around, doing all the things you did. And then those things were sucked into nothingness. There was a small book her mother had left on her bed when she was fourteen or fifteen. Her mother had left the book without speaking about it and never mentioned it. The book talked about 'urges'. Mary was a slow developer—was that what you said back then? She laughed about the book with her friends. *Urges! Have you felt any urges today? How are your urges?* One or two girls just stared at her, knowing more perhaps. Now she liked the word. It described something or covered it up while letting it exist. She still liked to touch this person who'd shared her life for so long, to touch him and be touched. It was very sudden now. In the old house, the previous house, they'd made love in their upstairs bedroom with the curtains open to the morning sky. No one could see or hear them. They'd not tried—dared?—to have sex in the village. What were they afraid of? The absence of this part of their lives was another reason for their unhappiness.

How they'd thirsted for each other's young bodies! They'd make each other late for everything. They stayed in bed. They washed each other, showering together, using all the hot water in her flat so her flatmates complained. She didn't care. It was a period of beautiful thoughtlessness.

She'd not really understood sex until she met Pete Brunton. Not that he was any kind of savant. Plainly he was not. She had done it a few times before they met—three times to be exact. The first with a boy from another school whom she never saw again, and it was like passing a multi-choice exam. Is it a: your hand, b: his leg, c: your mouth. The parts were separated and they swirled. She didn't want to look. They were a little drunk too, and it was very dark. The next two times, at university, were more in the line of basic practice, like role play in French class. *Avez-vous un baguette, s'il vous plait? Non, Mary, une baguette! Féminin pas masculin!* It was still a form of study. Good, one of the boys told her. *Very good*. She was grateful for the encouragement. She grew conscientious. The parts worked more together. Following a set of instructions, she had learned the basics. It helped that she had only pretended to be drunk. Otherwise, the embarrassment of taking off her clothes was too much. But you couldn't say it flowed. The puzzle of her own pleasure remained. A girlfriend had once told her that a boy was just a length of garden hose: you turned the tap the right way and eventually stuff came out the end. What are we then? Mary had asked. The friend said, We're like the underground pipes of a city. No one really knows what's connected to what and we might spring a leak at any minute. We might flood the streets!

Pete, it transpired, was a virgin. He admitted this only later. They were hardly talkers when it came to sex anyway. After she'd found out, she thought it added up. He seemed very happy for her to take the lead. What had first seemed 'gentlemanly' was really cluelessness, utter ignorance. She quickly realised he was ready to follow her instructions. *Is that—? Lower. Lower. Faster. Faster.* He was studious, her little librarian. More than that, he was ravenous. He'd been waiting and waiting. When she'd first taken off her bra in front of him, she saw his eyes literally widen and she burst into laughter, covering herself up. You look like you could eat me, she said. He was blushing. He didn't know what to say. He was completely tongue-tied. She wondered then if he was going to last. Would she just overpower him? She had liked talking to him with their clothes on. He knew about the world. General knowledge was the boring word for it, but this was different. He had a ready understanding of things which she suspected were of great value. He knew about other countries. Periods in history. Did it all come from books? Well, who cared. He'd got it in him, hadn't he. He made the other young blokes she'd met seem lacking. He wasn't conceited at all. Perhaps that was as much as they needed from each other. But no. Quite easily he got over his fright. With great ease she was convinced.

She remembered her sister being less convinced, at least at first. Mary expected that. Showing him off was always going to be a trial. And sure, from an objective viewpoint, Claire's cutting inventory had something to it. If you stared at it, Pete's chest was indeed 'narrow'. Yes, his chin was, at first, a bit small for his face, until he smiled. His ears? Not massive but not modest either—granted. All the better to nibble on! Okay, really his legs were ridiculous. Where were his calf muscles? Claire was right, sort of. And it didn't matter. None of it mattered.

Before anyone had even met Pete, Claire was typically on the alert.

They were in their parents' living room one Sunday evening after dinner when both daughters were home for a visit. Mary was in her last year of her BA in Education; Claire was working in an office, desperate to head overseas. They were all looking at the television and not at each other.

It was a phenomenally boring programme. Their father had come into some money from a great-aunt, and since the money was unexpected he'd done something unexpected with it—and bought a television. It was very expensive and very temperamental—a bit like your mother, he liked to say. A lot of the time was spent adjusting the bunny ears to steady the picture. Can we adjust Mummy's bunny ears too? Claire said. And she'd reach for her mother's head. *Get off me!*

'Who is this Peter fellow anyway?' said their father.

'Pete,' said Mary.

'Pete,' echoed her sister with a smile.

'Eh?' said their father.

'No "r",' said their mother. 'He's dropped the "r".'

'Odd,' said their father. 'It's hardly a long name to begin with.'

'Says the man who named us Mary and Claire,' said Mary.

'I wanted Genevieve for one of you,' he said.

'Thank god sense prevailed,' said Claire.

'Give it a fiddle, will you, dear?'

Mary was nearest to the television. 'I don't like touching it,' she said. 'It gave me an electric shock last time, Daddy.'

Claire looked at her. 'A bit like Pete?'

Mary swung a cushion at her sister.

'Will you two stop it!' said their mother. 'If that television is damaged, you'll pay for it and it'll take you a long time to clear the debt.'

'Oh, can we not just turn it off,' said Claire. 'I can't fill my head with any more fascinating information about the trade routes of English cargo ships!'

'Do you not want to learn anything, Claire?' said their father.

'Yes! Yes, I do! I want to learn about Mary's Pete!'

'There's nothing to learn,' said Mary.

'Is it hot in here?' said Claire.

'It's fine,' said their mother.

'Then why is Mary turning red?'

'Ha ha,' said Mary.

Their father said, 'If we're continuing to speak over the television, we should turn it off and save the money.' That was another theme—how much the TV cost to watch.

Claire lunged towards the set and turned the knob. They all watched the picture fall into the middle of the screen and disappear. It was always worth watching it happen. It gave Mary a funny feeling, as if their lives were being sucked into the hole.

Claire said, 'He's completely smitten.'

'How do you know?' said Mary.

'I have my spies.'

'Where is his family from?' said their mother.

Claire snorted. '"Where is his family from?" "Where is his family from?" They're from planet Earth, Mummy! Fellow humans. Why would you think that's an interesting question!'

'Claire,' warned their father.

'They're from Masterton,' said Mary.

'Masterton!' said Claire. 'Are you sorry you asked?'

'You met him at university?' asked their mother.

'She met him on a dark night outside the Union Hall!' said Claire.

'Claire, I don't know what's wrong with you tonight,' said their father.

Mary said, 'She's trying to deflect attention from her own trysts.'

Claire clapped her hands and shrieked, 'Trysts! Don't

women have trysts removed?'

Their father said, 'If I could send you to your room, Claire, I would. But since you're apparently twenty-five years old, I no longer have that power.'

'You must bring him around, Mary,' said their mother.

'Is he a . . . sportsman?' asked their father.

She thought of his skinny bare legs on his bicycle. 'No, not really.'

'Good,' he said.

'What does he like?'

'He likes her,' said Claire.

'Books,' said Mary.

'Oh god,' said Claire.

'He thinks he might be a librarian.'

'You're kidding us,' said Claire. 'Does he read you bedtime stories?'

'Enough,' said their father.

Their parents lapsed into a thoughtful silence. Having announced it into the room, Mary also felt unsure that it was a great aspiration for a man to be a librarian.

'Tea?' said their mother.

'Oh yes,' said their father.

She was glum. She'd betrayed Pete—not by saying he liked books, but by failing to indicate how wonderful he was and how he'd changed her and what they'd discovered about each other's bodies. Claire was on to it, of course. Mary hated her for knowing it. Oh, perhaps they all knew it, even their father, and it was best to leave it in the shadows. Perhaps she gave it all away in her manner. She expected she did. She was in love. Wasn't that obvious? She loved Pete— incredible to admit this to herself. More than that even, she had begun to think of him as a father, which must mean she would be a mother at some point, an idea that was very strange and startling. She'd had dreams in which they were staring into a cot but they couldn't quite see what was in the blankets. She woke and her breasts hurt. Incredible, the power of the mind! The notion of a baby—their baby—seemed to have nothing to do with her own parents or their example. They weren't in the equation at all. She and Pete would work this out together, would they? Just as they'd worked out sex. Not that there was any sense of a rush. Pete didn't rush. Steady Pete. Even Pete. Not Pistol Pete.

She walked part of the way back to her flat with Claire, who had to catch a bus across town. Claire had decided on a different approach and had hooked her arm inside Mary's arm. Friends. They skipped along for a few yards, like schoolgirls, though they'd never done this back then.

When they slowed down, Claire said, 'Is he great?'

'He is,' said Mary.

Claire squeezed her arm. 'You!'

'What?'

'You sly old dog! Nabbing the librarian.'

'He might never be a librarian. Who knows how he'll turn out.'

'True, he might be a mass murderer. We all take our chances.'

Mary laughed. 'And what about you? Talking of sly. What's happening there?' Her sister had let it slip a while back about someone. She was always so secretive.

Claire threw her head back and looked into the night sky. 'I think I'll marry him.'

'Claire!'

'Well, I might. Who knows.'

'Who is he? Have they met him?'

'Just someone at work. And no, they haven't met him. Daddy won't like him. He plays rugby.'

'Is he covered in muscles?'

'Completely covered. There's not an inch of him not covered in muscles. For a hobby, he tosses librarians into the air.'

'Shall we go on a double date?'

'Pete and Lance,' said Claire.

'Lance?'

They both burst out laughing.

Mary felt joyful and strong. 'I'm going to apply to join the police.' She'd not told anyone this before, not even really herself. And not Pete.

'And I'm going to join a nunnery!' said Claire.

'No,' said Mary. 'I really am. Last month we went to Trentham for our Crime and Society assignment. It's where they train. They said they need more women.'

'What are you talking about?'

'Claire, I want to do it.'

'You? But you're so . . .'

'What?'

'I don't know. I just don't see it. Cops aren't like you.'

'Why not?'

'Because.' She pinched Mary's biceps. 'Who are you going to arrest? This is the funniest thing I've heard all week.'

They walked on for a bit. 'It is quite funny,' said Mary. She was suddenly hurt and desperate not to show it. 'Of course they'd turn me down.'

'I expect they would.'

'If I ended up applying, I'd be realistic about my chances.'

Claire smiled sympathetically. She'd scored her hit and now she knew it was time to be kind to her little sister. 'It would be so hard for a girl. And anyway, you'll be off teaching next year, earning some money, hanging around libraries.'

'Probably,' said Mary.

They'd reached the bus stop. A man in a hat and raincoat was waiting in the shelter. He was smoking. He nodded at them. Mary said, 'Shall I stay until it comes?'

'No, no,' said Claire. 'I'm a big girl now. We're both big girls.' She gave Mary a quick hug and they said goodbye.

Near her flat, Mary saw a figure on the footpath. A man, loitering. She slowed down and tried to see who it was. The streetlights ran out at this point and there was hardly any moonlight. She felt her heart quicken. Her parents always told her to walk with a friend at night. She thought, If you are going to be a policewoman, don't lose your courage now. Walk on!

The figure stared down the street in her direction. Then he started waving. It was Pete. 'Hello!' he called.

She ran to him. 'How long have you been waiting here?'

'I don't know. An hour or so. Maybe longer.'

'An hour!' She was thrilled. A person had waited an hour for her.

'At least it wasn't raining.'

'Are you freezing?' He liked wearing jandals, no matter the weather. It seemed to speak of his readiness. He wasn't buttoned down at all, for a librarian-in-waiting.

'I'm okay. How are you?'

'I'm okay,' she said. They kissed quickly. Next she was embracing him and crying.

'Hello, what's wrong? Mary, what's happened?'

'Nothing,' she told him, wiping her eyes. 'I'm just happy.'

'Okay.' He was smiling at her. Now his eyes were moist. 'Me too.'

'Tell me,' she said, 'why did you drop the "r"? Peter to Pete.'

'Oh, I can't really remember. Friends just started calling me that. But when I go home, I'm always Peter. They find it awful, Pete. My mother especially.'

'Is she strict?'

'Strict? I don't know. I find her . . . inscrutable.'

'Inscrutable?'

He laughed. 'Maybe most people are inscrutable.'

'No,' said Mary. 'Most people are scrutable.'

'Really?'

'Yes. My family, for starters. And you, for instance. I can tell pretty much for certain what you have in mind right now.'

He pressed her close again. 'I missed you today. My little teacher.'

She'd not told him about her trip to Trentham, her sudden piercing dream of joining the police. She'd told her sister first. She felt this was the wrong way around. Still, she couldn't do it this minute either. She didn't want to spoil the night. 'My little librarian.'

He said, 'Can you read me like a book?'

'It's a short book all right,' she said. 'And not suitable for children.'

She knew that people said Mary Brunton's kid was killed in that accident and after that she had to leave the force. Such a shame. She might have gone a long way. First female this, first female that. A real pity.

Not true.

1981, the year before Will died, you had to put that in the mix too. The cursed Springbok Tour. She couldn't stand to even hear the words. If people worked out the dates of her police career and asked about the Tour, Mary would mumble about back-office support. In truth, it was probably the only argument of any substance she'd had with Pete, and that lasted more than a day or two. Mary knew it was a replica of any number of such arguments happening across the country. Not that this helped. Did it start then, the beginning of the end? She thought that if she dug, she might find plenty of other moments when she wondered if the job was worth it, the job she'd loved and was good at. Really you were always on that edge. She'd seen plenty of colleagues chuck it in, finally crack and just walk out on a Friday, saying, Nup, nup, blow this for a laugh.

For the Tour she wasn't Red Squad or anywhere near it. There was only one female in Meurant's lot.

You went to the briefings and it was Them against Us, with no clear idea who the Them was apart from everyone not in the police. That pretty much covered it. At the police bar the drinking sessions of those weeks were off the charts. Mary usually stayed for one round only, and when she tried to sneak away someone would always yell out, 'Mumsies! Last drinks for all the Mumsies.' Normally by then there was a pissed constable going from table to table, compulsorily sculling, a cardboard penis around his neck reading 'Dick of the Day'. There was already someone with a 'Dumb Hori of the Week' sign around their neck.

She used to repeat to herself, On the Tour you broke no one's head open. Pushed your baton into no student's ribs, nor shoved a church minister to the ground.

And she did not, thank god, see Pete and Will among the protesters that day.

She remembered she was scared. Was she the only one?

No, they were all scared. At a point she saw it, even the hardest of them with a kind of fright in their eyes at the scale of what was coming at them from all sides. An agreement had broken down and here were the broken pieces gathered up and brandished. All bets were off.

Outside Athletic Park at the height of the protest, when the barbed wire was pulled away, Mary, alongside her fellow female officers, was at the rear. They were leaning against their male counterparts like rugby backs joining a scrum to get it over the line. The crowd pressed forward, chanting. She felt the push, then a little stumble from the bloke she was pressing against. He recovered his footing and they all pushed back again, just holding. It came in waves. Next she was handed a child. Couldn't believe it. The kid, aged five or six, was passed over the heads of the frontline into Mary's arms. She was pissed off. What was she running, a crèche?

'Who are you, sweetie?' she asked the girl.

'Debbie,' she said. She looked utterly startled. Who was this person in a visor and padded vest?

The senior was shouting instructions. The protesters had their own loud hailers. Barking away. From the stadium came waves of crowd noise: nothing one moment, then it was as if thirty thousand people were about to come over the rise and sweep them all away, cops and protesters alike. Hearing that sound made Mary think, finally, of the stupidity of everything unfolding. All this for a game of rugby. Her uncle and several cousins were in the stadium. The frightened little girl brought by her parents so she could witness history. 'Listen, Debbie,' she said, 'I want you to go and stand over by that tent, all right? Mum and Dad will collect you from there, okay? But stay there and don't move. It's a bit dangerous at the moment, eh.'

The girl nodded and failed to move.

'Go on then, you walk over there and you'll be safe.' Mary gave her a little push.

She never saw the girl again. Mary was deployed to MacAlister Park shortly after that, and once the game was over they had to line Adelaide Road to stop the rugby fans from attacking the protesters as they walked past the hotels. Again she was scanning the street for them. She'd told Pete to leave before the game finished. He'd not liked the idea she was issuing that order. It wasn't an order, she said, it was common sense. Common sense, he said, was already a non-starter when you had to deploy the full force of the state's law-enforcement resources to guarantee a game of rugby could take place as an advertisement and endorsement of an evil regime. She told him, Wait, let me get a pen. I want to write that to my boss as my excuse me note.

A beer bottle hit her on the shoulder and gave her a dead arm for a while. She stepped in to break up a fight and was clipped on the ear by a wild swinging fist. She had ringing in that ear for days. They were protecting the Mongrel Mob and Black Power, which was odd. She assisted in two arrests for disorderly conduct among the rugby lot and was spat at by a woman. The third time Mary was back-up, Ross Hayes was there and told her she was the arresting officer and she'd be going back to base in the paddy wagon. She said that wasn't her role, but he simply repeated what he'd said and moved off. He probably just wanted to get her out of harm's way. He was doing what she had done to the little girl. *Wait over there, love.* Later, colleagues who'd been on the frontline all day came back, saw her, didn't know what to say. One of them tried to get things back on keel: 'How'd you swing this cushy number?' But mostly they were pale, silent, in shock.

When she arrived home, Pete pointed at her uniform. 'What's that?' he said.

She looked down and saw that there was blood on the arm of her blazer. 'Not mine.'

Since watching what happened in Hamilton, where the game was called off, and people looked ready to kill, Pete hadn't wanted Mary to be anywhere near the action. 'Get yourself into the back room for this one,' he said. 'Operations or something.'

'We don't get to choose.'

'It's too dangerous, Mary.'

'Not everyone gets to work in a library,' she said. That was unfair, she knew.

He'd walked off.

A few days later he told her he was marching against the Tour. They'd been talking about it at the library and quite a few of them were committed to joining the protest.

'It's your right,' she said.

'And Will wants to come along too.'

'Hang on,' she said.

She had a shower, inspected her shoulder where the bottle had hit, and other body parts. Just bruising. One large purple patch on her thigh. She'd been shoved around a fair bit. Her ear was still playing its tune.

Downstairs she found Pete at the front door, talking to one of their neighbours, Alex, an Englishman who worked in insurance. Slimy fellow, always reaching across the boundary hedge with his long clippers and depositing the cuttings on their side as an excuse to pop over.

'Here she is,' said Alex, smiling. 'Apologies for barging in at dinner time but I just wanted to thank you, Mary.'

'For your great work today,' explained Pete.

'Okay,' said Mary.

'I watched it on the telly and securing that test match was a victory for democracy over mob rule. Plus, a bloody good result on the field too!' He was reaching forward, past Pete, extending his hand to her. She was reminded of politicians at awards events who always wanted to touch her.

She held up her hand. 'I have all this hand cream on—just washed.'

He withdrew his arm. Pete wasn't letting him in the door.

'Thank you again, Mary. I was just saying to Pete that it takes courage to stand up for something.'

'Uh huh,' said Mary.

'How did it go? It must have been tense.'

Mary shrugged.

Alex pushed on. 'Anyway, to live next door to a police officer, it's a privilege and an honour.'

Pete said, 'We feel the same about English insurance salesmen.'

Alex let go half a laugh.

'Good night then,' said Pete as he closed the door. He turned to her. She saw he wanted it fixed between them. 'How are you, seriously? How did it go?'

'No one was killed.' Somehow she didn't want it to be fixed quite yet. There was too much adrenaline flowing through her. She felt combative still, tensed in the legs and arms, as if expecting to duck, to run, to stand firm in the face of attack. If she'd taken their neighbour's hand, she might have pulled it off. Clearly, the shower hadn't worked.

'I was really worried about you,' said Pete. 'We stayed at the back, well away from trouble. But I saw things were getting hairy. Are you okay, love?'

She'd been in crowds before but nothing with battlelines. She managed not to burst into tears. 'I stayed at the back too. Can we eat?'

At dinner, Mary asked Will what it was like to be on the protest. She managed to keep judgement out of her voice. She was still mad at them both.

'It was fun,' said Will.

'Fun?'

'We had hot chips.'

'Afterwards,' said Pete. 'It's hungry work fighting apartheid.'

Mary looked at Will. 'Is that why you're not eating your dinner?'

Pete had made Will's favourite white meal: macaroni cheese.

Will stuck his fork into the pasta and brought up a long twist of cheese. 'I don't like strings, when it's too long like this. I feel like I might choke.'

'Cut them up then,' said Pete. 'Use your knife to cut the strings up. Here.' He leaned over to show him.

'Don't help him,' said Mary sharply. 'Don't baby him.'

Pete glared at her.

They ate without talking. Will was pushing the food around.

'Leave it alone if you're not going to eat it!' said Mary.

Will put his fork down. After a while, he said, 'Who is Amanda?'

'Who?' said Pete.

'Amanda. Everyone was calling it out today on the march.'

'*Amandla*,' said Pete. 'It was Amandla Ngawethu.'

'That's the name!' said Will. 'Amanda Noweto. I think she was locked up in her own country, in South Africa. She should be freed, shouldn't she. Do you agree, Mum?'

Mary had a mouthful of food.

Pete said, 'Amandla Ngawethu is a Zulu phrase, it's African. It means the power is ours.'

'Poor old Amanda,' said Will.

Pete reached for his son's plate, whipping it away. 'Okay, you've had enough. Why don't you get your pyjamas on? Been a big day for everyone.'

Will stood up from the table and raised his fist in the air. 'Amanda!' he chanted loudly. 'Amanda!' He waved encouragingly at Pete.

'Amandla Ngawethu,' Pete responded faintly.

Marching from the room, Will called it out again, 'Amanda Noweto!'

'Jesus,' said Pete.

When Will was in bed, Mary came and sat with Pete on the sofa. 'Foot rub?' she said.

He put down his book and took her feet into his lap. He peeled off one sock.

'Be gentle,' she told him. 'They were stomped on a bit. Mostly friendly fire, to be honest.'

'Poor love,' he said.

After a while, she said, 'I don't know if I want to be on the job anymore.'

'It must have been a hell of a day.'

'Yeah. But generally. I don't know. I want to quit.'

Pete said, 'Seriously?'

She saw at once he was excited by this, which was sort of disappointing. Had she been hoping he might tell her no, no, you can't quit? You're a great cop. You need to stay and fight for change.

'But what would I do?' she said.

'There are lots of other things you could do.'
'Like what?'
'Teaching. Remember that? That was the plan once.'
'I don't have any patience with kids.'
'That's not true.'

She told him about the little girl who was passed over the heads of the cops in front of her and how she, Mary, got rid of her as fast as she could.

'Come on, that was a highly pressured situation.'

'I said, "Go on, move over there, go on." I really resented that the females again had to deal with the kids. But it's not even about that. You're better. You're better with him than I am. With Will.'

'What?'

She felt him press harder into her heel. It was just on the right side of pain. 'You know.'

'I get to hang out with him more than you do. I don't have nightshifts. I don't have the stress you have. Mary, I deal with library fines. Occasionally someone is upset a book is not in place when the catalogue says it is. Or they come and tell me off for having such a terrible book on the shelves. Sometimes I have to wake up a person who's snoring. It's a doddle.'

'You could still get annoyed at him more than you do.'

He put her sock back on and smiled at her. They both knew what she'd said was true. He was quite happy. Her incompetence was a boost. Free Amanda Noweto, she thought.

She pointed. 'Are you doing the other foot? These are the feet which have protected the rights of racists to play a game of footy, you know. My calves are sore too.'

He started, and she remembered how he'd rubbed her feet

when she was in labour in hospital. He'd asked her if he could help in any way and she'd had absolutely no capacity to direct him. The contractions were coming closer and closer. Why was he even around? Because they'd agreed beforehand. But now? She really didn't think it was her job to give him a job. Had he always been like this, a little removed from the action, a kind of deputy? Someone waiting to receive orders. Sweet and hopeless. Mostly she'd been the boss. He'd begun doing something at the bottom of the bed. She only found out later he'd been massaging her feet and legs. At one point, he asked, 'Is this good?' And she'd said, 'Is what good?' They'd both found it funny later. It was the birth story they told people.

She didn't tell anyone, not even Pete himself, that when she found out she was pregnant, she kept it to herself for a long time. And if he'd suspected this was the case, he'd never asked her about it either. She had to consider her options. That was how it appeared to her. Look what you've got yourself into. Now what are you going to do? He seemed peripheral then, poor Pete. Aghast, she saw herself as her sister, making a flip judgement on men, that they were good for such a limited number of things.

To go through with it, what would that mean? Immediately she felt it was the end of her career. Female officers didn't come back from this. It may as well have been a criminal conviction. Guilty of procreation. You were toast. She'd been to the farewells. She loved her job back then. And while a baby wasn't not in the plan, they'd also not committed to it, not now anyway. She replayed all the 'nots' in her head. There were so many negatives sloshing around.

Her GP told Mary she was around twelve or thirteen weeks. She asked how Mary felt about it. Here was the opening for her to be assessed as at risk. She was at risk, though not of the right kind, she knew. Still, her GP might have made it happen. The look on her face was frankly sympathetic. Mary remembered her doctor liked to chew on the end of a pencil and her clothes smelled of cigarette smoke. 'Can I think about it?' said Mary. The answer from her doctor was that she shouldn't take too long.

The other negative was that Mary hadn't taken her contraception pills for a month. That was why this had happened. Then had she wanted it to happen? Or had she believed it would never happen? Several things were true at the same time.

In the next few days she began to feel queasy, and then one morning Pete heard her being sick in the bathroom. He called out, asking if she was all right. It would have been straightforward to pretend it was a bug and secretly to make an appointment that week. Instead, Mary walked out of the bathroom and told Pete she was feeling fine. 'In fact,' she said, 'I feel wonderful.' He studied her and she rubbed her tummy meaningfully, smiling at him. Immediately his eyes filled with tears. His emotion was lovely, persuasive. It could all work, could it? He was holding her carefully, the thing between them.

After a couple of hours, Mary tried the Andersons again. This time she got the daughter, who said her name was Vivian. Yes, Vivian—that had been on the file Dave Monk had given her. Mary hadn't wanted to retain it, yet it lodged, like everything about that time. Old habits. On the phone Mary was explaining who she was and how the police had passed on the details. When she finished there was a long pause. Finally, Vivian said, 'Kia ora Mary. Dad died last month.'

'Oh,' said Mary. 'I'm sorry.' She was completely deflated. She sat down.

'It was a long journey,' said Vivian. 'He did well.' The delivery was slow. 'And it was a blessing for him to be released.'

'I see.'

'He came to a point, Mary,' she said, 'where a lot of the things in his life . . . made sense. He said something like that.'

'Did he.' She was finding Vivian a bit irritating.

'You'll hardly be gripped by the story of my father's life. I know that, Mary.'

Mary felt pricked by this woman's sudden understanding. Her tone must have given her away. Good for Vivian. They knew where they stood, Mary hoped. Let's not have too much more about dear old Dad's blessed release.

'No, no,' said Mary, 'my husband and I, we were surprised to find out about your family's approach. Out of the blue.'

'Us too, Mary, us too.' Vivian put in the pause again. 'We had no idea about a lot of Dad's past until quite recently.'

'He suddenly wanted to unburden himself, eh?'

There was yet another pause. 'I'm not sure. I'm not sure about that word "unburden".'

Mary waited but Vivian was waiting too. 'What would you say then?'

It was strange how this was going, to be interviewing this person about Shaun Anderson, as if anyone cared, outside his family. She thought of the list of convictions he'd accumulated, the misery he'd caused all those years ago. If he'd become a reformed character, Mary was happy—but mainly happy if this meant he'd stopped inflicting pain on others through his recklessness. Otherwise, it was meaningless. He'd been involved in her son's death. Had justice been served? Periodic detention for that? Oh well. A judge had made the call. Win some, lose some. But Anderson had not made an approach to Mary and Pete at the time or since—not until now, and he'd left it too late. His lawyer back in the day had probably advised him on that. No apologies, no culpability. Sadness was fine. Sympathy was good. His other convictions couldn't be admitted into the trial. Fair enough. She understood the law. And okay, he had a daughter and she was talking about him, not disowning him, wanting Mary to be interested. That was worth something. She wouldn't hang up quite yet.

'I reckon,' said Vivian slowly, 'that Dad needed something. Was missing something. Rather than he wanted to lose something, to unburden. I think, Mary, he wanted to gain something.'

'What?' said Mary. 'Gain what?'

'Gosh,' said Vivian. 'Where to begin?'

Mary could hear Pete moving around in the garage. The connecting door was flimsy. It was true of a lot of the house. Things were solid and then they weren't. Those first impressions of vault-like tightness hadn't been accurate. They'd already paid for someone to come and secure the bathroom vanity to the wall. A couple of screws had never been fitted. Now they tested everything. The long bench which served as a desktop in the study alcove had movement. The handle of their wardrobe was loose. The newness of the place didn't guarantee anything. It was like they needed to apply a giant spanner to the whole place and tighten. A bit like her brain.

Mary waited Vivian out.

Finally, Vivian said, 'We'd like to meet with you and your husband, Mary. That was the plan before Dad passed. He talked about it with his brother. Maybe my uncle was even the one who pushed Dad a bit.'

'So your father didn't really want to contact us?'

'No, he did, but he was, you know, ashamed or worried. But then he was determined. He was hoping for it, for sure. My uncle promised him we'd get in touch with you and invite you to the river.'

'To the river?' Mary couldn't think what this would achieve. She was suddenly very tired. It was time for her afternoon nap. 'Oh, I don't know, Vivian. It was all such a long time ago. Ancient history. And with your father no longer around.'

'Yep.'

'You know.'

'Yep. My uncle says it would be good.'

'Does he?'

'I'm listening to the family on this one. My uncle is the one with the knowledge.'

The word irritated her. 'Well, we went there. To the river. At the time, we went to the camp. The day after.'

'Yep.'

'I'm not sure if going there again would achieve much.'

Vivian didn't speak.

Mary said, 'Our son Will was thrown out of the vehicle your father was driving. Five boys on the back of the ute, off to shoot possums at night. Maybe you know the details? Anyway, Will was knocked unconscious, they think, and he went under the water. The other boys were more fortunate. Cuts and bruises. The ute flipped on the bridge. In the dark, it was hard to see what had happened and how everyone was. Your father had a head wound, banged his head in the crash, not serious.' Mary wasn't convinced she should carry on. No, she needed to state things, for the record. Maybe dear old Dad had sanitised the story. 'Will was taken downstream. It was ages before they knew he was missing. Maybe your father didn't even know how many kids were on the back. He was probably also disorientated. It was too late anyway for Will. Certainly, we blamed people. There was a complete lack of care shown to those boys by the school and, I'm sorry to say this, by your father, by everyone who thought the night-shooting expedition was a good idea. Who thought putting all those boys in the back of the ute was a good idea. And because the charges against your father were downgraded, on what we still regard as dubious grounds, the questions we have about what happened that night have stayed with us. That's almost forty years of wondering. Speaking frankly, Vivian, we believe your father escaped justice. He had no intention of causing harm, of causing death, but intention is only part of the law and only part of everyone's responsibility to one another. It doesn't feel great to be saying this to you at this time. But . . .' She stopped, listening to Vivian's breathing. Then she went on. 'I hope I'm not giving you new information when I tell you that your father had a long list of traffic convictions. He took risks on a regular basis. He endangered himself and others frequently. He liked cars and going fast and alcohol. He liked them together. It was a pattern when he was younger and even not so young. He was never breath-tested at the camp after the accident. He should have been. It was overlooked. I'm not saying he had been drinking. Someone told us he hadn't. Okay. I don't know. It was a big thing for the school, for the camp. But I'm just saying that this also adds to the questions we've carried all these years. Will was our only child. He died alone in the cold, in the dark, in a place he didn't know and, to be honest, where he never wanted to go in the first place. He was scared of the camp. We told him he'd be safe. He wasn't.'

Now the silence stretched out. Was Vivian even still there? Was she so offended by Mary's speech she'd walked off? Then Vivian cleared her throat. 'Tēnā koe Mary. So hard. So hard for you eh. If you don't want to come, that's all good. That's all good. For a lot of reasons, the people who should have known what happened at the camp never knew about it. Tikanga wasn't observed. This is all very late in your eyes, I understand. But it's something the old people see as important.'

'Say that all again, please. I missed it.'

Vivian repeated what she'd just said.

'I didn't know your father was Māori.'

'He hardly knew himself. Not until much later, when he started looking. I grew up with Mum, so this was all before I got to spend any time with him.'

Mary said, 'We didn't know any of this. Does it make a difference? I'm not sure.' She felt ambushed somehow.

'Back in the day, I suppose things like this were harder.'

'He never approached us back then.'

'No.'

'He could have but he didn't. Now we get this approach.'

'It's too long,' said Vivian.

'It's too late,' said Mary.

Vivian waited again. 'If you and your whānau come, there'll be a blessing. My uncle will do it. I'm no expert in any of this. Like I said, I grew up with Mum. She's Pākehā. We're doing it anyway. It's important.'

'Then it doesn't matter if we're there or not.'

'Uncle said that if you called, to give you the invitation.'

Mary thought for a moment. 'We don't know anything

about it. A blessing. We wouldn't know what to do.'

'We'll be in the same boat eh. I have to do a bit and I'm terrified. Uncle says to me, "It's not about you." Mary, you don't need to do anything except be present. You're very welcome.'

'I don't know. I'd have to check with—' She was about to say 'my people' but that was odd, as if she was conducting some kind of business. Who were her people?

'Yep,' Vivian said.

'And when? When would this be?'

'We'd arrange a good time for everyone.'

'I see.' The invitation had flummoxed her. She didn't know how to sound. She was coming off as ungrateful. Yet why should she be grateful?

Vivian was leaving another large silence, full of a kind of pressure.

No, that wasn't it.

She tried not to be flustered.

After another few moments, Vivian was speaking again. They'd be in touch whenever Mary wished. 'Yes,' said Mary. 'All right.'

After the call, she felt immensely tired, as if she'd run after someone and had failed to catch them, or to catch up with them—she didn't know which was correct. She walked around the house, looking for a place to sit down, trying various spots. None was quite right. Finally, she went into the garage and told Pete what Vivian had said.

'Gosh,' he said.

'Yes, gosh,' she said. 'I mean, after all this time.'

Her own exhaustion, she saw, was immediately infectious. Pete sat down on a box.

'We don't need to make a decision right away,' she said.

'Right,' he said. He looked up at her. 'What do you mean?'
'About going.'
'Why wouldn't we go?'
'You didn't even want to speak to her.'
'I would have spoken to her. You were in charge.'
'In charge? In charge of what? Anyway,' she said, 'blessings. You bless this, you bless that. A new motorway, a toilet block. Fine. Whatever you like. The uncle is behind it all.'

He was staring at her. 'This is for Will.'
'Yes, yes. Very nice.'
'Mary, what's the matter?'
'Nothing,' she said. 'Nothing.' She looked around the garage, all their possessions yet to be assigned places. It was overwhelming. 'Look at all this stuff!'

Pete stood up and moved to her. When he took her in his arms, she let her weight go and he had to readjust to hold her. She dragged at him and he stood firm. She recalled things: Colin falling against her when he and Claire came around to the house after Will died; the way her hair had been stroked by Alice, the woman she'd helped get to the church service in Lower Hutt; her own mother's embrace the day she married Pete and she'd whispered in Mary's ear, *You'll be all right, you'll be all right.* Up to that point she hadn't considered she'd be anything but all right. She'd been flying that day. How she laughed then, and her mother joined in, still gripping her.

Fourteen

He'd missed Gus. The dogs around the village were tiny indoor types, not much bigger than some of the birds who lived around the estuary. He needed to pat Gus's solid body. He needed to talk to him and listen to him.

Walking up Jan's drive, Pete met a woman dragging a large branch down to a skip on the roadside. He knew she was the wife of a man called Jack who knocked on doors and offered cheap tree cutting, cash jobs. He'd had a few conversations with Mary and Pete over the years and they'd once got him to take out an old tree stump. Now the sound of a chainsaw started as Pete passed Jack's wife. They greeted each other. She often helped Jack on these jobs, as did his children. Pete saw that Jack was taking off the branches of the tall pōhutukawa in Jan's back yard. He wore earmuffs and safety glasses. Soon there'd be nothing much left of the tree except a trunk.

Jan waved to Pete from where she was lying on the divan in the sunroom. She motioned that he should come in. When he stepped inside, Jan said, 'Oh Pete, don't hate me.'

'For what?'

'The tree. It grew there by chance and its roots were heading my way. Wonderful tree, wrong place, I'm afraid. I've ummed and aahed for ages, and then Jack turned up. He's so persuasive.'

'He is. And it sounds like a sensible move.'

'Sensible?' She looked out the window, where Jack's wife was passing with another bushy branch. 'I've been lying here full of regret. Who am I to kill a tree? This broken-down lady. Please sit down, Pete.'

He heard a shortness of breath in her speech. It was hard to tell when she was lying down, but she seemed more bent over than the last time he'd seen her. It was the first time they'd sat together. Usually there were a few words exchanged at the door or she would call out from wherever she was. She used a stick and then a walker.

He was about to sit on the cane chair by the window but noticed there was an envelope on it.

'That's Jack's cash,' said Jan. 'When you go, would you mind handing it to him? I don't think my body is working very well today. He's from Vanuatu but his wife is from Niue. He says he's sending the money home to his sick mother. People's lives.'

'Sure.' He put the envelope in his jacket pocket. 'How's Gus?'

'Oh Pete.'

'What?'

'Gus is gone.'

'Gone where?'

'No, he died, Pete.'

His heart skipped, making him draw a short breath. 'He died? When?'

'The same week you moved.'

Now it was running along, arrhythmic, hectic. 'But I saw him not long before that.'

'He was old. He had a number of issues, poor Gus. I was dreading having to take him in, you know. But in the end, Gus helped me out. Like he always did. One morning he didn't come when I called. I went in and found him. He might have just been sleeping, although his sleeping was never as still as that. I miss him so much.'

'Yes.' He sat slumped, trying to settle his chaotic heartbeat, unable for a moment to offer Jan condolences on her loss. He remembered the dog hungrily licking his bowl.

Gus was hers. She had no one else. There were some nieces and nephews who occasionally used the house if they felt like a beach holiday. Nice young people, moving through. One time they'd carried Jan over the dunes and then down to the water's edge. They'd hugged Gus. They tied a spotted handkerchief around his neck. One summer they hung fairy lights in Jan's garden, extending them to Gus's kennel. Pete hadn't seen anyone visiting in a while apart from Jan's carers. Busy lives.

'Jan, I'm so sorry. I don't know what to say.'

'You were a great mate to him, Pete. He always enjoyed the walks.'

'The walks were for me.'

'Anyway, it was mutual.' She adjusted the blanket covering her legs. 'I'm sorry I wasn't in touch, but I knew you were busy with the move and everything. To be honest, I couldn't find your number. It's always been a casual arrangement. You'd just show up, like today.'

It sounded a bit like an accusation. Jan was right. He saw Gus when he wanted to. He used him. The flutter in his chest was awful now. He drew a longer breath and let it out. 'No, Jan, it's all fine.'

She looked completely done in. Now that the reason for his visits was gone, he found he didn't know what subjects they could move to. He didn't want to talk about the retirement village. He needed to leave and regain himself.

They listened to the chainsaw, the thud as another branch fell on to the ground. It made Jan flinch.

'Pete, if I could ask another favour?'

'Of course.'

'Gus's things, they're still here. I don't know if op shops take stuff like it. Leads and bowls. Probably we just need to dump the remaining food. I haven't been able to face it and I don't feel I can ask my carers to . . . There's the kennel too, but that's quite large.'

He took another breath. 'Leave it to me.'

Jack turned off the chainsaw when he noticed Pete was by the dog kennel. He walked over.

He pointed at Pete, smiling. 'Stump.'

'That's right, you took out our stump. I'm Pete. How are you, Jack?'

Jack waved his chainsaw. 'Busy, very busy.'

Pete explained about Gus and the kennel.

Jack said, 'You need to lift that?' He took off his safety glasses, the earmuffs hung around his neck. 'I'll get my wife. Me and her will do it.'

Had Jack seen his discomfort? Standing and moving around was actually better. His chest was settling down. 'No, no,' said Pete. 'We don't need to involve your wife. She's got her hands full. Maybe if you and I could take a side each?'

Jack was already calling her. He put the chainsaw down and turned back to Pete. 'You don't want an injury. You don't want to end up like her.' He gestured towards Jan's house.

Jack's wife was powerfully built—broader than Jack—and Pete watched as the pair hoisted the fibreglass kennel into the air and carried it down the drive to his car. Pete opened the rear door, folded down the seats, and they slid the kennel inside. It just fitted. He thought of a hearse, with Gus inside this dog's coffin. Pete placed the leads and the bowls beside the kennel, and finally a few bags of dog biscuits. He shook Jack's hand and then his wife's hand. He could feel their calluses.

'All right, boss,' said Jack.

'So kind of you,' said Pete.

'Anything else?'

'No, you've been great.' A wave of guilt washed through him. They should have given him more work. Jack wasn't a trained arborist, though Pete supposed he knew enough. He'd identified most of the trees on their property when he'd done the stump work. And he worked hard. 'Oh, I almost forgot,' he said. He handed Jack the envelope containing Jan's payment. 'From Jan.'

Jack looked annoyed for a moment. He stepped back and gestured for his wife to take the envelope.

'Sorry,' said Pete, confused.

'She's accounts,' said Jack, smiling again. 'Money.'

Jack's wife took the envelope and put it quickly inside her dress pocket. She gave him a quick nod and stepped back again.

'Excuse me,' said Pete, 'what is your name?'

Jack said, 'Her name is Salilo. But we make it easy for you. Sally.'

'I'm Sally,' she said.

'Hello,' said Pete. 'But I hope I can say it correctly, Salilo.'

'Oh, boss, listen to you! Are you also from Niue?' Jack laughed and Pete joined in. They were laughing and looking at Gus's coffin. Pete glanced up at the house, where Jan was peering from the window.

*

When his mother was first admitted to hospital with delirium it was just before Christmas and she got stranded in a general observation ward while they waited for a bed in the geriatric ward. The doctors were deeply apologetic and completely powerless. His mother got worse and worse in this setting. Her main care came from nurse aides who sat watching a row of patients and were trained only in the basics: lifting, washing, walking. The ward was large, with about fifty beds surrounding the central nurses' station. It was a holding pen for all sorts of patients awaiting their next move. It was precisely the wrong place for Margaret. The gold-standard care for delirium patients was connected with reducing noise, light and all environmental stimulants. The brain needed to restore itself away from stress. It also didn't need to be challenged. The usual orientation questions a doctor might use were known to be counterproductive. *Do you know where you are? Do you know why you're here? Can you tell me the name of the Prime Minister? Can you tell me your birthdate?* Despite the geriatrician's advice, nearly every doctor who approached Margaret's bedside began with this interrogation. If Pete or Mary was there at the time, they'd try to head this off. Frequently the doctor would carry on regardless. Margaret's usual answers were: *I am in hospital. I am here because my son is trying to kill me but he is also under threat so the real enemies might be other people entirely—you, for instance. I don't want to tell you the name of the Prime Minister since it might be used against me. I was born in the year of our Lord, anno domini we called it, not that I would expect you to understand that. My son did Latin and will assist you in the translation, if he feels that's appropriate.*

Suddenly she lived in a terrifying world of assassins and

plots. Her old world of running a household, doing the shopping, reading crime novels and going for walks was gone. She'd been chosen to work something out. Everything was connected, she told Pete, and it was a matter of solving it. She spoke non-stop to visitors.

'It must be exhausting,' he said to his mother one day he was with her. 'You've got so many things to work out.'

'It is exhausting,' she said. 'But I quite enjoy it.'

Sometimes she cowered and tried to pull the sheet over her head when she saw a doctor she didn't like moving towards her. Almost without fail she took against the doctors of colour. She shrank from their touch and began shivering uncontrollably. 'I'm shaking, I'm shaking! I can't stop!'

'Margaret,' the doctor would say, 'can you look at me for a moment?'

'I'd rather look at the devil. Are you the devil?'

'Margaret, I'm a doctor here at the hospital.'

'We all have our crosses to bear.' She'd shoot a look at Pete, almost mischievously, but then she might shriek if the doctor tried to get any closer.

The hospital would ring them in the evenings when Margaret was refusing to leave the toilet or the shower cubicle. They'd drive in, always together. It was a two-person job. Pete would talk to his mother through the door. She once bit a nurse aide's hand, and when they got to the hospital they felt they were being judged. Here they come, the terrible people who've dumped their mother on us. Eventually the door would open and Mary would go in and help Margaret get dressed. Suddenly she would be compliant and they would lead her back to bed.

'Is that my pillow?' she would ask. 'I think they've swapped my safe pillow for their poisonous one.'

'That's the pillow we brought from our place, Margaret,' Mary would say.

'Is it?'

'Yes.'

'Is it, Peter?'

'Yes, Mum.'

'Okay.'

Why did she have so much trouble walking? She had to be assisted everywhere. Soon she was in a wheelchair. There was no physical reason, they were told. There was no reason for any of it. The delirium had arrived like a lightning bolt. It was expected to last a few days. Probably the result of some infection. But they couldn't locate any infection. Still, the symptoms would slowly recede, everyone felt. None of the scans showed anything especially unusual or troubling. They tried three times to insert the lumbar-puncture needle into her spine but there was too big a build-up of arthritic material. They were trying to rule out encephalitis.

'You've got to get her out of this ward,' Pete would tell the head nurse.

'We're really trying,' she'd say. 'It's unsafe for everyone.'

One day he'd wheeled her downstairs for a change of scene. The lift doors opened, and his mother feverishly scanned the lobby, sensing her freedom for the first time in weeks. The Christmas decorations were up. He knew she was capable of making a scene, or perhaps she'd leap from the wheelchair and run through the exit. The security men would have to intervene. Already that morning she'd lashed out at an orderly, striking him on the arm with the side of her fist; she'd also pinched the hand of a nurse.

'There!' she told him. 'Take me over there!'

He tried to turn her in the direction of the large Christmas tree near the café, but she said loudly that he was heading the wrong way and she pointed again. Pete wheeled her across to a desk marked 'Welcome! Volunteer Inquiries Desk' where a young woman greeted them with a smile.

His mother said, 'I would just like to thank you for all the great work you do in this place. It really is marvellous to have such dedicated people here.'

The woman said, 'Oh, that's so lovely. Thank *you*!'

'No,' said his mother, 'thank you. I've experienced only kindness since my time here and, further to that, I have something to offer you in recognition of your service.'

'What a sweetie,' said the woman, smiling at Pete.

He tried to suggest that all was not well with this sweet person, but it was difficult to communicate much with an eye-roll.

His mother said, 'I am offering you an all-expenses-paid cruise to a destination of your choice.'

The young woman blinked and looked from his mother to Pete. 'Okay, ha! Gosh.'

'We're finalising the details. This will be the opportunity of a lifetime.'

'It sounds amazing.'

'It is amazing,' said his mother.

'How kind.'

'Now I'll need your answer pretty soon. Later today if possible. Will you need to ring your mother?'

'Yes,' said Pete. 'She'll need to sort out some things to see if she can go on the cruise. It's hard to just drop everything.'

'What?' said his mother.

'I will,' said the woman. 'It might be quite tricky.'

'Tricky?' said his mother. 'Do you realise there are people who would jump at this chance? Tricky.'

Pete had started to turn the wheelchair away.

The woman at the desk said, 'It's been lovely meeting you.'

'How stupid can people be?' His mother was suddenly furious. 'Take me over there!'

'To the Christmas tree?'

'Yes, I want to see if we can smash it.'

'We're not smashing anything, Mum.'

'Then why are we here?'

He spun her around again. 'Would you like to go outside for a bit?'

'Where? You're making me dizzy.'

'Just through the doors there. Just for some fresh air.'

'No!' she said loudly and fearfully. 'Take me back, take me back! I can't go out. Everything is gone. It's all gone! There's nothing left.'

Finally, she was transferred to a short-term closed psychiatric geriatric unit, with specialist care and her own room. The medication appeared to start working. Margaret began to sleep better, eat better. Pete tried to get there every day but there were some days neither he nor Mary could make it. He was also able to return to more regular sleeping. Relief surged through his body. For the first time in two months, he felt as if he'd handed over his mother to people with expertise. Hours went by and he realised he hadn't thought about her. He told this to Mary, and she assured him that this was a good sign. When his mother did come to his mind, however, it was always with a pang of guilt.

At the first meeting with the psychiatrist and the medical director, he was encouraged to talk about his mother—not only about when she'd become ill but also her life before then, her life with his father, what she enjoyed doing, what a normal day consisted of—and when he got back to the car, he sat in the carpark weeping. They had asked about his mother's two older siblings, who were both dead, and he thought at first they were trying to piece together his mother's childhood and build a psychological portrait of her. Of course, they were simply seeing if there was a pattern of dementia or other illness.

But to be listened to like this by people with skills and understanding was so powerful he had to get out of the car again and walk around for a while, his legs shaking. He remembered the moment when the psychiatrist, for the first time, began to write as he spoke. How strange he felt! Like a president, or a person of importance. Someone was valuing his words, someone was valuing her.

One afternoon, Pete entered Margaret's room and found her sitting on the edge of her bed with a life-size toy dog on her lap. She gave him a curious smile, which seemed to say, I know, I know, look at me. Isn't this ridiculous.

'Hello Mum,' he said. 'Who's this?'

She pushed the dog away from herself slightly. She'd never had anything to do with dogs in her life, not as a child nor as an adult. His father had an antipathy towards them. Pete recalled times when they'd been at a park or on a beach, when his father started muttering about 'damn animals'. Away in the distance someone would be walking their dog off the leash. His mother told him to calm down, they were miles away and not bothering anyone. But his father's agitation would grow. Sometimes he'd walk towards the dog owner and have an argument. Men would shout at his father, give him the fingers. As a boy, Pete knew to avoid any interaction with dogs if his father was around. He had no idea why his father was like this.

His mother's possession of this dog felt like an answer

to her husband. Now finally she could enjoy a companion animal.

Pete reached out and stroked the toy dog's head. 'Hey boy.'

'Have him if you want,' said his mother, offering it to him.

He took the dog. 'He's got soft fur.'

His mother stared at the dog who was now facing her. 'He has very black eyes.'

This was true. The black glass eyes gave the dog an odd look. Not unfriendly exactly, but mysterious and withholding. Sometimes Pete had thought the psych geriatric unit imbued even the most ordinary objects with a kind of uncanny force. His mother had a fear of the electric plug on the wall opposite her bed. It had a reset button which glowed red. He reassured her about it but certainly he could see why it might appear malevolent. The red eye was piercing if you looked at it long enough—and this is what she did, of course, lying in bed. There was a basin in her room and the taps were operated by a long narrow metal wand. Margaret believed this was something that the staff used to impale patients on. She warned Pete whenever he got too close to it. She didn't like getting out of bed from the side but preferred to crawl to the foot of the bed and leave that way. She received electric shocks if she went the other way. Pete saw that where she might normally step on to the floor they'd placed an alert mat which let the nurses know Margaret was out of bed. His mother saw that this wasn't normal and provided the interpretation. She looked at the name labels Mary had sewn on her clothes so they wouldn't get mixed up with other patients' clothes, and she said, 'These aren't mine.' And she was right. Since when had her shirts carried her name? Did they think she was a schoolgirl?

Now Pete held the dog out to her. 'Would you like to hold him again?'

'Put him down there,' she said, pointing to the end of her bed. 'He's had far too much attention.'

The nearest op shop couldn't take the kennel, and for a moment he thought he might bring it home with him and—do what with it? Get a dog? Build it and they will come? No. They'd never had a dog. From time to time they'd discuss it. But they worried about the times they would have to leave it—when they went away on longer holidays, or even just overnight. Mary remembered the dogs her family had owned and the desperate act of dropping them off at a place, usually in some rural setting with chain-link fencing, and the uncertainty around the kind of care the dog would receive. She would usually be in tears, her mother too, while Claire and her father went silent.

Pete ended up driving north for thirty minutes and visiting two more places before somewhere agreed to take the kennel. One of the volunteers, a young woman, helped him lift it from the car to outside the shop's storeroom behind the building. For some reason he decided he needed to check inside the kennel, and he put his head through the opening. A powerful smell of Gus was present. Even though he'd never considered Gus to have a strong odour, this was his sleeping place, no doubt. He saw in the far corner a series of lumps under Gus's mat. He reached in and lifted the mat. Five or six old tennis balls rolled free. Gus had been storing them there—not, Pete thought, to play with at a later date, but so that no one would throw them and expect Gus to run after them. The next dog could do that.

He stood up too quickly and felt faint. The woman who'd

helped him had gone back inside the shop. He put his hand against the nearby gate, steadying himself, and touched his jacket in the area over his heart. Let me not collapse here, he said to himself. Mary thought he was walking a dog on the beach forty kilometres away and she would need to spend an inordinate amount of time working out how he'd got to this location. He would have posed her exactly the kind of puzzle she dealt with in her career as a policewoman. Probably it would be easily solved. Still, to end here, behind an op shop, a place full of old stuff, run by kind people, wasn't so terrible. He saw them carrying his body inside, into the storeroom. He'd lie there, with the washing machines waiting to be tested, with the three-legged stools, among the banana boxes of clothes needing to be sorted on to the labelled shelves. *Men, women, children.*

In a flash he saw Will after the accident, laid out on the table in the cold room at the camping place.

His blood achieved equilibrium once more. There was no pain from his heart, only a mild run of palpitations which no longer scared him.

In the car he felt his thumb throbbing. He inspected it and saw it was quite swollen. He'd jammed it getting the kennel out of the car. It was on his right hand, and backing the car out he learned it was too painful to use for steering. His lower back had twisted awkwardly too in bending with the kennel, and now it gave a twinge. Truly he was falling apart. On the road he was followed closely and then overtaken by numerous cars. One gave him a hostile blow of the horn as it went by. He didn't feel like he was going too slow for open-road driving. He used to enjoy driving and now it was stressful. How long before he gave it up? The idea depressed him. He opened the window to feel air on his face—he had to be alert—and to let the smell of the kennel leave, blow out over the farmland.

When he got back to the village, he said to Mary, 'Gus died.'

'Who?'

'Gus, the dog. Jan's dog.'

'Oh,' she said, 'that's very sad. How old was he?'

'Pretty old.'

She nodded and walked out of the room.

Truthfully, he didn't mind this. He was too tired to talk anyway, and how could he tell Mary the story of the kennel and his turn outside the op shop without worrying her? She was too fragile. No, she had never been fragile. Erratic maybe. He could no longer guess at her reactions to things. She would move about the rooms with a new listlessness and then be taken up with a purpose. She was slack and then everything was urgent. She seemed always to be looking for something. *Have you seen it, Pete?* Of course, things were hard to locate now after the move.

What did you say? She wore her hearing aids only if they were out at the shops or away from the village. He thought at first she wanted him to be her ears, but that wasn't it either. She would cut him off if he tried to repeat things. She appeared content not to have heard a lot of what came at her, though she was hardly floating in some blissful silent space. Often she slumped in her chair, looking annoyed. He was torn between staying in the same room with her or leaving her there for a while. In time she'd revive, coming to find him.

In the new place he was also first out of bed and had to remind her to take her pills. She seemed grateful to him for this. It was soon their ritual. *Look at you*, she'd say. He would place the tiny pills in her palm and wait for her to swallow them with the glass of water he'd brought her. *Thank you.* Touching the soft pad of flesh by her thumb became a highlight of his day, their one reliably intimate connection.

Fifteen

The year after her sister died, Mary would be visited by Claire in a recurring dream. They'd be at a dinner with a large group of people, though Mary never remembered who these people were, just that everyone was friendly and the atmosphere was festive. A kind of reunion, she thought. Mary would look down the table at her sister and they'd exchange secret smiles, listening to whoever was talking, having a gentle unspoken joke at their expense. *Will you listen to this guy!* It was all lovely and bathed in a soft light, as if the evening was gradually coming to an end. The dinner had been a success. Whatever anxieties people had carried in were now dissipated. Mary was already looking forward to the debrief with Claire on the drive home. In the dream it was understood the sisters lived together and had no others in their lives. Pete didn't exist and nor did Colin. They didn't have parents. It was perfect. The dining table was covered in wine glasses and candles. Everything shone. You are dead, dear sister, Mary said to herself in the dream. But you are okay. It was beautifully reassuring, since Mary within the dream was able to step outside the dream and experience this feeling.

Claire was smiling but then she also started yawning. She yawned widely, hiding it behind her hand too late. She almost giggled at Mary, who'd seen the yawn. *Oops, sorry.* She yawned again. She couldn't stop.

At first Mary thought this was all fine—of course her sister would be tired. It had been a long evening. Time to go home.

Then she began to worry. She didn't like Claire's face when she yawned. It was pulled out of shape. Claire wasn't bothering now to cover it. Her mouth opened wide and then closed. It was out of character. She gulped and gulped. Soon the others at the table would notice. The mood would be ruined. The evening would be remembered for this behaviour. From the end of the dining table, Mary began to frown at her sister. *Stop that*, Mary sent the message. *Enough*. But it didn't work. Claire was helpless in her tiredness. She yawned and yawned, trying to get air. The dream always ended at this point. It was stuck.

For a long time after he died she would still wake in the morning and have as her first thought, I must get Will up and ready for school. He'd never liked leaving his bed on a school day. It was usually a struggle to convince him to get dressed, eat breakfast, pack his bag. He wouldn't throw tantrums or physically resist them. Pete called him Little Gandhi, the resident prince of passive resistance. Everything in the morning took such a long time, and often Mary would have left the house before Will had even made it to the kitchen. Pete was in charge, if it could be called that. He started at the library later, had more flexibility there. Closing the door behind her, she used to feel guilty. Over time she lost that feeling, knowing that if she hovered and tried to help, tried to hurry things along, it would all become much more stressful. She saw Pete was now reconciled to Will's pace. Mostly he just laughed at his son's inertia, and slowly found ways to dilute the tension they'd created. That was how Pete framed it—as something they were doing to Will, rather than the other way around. At first Mary found this irritating. She would sometimes think, What if I had had a daughter? The loneliness of being in a household with these two males could strike her. She saw how, when she was growing up, her mother and her sister had completely defined life.

Pete came up with incentives. Will was allowed fifteen minutes outside once he'd eaten breakfast. If he didn't use the fifteen minutes at home, they would use the same amount of time on their walk to school—to explore the nearby park, or simply to take another, longer route. It seemed Will needed to put his hands in the earth or to observe close-up the lives of other creatures. If they stood quietly amongst trees, listening to identify birds, or crouched down to see insects, examine tracks made by possums, look into the stream which crossed the park—this was usually enough. Will could carry it with him through the school day, perhaps, and not feel totally isolated from what mattered to him. And at school, by all accounts, he was not vastly unhappy. There were a few kids drawn to him, and they mostly kept away from the bullies.

Mary remembered she'd once brought up the idea of home schooling with her sister. Claire was horrified. Did they want to make Will even more of an outsider? And how would they manage? Mary would have to leave work, or Pete would. They had a mortgage. Kids had to make their way in the world, she said.

'You make them sound like little . . . employees!' said Mary.

'Employed by the world maybe,' said Claire. 'Engaged there, yes.'

'Will has found the bits of the world he wants to engage

with. They just don't happen to be at school.'

'No, no, no.' Claire was shaking her head. 'Mary, the other thing is this. You need him away from you. You need him away from the house. You need time out. For yourselves. When Colin leaves for school in the morning, sometimes I dance a jig. I literally do a little dance. Do you not do a little dance?'

'I do,' said Mary. 'I do.'

Mary's last real case as a cop had the feel of an hallucination. She knew it had happened, though she also doubted her recall and she didn't like to think of it.

There was a career crim called Barry Must. Mary had arrested him before, years ago, for a burglary. Back then she was a newish constable and he'd been fairly harmless, in and out of prison for stretches of one or two years. No one got hurt when Barry Must broke the law, broke into people's houses and businesses, leaving clues. *Must've been Barry*, cops liked to say. Barry himself somehow encouraged this comic touch, she thought. He was jokey, hapless, took what was coming to him. He inhabited his tall and large body with a kind of apologetic goofiness. He lumbered. He crashed through windows. There was nothing slippery about him. He seemed uninterested in evasion. She'd arrested him at his mother's house. When she arrived, they were watching TV together and Barry was wearing a kitchen pinafore. His mother had put it on him so he didn't get food down his front. He asked if he could finish his dinner. Mary sat on the sofa with Barry Must's mother, watching *Coronation Street*. Cops went, *Where's the pinny, Barry?*

Then it all changed. Apparently Barry fell in with some heavy types in prison and the next lag was eight years for an armed robbery where a bank teller was shot. Barry was the driver and was out early, but now he was quite far down the slide. Mary found it hard to believe but he'd become a nasty fellow and somehow an enforcer. The drug squad had him in their sights, but he was too low to pull in just yet. They figured Barry wasn't that bright and soon he'd stuff up and allow them to swoop on the big boys in the ring they were targeting.

All of this meant Barry had left Mary's orbit.

Then one night she attended a possible domestic. She was a sergeant now and should really have had her feet under the desk in her office where there were rosters awaiting her attention and where it was vaguely warm and someone occasionally brought you coffee. But that week was the first week for a young constable called Sarah Hunt, and Mary decided she might tag along. Mary always remembered the name because when they first met she'd said that Hunt was a good name for a copper, and Sarah had told her it wasn't such a good name because of what it rhymed with. 'Punt,' said Mary. And Sarah said, 'How'd you guess?' Instantly she liked Constable Hunt. Sarah had grown up on a farm, played rugby for South Canterbury. She wanted to be a dog handler eventually. Her boyfriend was at their house right now, she said, with Sonny, their Alsatian. The love of her life, she told Mary—Sonny, that is. She wasn't totally convinced by the boyfriend. Sarah had a big outdoorsy laugh.

The house was in Houghton Bay, down a steep and mossy driveway. Mary and Constable Sarah Hunt shone their torches on the ground and stepped carefully. A cat fled past them, disappearing into the bush. They waited at the front door. The call had come from a neighbour. Reports of shouting and screaming, things breaking. The house was silent. On the porch were gumboots, a bucket with a fishing rod in it. Raincoats hung on a hook.

Mary knocked.

Her mentor and now her boss, Ross Hayes, had drilled her on this moment. Entering a Scene. It was not just that you had to keep your wits about you. Ross said some coppers, experienced ones and new ones, believed it was all about what you arrived with and carried with you—confidence, focus, all that. But he liked to turn it around. It was what the Scene gave you, not what you took into it. Be receptive until it hurts, he told Mary. Be open until you think you'll burst. When she'd looked at the fishing rod, she thought of a man bending down and gutting a fish. She shone her torch into the bucket and, sure enough, there was a long filleting knife. If, say, a person was to rush through this door, he would know where to reach for a knife. She nudged the bucket with her foot until it was hidden by the raincoats.

Someone was coming. The porch light came on. Mary blinked to clear her vision.

'Here he comes,' said Sarah. There was tension in her voice. She'd graduated only the previous month. She stood behind Mary.

'Take it easy, Constable,' said Mary.

'Yes, Sarge.'

A man's ugly voice came through the door. 'Who is it?'

It was good to have Sarah Hunt with her. 'Police,' said Mary. 'Can you please open the door and step back.'

'Fuck off,' said the man.

'Sir, can you open the door now.'

'What do you want?'

'We want you to open the door, sir.'

'Where's your warrant?' His words were slurred.

Mary said, 'This isn't a search. We've had reports of some noises coming from this house.'

'Who the fuck reported it?'

'Open the door.'

There was a pause. 'Nah, fuck this. You can fuck right off.'

They heard him walking away from the door. Mary pointed her torch at the nearest window, but the curtains were closed. She knocked again on the door. No answer.

'What now, Sarge?' said Constable Sarah Hunt.

They followed a path around to the back of the house. 'Have a go,' Mary told Sarah, indicating the back door.

'Break it down, you mean?'

'Well, no. Try knocking.'

'Yes, Sarge.' She bashed at the door with the side of her fist.

'Shit, you have a good knock.'

There was no movement from inside the house.

Mary asked, 'What was on your farm?'

'Sheepandbeef,' said Sarah.

It came out as one word.

'What do you think we should do, Constable Hunt? There could be someone in danger in that house.'

'Smash the door in,' said Sarah. 'Looks pretty flimsy.'

'Or call for backup?'

'Oh yep. Backup, yep.'

'We don't know what we'd be walking into.'

'He's been on the piss. A single male occupant.'

'You sure?'

'No, Sarge.'

Mary directed her torch around the back yard. Three tea towels hung on the clothesline.

Sarah followed her torch. 'His wife?'

'Men technically might be able and even willing to hang out tea towels but, you know, it's rare.'

She remembered then how a few years before there'd been a push to 'improve the lot' of female officers. They heard there were some exciting initiatives coming from the very top. The first one was the weekly distribution of recipes to every woman in the force. Apparently, the Commissioner's wife had come up with this. She thought it would take the stress off them if they didn't have to think of what to cook their husbands every night. Mary wrote a letter about it which sort of became famous. She was bumped from guest lists she'd previously been on. No big deal. Other scrapes followed. They all seemed minor. You had to pick your fights. There was a lot she let slide. Sometimes she dug her heels in.

Mary continued to scan the area. There was a lean-to shed, possibly the laundry, and a child's bike against the fence.

'One kid?' said Sarah. 'Where's the kid? Inside.'

'I'd love to have your Alsatian with us right now. Sonny?'

'Yeah, Sonny would be good. He likes kids.'

They waited in the silence. It was a still night. Far off they heard a sort of static—the sea? Mary had never associated this area and all its dips and hollows with the sea, but it was close.

She was about to radio for assistance when there was a noise from the shed. She took a few steps towards it. 'Hello?' she said. Perhaps it was the cat they'd seen.

She peered inside and her torch fell on the face of a boy, about nine or ten. He was barefooted, sitting on a pile of firewood.

'I'm Mary, and this is Sarah.'

The boy stared at them, shivering. He was wearing shorts and a singlet. It was about five degrees.

Sarah said, 'What's your name, bud?'

He continued to stare. Then he looked down at his right hand. Mary shone the torch. He was holding a small axe. It was rusted and blunt. She saw now that he was also bleeding from his nose, which looked broken. He looked thoroughly beaten up.

'You've been in the wars, eh,' she said.

He sniffed and wiped at the blood with his left hand, smearing it across his face.

'Must be cold,' said Sarah. 'Come and we'll fix you up.' She took a step towards him, and he raised the axe. 'Steady there. You're good. You're safe. We're gonna help you.'

'He'll kill me,' said the boy.

'Don't worry about him,' said Mary. 'That's all over. We have that right under control.'

The boy was assessing whether this was true or not. Finally, he said, 'I can't walk.' He looked at his left leg.

'No worries, bud,' said Sarah. 'I'll give you a piggyback.'

He looked again at the axe. 'What about this?'

'Nah,' said Sarah, 'just leave that here, eh. Don't need it now.'

The boy let go of the axe.

Mary moved closer to the boy. Quickly she reached in and picked up the axe.

Just then the back door opened and the man from the house came rushing at them. He roared and held something above his head—a piece of timber. He brought it down on the arm Constable Hunt raised to protect herself. She screamed in pain and staggered away. Mary stepped from the shed as he raised the timber again. She ducked down and slammed the axe into the man's shin. The timber landed on the ground beside her head while he slumped to one knee, yelling. 'That fucking hurt! Bitch, that fucking hurt!' He spun around, trying to work out what had happened. Mary had lost her torch but there was enough light to show the features of Barry Must.

It was a strange moment, almost as though it was a case of mistaken identity and she'd have to apologise. Barry! Sorry! *Must have got the wrong man.*

She doubted he knew who she was, though, and he'd somehow grabbed Sarah's leg. He seemed possessed. Sarah kicked out at him, but he held on, growling. What was he going to do—take a bite? Anything seemed possible.

Then the boy came out of the shed, hobbling on one leg. Barry saw him and cried out, 'There you are, you little bastard!' He let go of Sarah and lunged at the boy.

Mary brought the axe down on the back of Barry Must's head. In her report she would say she was aiming for his arm, the one threatening to grab his son, whose name was Scott. But because it was a dynamic and evolving situation and they were almost in darkness, her aim was compromised.

Why hadn't they called for backup?

Because it was a dynamic and evolving situation.

Ross Hayes told her to use the phrase. There had to be a police investigation, which Ross assured her she would fly through. He was odd about it, though. As if he didn't want to know the details. As if she'd killed plenty of people before as a police officer and knew the ropes, knew the hoops—now jump. She thought it was off, how Ross acted.

She believed she handled the oral part of the investigation well. Two hours in a large bare room, facing three men at the end of a long table.

Why hadn't they found and removed the boy from the scene earlier?

Because he was hiding and because he was injured.

Why hadn't they attended to Mr Must or attempted CPR while they were waiting for the ambulance?

Because I was attending to the injuries of Scott Must, having ascertained that Mr Barry Must was deceased from a massive head trauma. Also, Constable Sarah Hunt had suffered a severely fractured forearm and was in shock.

The three men thanked her. True, they didn't give anything away, but no one was going in to bat for old Barry Must, career crim and child abuser. It seemed that the process was concluded.

Then, while still on leave, Mary found out there were possible charges against her. Who'd brought the complaint? That was unclear.

Mary met with the police lawyer, a small man with a birthmark on his neck which deepened in colour as he got into his work. It was important, he said, that Mary understood how this might go if it went further. She asked him how much further it could go, and he said it was hard to say, possibly court.

She was in a daze.

He would, if she allowed it, conduct a little role play. She didn't need to take part, just listen.

She should have walked out then.

Sergeant, do you consider the force you used against Mr Must to have been reasonable and appropriate?

She went to answer, and he held up his hand. He was doing both parts.

I do, he said.

This was a force sufficient to almost completely split open the back of Mr Must's skull, Sergeant. A force which resulted in brain material being found on your own clothing. Why do you consider that to be reasonable and appropriate?

Because it was a dynamic and evolving situation.

Mary was in a dream, she felt.

Have you ever used such force before in the line of duty?

No.

So this was extreme?

I've never had to use that much force in the line of duty because I've never been faced with what I was faced with that night.

So it was extreme, yes. Sergeant, had you previously had any interactions with Mr Must?

Yes, I arrested him for burglary a number of years ago.

And when you arrested him, did you consider Mr Must a violent and dangerous man?

No, not at that time.

Indeed, you arrested him at his mother's house, is that correct?

Yes.

He was sitting having dinner with his mother, yes?

That's right.

Mary interrupted the lawyer. 'How do you know this? They won't know it.'

'If I know it, they'll know it.'

He went on:

And you sat beside Mr Must's mother, as her son finished his dinner, is that what happened?

Yes.

A nice calm scene.

It was a long time ago. I believe Mr Must had hardened in the intervening years. His record of violence speaks to this.

Sergeant Brunton, do you consider the comparatively recent loss of your own son before this incident at the house of Mr Must a factor in any of your decisions that night?

'What?' said Mary.

The lawyer put a finger to his lips for her to be quiet.

What?

I repeat, do you consider the tragic loss of your own son before this incident at the house of Mr Must a factor in any of your decisions that night?

No.

Relevance, your Honour!

'There's a judge here?' said Mary.

The lawyer held up his hand to her again.

Please get to the point.

I'm asking, your Honour, if the discovery of the boy Scott Must in the shed that night connects with Sergeant Brunton's emotional and traumatic memory of her son's death—

Objection!

—and if she lashed out in some way at Mr Must as a result of unprocessed and deep-seated grief at that terrible loss. The question, your Honour, goes to a lack of judgement which had catastrophic results.

Objection, your Honour!

Sustained.

'You're joking,' said Mary.

The lawyer shook his head. He was enjoying playing all the voices. He was taking pleasure in being her. She should have walked out then too.

Is it true, Sergeant, that you failed to complete the required sessions with the police psychologist in the wake of your son's death?

Mary told the police lawyer, 'How the bloody hell would they know that?'

'I know it,' he said.

'I don't like that you do. Those are confidential sessions. Is this legal?'

And is it true that since your son's death your performance as a sworn officer has been the subject of some speculation?

'Speculation!' said Mary.

Were you not transferred out of your regular role, spending time in other districts?

'That wasn't a disciplinary measure!'

Sergeant, there was a transfer, and were your superior officers not looking for ways to minimise the disruption around you?

'This is all a joke of course,' said Mary. She walked out then, with the little lawyer's face now pretty much one big birthmark. She went to see Ross Hayes, but he was unavailable. He'd been called to a week-long top-brass shindig in Auckland. She left him messages he never returned. She fumed. She was lost.

Constable Sarah Hunt was transferred out of the district. Mary phoned her one evening but then she didn't know what she wanted from her. Sarah was a complete newbie, with a future to think about. On the phone, Sarah was guarded, strange. Yes, she was recovering well, trying to put it all behind her, moving on. She'd had some good advice. What advice? Mary asked. Oh, just some wise voices. The South Canterbury farmgirl had evaporated. You move on, Sarah said again. Don't dwell. Yes, it happened. It's over. Mary wanted to yell at her. Instead, after a brief and meaningless exchange, they said goodbye.

Then she was told that the complaint, if it really had been a complaint, had gone away. Dropped. No reason. On balance it had been decided, etc. No real debrief from her superiors. Ross Hayes told her it had all been a mistake. *Time to move on*. Could she? She was in the clear, not because it was shown she'd acted properly, only because someone had made the call. As though the paperwork had gone missing, fallen behind the filing cabinet. She felt she was now in the middle of a cold case. There was a file someone else might discover one day. *This guy Barry Must.* She wasn't really in the clear. The stain remained. She knew it would go with her wherever she went.

'I'm done,' she told Pete. 'They want me out and I'm out.'

He could only show her his relief. He'd wanted her to resign before, and after Barry Must died he was even more adamant it was the right call. He couldn't follow the machinations she was inside. It was a secret closed world he'd never cared for. He was still grieving too, of course.

She posted her resignation letter in the final week of her leave and never went back. No one rang her or tried to make contact in any way. She boxed up her stuff. Now what?

In the weeks after she left the force, she met her sister for lunch. Mary hadn't told Claire any of the details of what had happened the night she and Sarah Hunt went to Barry Must's house. It was a matter of pride that she had almost never given in to Claire's hunger to learn whatever was most lurid about her police work. Not that she wasn't tempted. It took a great deal of effort to withhold stories from her sister, not least because she knew she would grow in Claire's eyes if she were to talk about some of these things. A story was a magic bean, and Mary saw that she could scatter a few and soon be high above her sister. Also, she didn't trust Claire with confidential information. Anything she said would travel. Perhaps not telling gave her an edge anyway, since Claire was left to imagine all the terrible and fascinating stuff her little sister got up to.

They sat in the railway station café. It was bizarre to meet like this. They'd tried a couple of times to arrange lunch and it hadn't worked. On this day, Claire was catching the train up the island to meet a man. She didn't want to drive all that way. Colin was staying with his father. Mary had suggested they could postpone again, but Claire had insisted it would all be too difficult when she came back because of various commitments and why not grab the time they had? Mary was jobless anyway, Claire pointed out, and was a free bird.

'Who is this man?' asked Mary.

The café was crowded. People had their suitcases around them. It was hard to get to a table without spilling your tea.

'No one really,' said Claire.

They looked at an elderly man struggling to collapse his umbrella. Outside it was wet and cold. They hadn't taken off their coats. The smell of burned and rusting stones entered the café in sharp gusts from the tracks. Mary had a sudden desire to buy a ticket and go somewhere.

'He lives up there, does he?' said Mary.

'His holiday place.'

'Fancy.'

'I think it's very modest. Belonged to his grandparents or something. But there's a lake.'

'A lake is good.'

'If he goes fishing, I'll scream.'

'Teach a man to fish.'

'And he'll be very boring,' said Claire. She sipped her tea and prodded at her sandwich. 'God, I hope there's a supermarket nearby.' She pointed at Mary's sandwich. 'What's in yours?'

Mary lifted a corner of the white bread. 'Egg?'

'Ugh,' said Claire.

An announcement came over the loudspeakers. Claire listened and checked her watch.

'Are you okay for time?'

'It would be ironic to miss it, just sitting here, talking away.' She nibbled her sandwich and put it down again.

'How's Colin?'

'Oh, you know.'

A young mother was trying to manoeuvre her pram past their table. Claire moved her suitcase and smiled up at her. The mother nodded her head. She looked completely shattered. She'd been caught in the rain. You can't hold an umbrella and push a pram. Her hair was plastered to her head. The infant stared out at them from behind its plastic hood beaded in rain. Once she was past them, Claire said, 'Poor thing but, you know, bad planning.'

'How?'

'Listen to the weather forecast maybe? Make alternative plans?'

'Maybe she couldn't.'

'Yeah,' said Claire. She looked closely at Mary. 'What are you going to do?'

'What do you mean?'

'Now. Mary, what are you going to do? Speaking of plans. Now you're unemployed?'

Mary looked around the café. 'Not sure.'

'Not sure! Okay.' Claire laughed. 'No hurry, I guess. Pete is still pulling in the big bucks.'

Claire liked Pete—everyone liked Pete—but she also enjoyed mocking him.

Mary said, 'I might need some time.'

'Mary, you do look tired.'

'I am tired.'

'You look it.'

'Thanks, sis.'

'Am I allowed to be concerned?'

'Sorry,' said Mary.

'No, of course you need to take some time. It's a massive thing, to leave a job like that. It's been your life.'

'I remember you weren't a believer at the start.'

'I wasn't. And you proved me wrong. Hats off to you, Mare.'

'Turns out you were right.'

'Hardly. What are you talking about? You won bloody medals!'

'Medals, well, yes.'

'Your achievements were recognised. I was constantly amazed.'

'Were you?'

'Yes! We all were. Brave Mary. Fighting the good fight.'

Mary leaned in close to the table. She pushed away her plate with the uneaten sandwich on it. 'Claire, someone died because of me.'

'Who did? What are you saying?' Claire came forward. Their heads were close together now.

'Someone died by my hand. On the job.'

'But how?'

She regretted telling it at once. 'A man was trying to hurt someone, a boy, and I reacted.'

'Okay. That sounds like you were acting to protect the boy.'

'I was.'

'Then that sounds like you were doing your job, Mary.'

'I think I was.'

'How horrible for you though.'

'It wasn't too good for him either, the man who died.'

'But how did you—?'

'I prefer not to say too much more.'

'No. I understand.'

Mary saw her sister was disappointed. For a moment she wanted to tell it all. *I smashed an axe through his skull. Parts of his brain ended up on my uniform.*

It wasn't what she needed to tell.

'Claire,' she said, 'I saw Will that night.'

'The night when—'

'When I killed the man, yes. I saw Will.'

'You mean . . .'

'I don't know.' She pulled away from the table. 'I don't know. I haven't told Pete.'

'No, because he's not your sister.'

Mary smiled at this.

Claire said, 'Mare, you were protecting the boy.'

Mary said, 'It was a dynamic and evolving situation.'

'What was that, hon?'

'Never mind.'

Claire reached out and placed her hand on Mary's hand. 'Will you be all right?'

'I don't know. Probably.'

'One thing I know. You have so much of your life ahead of you. You have so much still to come.'

'I want to believe that.'

'You do! Oh my god. Mary, you're just starting.'

'Don't overdo it.'

'Okay, maybe I went too far.'

They laughed. They looked at their ghastly sandwiches.

'Pete said I could be a teacher.'

'Oh, fuck that! Really?'

'Why not?'

'Teaching kids all day? Jesus.'

'Wow. Okay.'

'I mean, it's not our thing, is it. Children. Not our own anyway.'

'Fuck, Claire! Speak for yourself.'

'Yeah? Righto. Sorry. Sorry, Mare.'

'Nah, you're good. Fair call.'

'This place,' said Claire. 'Whose idea was it again?'

They both watched the young mother at a nearby table reaching inside the pram and lifting the infant on to her knee.

'Is there really a lake?' said Mary.

'He said there is.' She touched the handle of her suitcase.

Mary had the sudden sense that her sister was lost. They were both lost.

Mary thought Claire had married only so that she might have a child. Of course, marriage wasn't necessary for this but somehow that's how it worked. Job done. Claire had wanted to see what it was like. She'd said as much to Mary in the past. Her living happened on waves of curiosity. What about this? And this? She didn't stay in the same job for longer than two years. More than that, Claire didn't particularly need men. In some profound way, she didn't take them seriously. Putting them in a separate and inferior category, however, had the effect of making them special too. She was drawn to physical strength and beauty. She was shockingly superficial, since there was no depth there, nothing to look for beyond the surface. Her love life was, Mary guessed, sporadically active. It was also mostly secret, waved away. To learn even this much—a bloke, a lake—was unusual. Whoever she was with and under whatever circumstances, it was not the future. Claire made it all seem incidental, almost accidental. Would she even get on this train today?

Mary said, 'Remember when I used to want to get rides on your back? When we were young.'

'What? No.'

'Remember?'

'Not really. Rides? I mean, you could be really annoying.'

'And you were so mean.'

'That's us. Annoying and mean.'

With one hand the mother fed a rusk to the child while she deftly brought a cup to her own mouth and drank. It seemed a miracle of coordination or just a miracle. Then it was as if the mutual calm of mother and child stretched over the entire café. Peace reigned. The trains were banished. No one was going anywhere.

'I remember when Will was that age,' said Claire, 'and he was very content just to take in the world. So settled.'

'Please,' said Mary, 'don't. Don't. Please.' She felt suddenly on the edge of some sort of howling. She did not want to scare the child chewing on its rusk.

'Okay, darling,' said her sister. 'Okay.'

They sat together without talking or moving. Then another announcement came through and it was almost time.

'When Colin was a baby,' said Claire, 'just six weeks or ten weeks, something like that, this one night he was screaming and screaming. That wasn't unusual. Oh, he was a shocker.'

'I remember,' said Mary.

'This night I went into his room and he wouldn't stop. It was about 2am. I was determined to break the pattern. Let him cry it out. Maybe it would take a few nights, but I'd win. I'd show him who was boss. I should have stayed out of the room. For some reason I went in. His face was totally contorted into this ugly mess. He wasn't recognisable. His whole body was wrenched with the crying, his little shoulders pulling forward each time his lungs filled and emptied. Christ, it was awful. I felt there was no connection between us. He'd severed it with this noise, this terrible act. Because I thought he was putting it on. No one really felt this bad. What was wrong with him anyway? He was fed. He was warm. I'd given him everything. I'd given him *life*. And he was throwing it back in my face, spitefully.'

'You were sleep deprived.'

'Of course I was.'

'I had the same moments with Will.'

'Did you?'

'He was a good sleeper actually, but he had his moments.'

'Colin was dreadful. Anyway. I need to tell you, Mare. I need to.'

'Okay.'

'This night, the horror of horrors night, I told him to be quiet. I said it into his unrecognisable face. But he didn't listen. He carried on. And I pressed my hands down on his tiny body, pretending to myself I was just tucking him in, wrapping him up more tightly in the blanket. I pushed harder and harder. Now I couldn't pretend. It would all be over soon. I knew what I was doing.'

'You were so exhausted.'

'I really pressed hard. Stop that. Stop now. I must have winded him, because he stopped and his eyes popped open and he stared straight up at me. This was what I longed for. Stopping was even worse, it turned out. We were looking at each other. Everything was clear.' Claire picked up her sandwich again and studied it as if it might have changed into something else, something desirable or at least edible. 'So. Ex-Sergeant Mary, you probably locked up people who were better than me. I think I could have killed my own son.'

Mary looked again at the baby with the rusk, now messed into its fat cheeks, the young mother staring hungrily into her teacup. The tide of Mary's own fearfulness rose in a blush right up one side of her neck. Then it rolled off again. There was something awry in her sister's story. Maybe something had happened that night. But it had been different, perhaps. Not as dramatic. With a wider margin for mercy. Claire was trying to be interesting, wasn't she? To compete with what she believed was Mary's old world, the dark place of mistakes, mayhem, the fateful sequencing of poor decisions. But what was she—Mary—doing? Only treating her sister as if they were in an interview room, doubting what she heard, working the angles, trying to get to the thing currently buried. She couldn't help it. Here Claire was, pursuing her canny pleasure, slipping out of Mary's reach again. Her bag literally packed. It was heartbreaking, perfectly familiar. They could pass through hell, they had passed through all the hell of Will's death, and nothing changed. In the end she admired her sister. Her gall was something else. She felt a bit sorry for the bloke she was meeting. He'd have no idea. He would be imagining a nice time on the lake in a boat, which was perfectly possible until it wasn't. She saw her sister laughing at him when he suggested a walk in the rain up a nearby hill for the spectacular views.

'What do you think of a mother like that?' Claire pressed again.

'No one's perfect,' Mary said.

Sixteen

It had been hot all week. All over the country temperatures were much higher than normal. Their house cooked behind its glass. They had to use the heat pump on its cold setting, though Pete was always turning it off and then on again. Even sitting in the shade outside didn't give much relief, and when the sun went down the humidity was still unpleasant. They found it hard to sleep or even eat. The blessing at the river was coming up.

The village delivered buckets of ice to everyone, and someone from the front office was checking in regularly. Then they heard that a resident had died from the heat. Underlying health conditions, they were saying. But it was someone from one of the independent units, not the hospital wing, someone they'd presumably had dinner with in the big room. Mary asked Pete how he was feeling. He said he was fine. On the news they heard about other elderly people dying. The announcer said, 'A warning, some viewers might find the details of this next story involving two dogs left in a car with the windows closed distressing.' Pete promptly left the room.

People were flocking to public swimming pools, fountains, the beach. Early in the mornings, Mary and Pete drove to their part of the beach. It was too draining to take their usual walking route through the estuary. If they walked close to the sea, the breeze took the edge off the heat. They swam or floated in the water. One morning, in the sea, Mary had an image of the retired rear admiral and his wife she used to see swimming. She asked Pete why it was called rear admiral.

'Because they were in charge of the ships at the rear of the fleet,' he said. 'They were of less importance, those ships, in least danger. In the front, leading the fleet into battle, was the vice admiral, higher rank.'

'How do you know that?'

'I don't know. When I was a boy I used to make model warships.'

'What? I didn't know that.'

'It's not a compelling part of my biography. If I'd told you, you might not have agreed to go out with me.'

'True. How long did this go on? How long did you make the ships?'

'Couple of years or three maybe.'

The water lapped under her chin and she pushed her head further back, closing her eyes against the sun. Her hair was in a bathing cap. 'Then you just stopped?'

Pete stood up in the water; it covered his shoulders. He was a head floating. She thought of the floating furniture their old house had been filled with. Was it the real Pete talking? 'Actually, a funny thing happened,' he said. 'A boy came to our house to play with me. He wasn't my friend, just a boy I knew at school. He'd heard I had this collection of warships and he wanted to see them. Anyway, he turned up one day. I doubt I'd invited him. Suddenly he was there. He came up to my bedroom and I showed him the ships. I had them set out on a big plywood board, which I'd painted to be the sea. He was very quiet, just staring at them. He was a bit stunned. They were impressive, I suppose. I'd put a lot of effort in, getting everything right. The little details, the paint jobs. Accurate, you know. Maybe he wasn't expecting all of that. Most likely he wanted to put his mind to rest that this collection wasn't really anything. That I wasn't worth bothering with. He didn't say much. He just stared. I didn't especially like him being there. After a while, I heard Mum calling out to see if we wanted a drink or something. The boy nodded, so I went downstairs to get the drinks. He stayed up in my room. Then when I was in the kitchen I heard him rushing down the stairs and out the front door. He was gone! Just like that. I ran up to my room and I saw he'd smashed all the ships.'

'What?'

'He'd smashed them. They were just in pieces, scattered everywhere.'

'Oh Pete.'

'It was very strange.'

'What did you do?'

'I was so shocked. I just stood there. And Mum came into my room. She looked at the mess. She knew I'd spent all that time, must have been hundreds of hours, on the collection. And she started picking up the pieces.'

'What did she say?'

'She asked me what the boy's name was. I told her. I can't remember his name now. Blocked it out. And then she asked where he lived, because, she said, she was going to go around there. But I said, No, please don't go around there. He was a slightly older boy, a bigger boy. He'd always intimidated me in some way. She told me she was going around to the boy's house to get him to take responsibility for his actions. It was unacceptable. He needed to apologise. I begged her not to go. I was crying. I told her she couldn't go.'

Mary stood up in the water. 'What happened?'

'She didn't go around to his place. But I remember how fierce she looked. How determined she was.'

'I can imagine that.'

'I remember she was a very strong person.'

'She was.'

'And she helped me.'

'She tidied up the mess.'

'No, I mean, in my life. She was always looking out for me and supporting me.'

She watched as he sank back down into the sea, his head disappearing. When he resurfaced, she said, 'She also loved Will.'

'Yes.'

'He was very special to her.'

'The birds.'

'Yes.'

'You know, Mary, if one of us gets ill or whatever—'

'In sickness and health,' said Mary.

'But if one of us goes completely la-la, like Mum—'

'Shoot me.'

'Okay, good. Sorted.'

'Take me out the back and shoot me, Pete.'

'Yeah, great. The back of where?'

'Or borrow a kayak and row us way out by the island, then shove me off.'

'Shove you off? Is there a struggle?'

'Could be. You'd need to take me by surprise.'

'But you'd want it, right?'

'I'd be too far gone to want it. I'd probably fight for my life. But ignore that.'

'Jesus, it sounds dangerous for me. Way out there in a kayak with a crazy woman. With all her police training.'

'It's not going to be a picnic for anyone.'

'What if you swam back?'

'By that stage I wouldn't know what swimming was. I'd think swallowing the water was the best way of surviving. I'd go down fast. Problem solved.'

'Right. I like it more than the shooting option.'

'Yeah, because obtaining a firearm would be an issue. Then the target practice.'

They'd started to wade in, meeting the heat once more, their bodies prickling with it.

Pete said, 'I'll be there, Mary. I'll be here.'

'Where?'

'With you.'

'I know. That's what I'm relying on. That's why I'm giving you instructions now.'

'Whatever.'

'Unless,' she said, 'we ask Colin to kill us both. With his access to drugs. We could go out literally on a high.'

By the time they got home from their swim, they were hot again.

Should they still go to the blessing? Would it be called off?

Mary had the sense that the heat was connected to the blessing at the river. That the temperature was being turned up and up and something would happen. Something or someone would flip the switch, or the switch would fall off in their hands.

The day before they were to make the journey, Mary suddenly remembered about Dave Monk. She spoke to Pete about it. Should they invite him? He would represent the police. Vivian had asked if there were others who would like to attend. Colin was coming—he'd drive them. But the police had played their role that day. The two officers who'd driven them up there, the investigation team.

'I thought you hated them all?' said Pete.

Did she? 'Well, it's unlikely Dave will be able to come at such late notice.'

'Do you want him there or not?'

'Someone should front.'

'It sounds like you still blame them. Dave Monk was hardly born.'

'No, I don't blame them. I don't even think I blame Shaun Anderson. Not now. Not much anyway. What are your feelings?'

'I don't know.'

'I suppose this might help us find out.'

'Maybe.' Pete looked at her. 'You could ask Ross. He'd probably have a gap in his diary.'

They'd never been back to the place. Sometimes, driving up the island, they'd see the turn-off and say something or say nothing but Pete would squeeze Mary's hand. Whenever someone squeezed her hand like this, Mary would feel terribly alone. She wasn't sure why. At Claire's funeral, her father had squeezed her hand and she tumbled into a deep hole.

The old school camp was gone.

That was a surprise. In their minds they'd imagined change, of course. The trees grown larger, the buildings upgraded perhaps or fallen apart. Instead, the road came to an end at a small carpark. An information board had been erected near the beginning of what was now a series of loop tracks. They walked over to it and stood in the shade of a small awning. A picnic table was set into a concrete pad beside a stream. The air conditioning in Colin's expensive car hadn't prepared them for the heat that hit them now. They shielded their eyes, trying to get their bearings.

There were two other cars. Mary and Pete were confused for a moment—had the camp been here on this spot? No, they looked at the map and read the instructions Vivian had sent through about the day. They needed to walk for about ten minutes and they'd come out in a clearing. They'd see the river then.

Mary said to Ross, 'Are you okay to walk?' She'd not digested the instructions, imagined driving right up to the camp as they'd done all those years before.

'I'm fine,' he said. He waved his stick in the air—and Mary saw he'd swapped the village one for a walking pole. He was prepared. He also wore proper tramping shoes and had tied a windbreaker around his waist. 'But go on ahead of me. I'm very slow.' She was surprised he'd agreed to come, yet there'd been no hesitation. Was he here, somehow, to make amends for his part in the affair?

'It's not a race,' said Pete. He was in a cap, tee-shirt, shorts and sneakers.

Colin, in new-looking creased cotton shorts and white polo shirt, had already disappeared around the first bend. 'It's cooler in here,' he called out. He was carrying a small pack with their provisions. Water bottles, fruit, chocolate bars. In a separate compartment of the pack was a framed photo of his cousin. Vivian had suggested bringing a photo.

'Don't lose us, Colin,' Mary shouted. 'You have the water!'

Mary was wearing a floppy straw hat she'd never liked but somehow always ended up using in summer. She'd tried to unpick the bow, but the stitching was threaded through the hat and she didn't want to put a hole in it. She'd chosen a pair of lightweight slacks, a V-necked top which had all those properties of staying cool in the heat and repelling odour. She wore her hiking sandals, made in Norway or a country like that. The straps had a funny kind of shine to them which she had hoped would fade but it hadn't.

She felt that all of them together looked ridiculous. Like a touring party from a long time ago. If she'd been dressed in a long billowing skirt, high lace-up boots and a white puffy blouse buttoned at the neck, she wouldn't have felt less out of place than she did. An image came to her mind of the family of quail which sometimes walked up and down their path at the old house.

In beginning to walk in the direction of the river, she knew that it was all a mistake.

They didn't have the faintest idea what they were doing.

Kindly, Vivian had sent them a link to a video of a karakia. The words scrolled up the screen as they were sung. They'd followed the English translation. It was a prayer of remembrance. Okay, good. They clicked on other videos. Pete had watched for longer than she had. She was too impatient. She was too old for it, she told herself. Her brain was frozen in its ways. Her tongue was that of an ox, an English ox. But he was excited, she saw. He repeated the lines, followed other links. Years ago, he'd enrolled in a reo class through the library. He went along in the evenings for a few months. He would come home, practising words and telling Mary about some of the concepts they were being exposed to. He was thrilled. He was convinced they had to make changes at the library. Then a Māori woman, who'd just joined, challenged the Pākehā in the class. She asked them what right they had to take her language. They'd taken her iwi's land and now they were back for more. Pete left the class. He was quite shaken by it. Mary remembered feeling secretly pleased about the rebuff. It was shameful to feel this, she knew.

How could it be true—that she felt their son was being taken away from them again?

Her bitterness fought through, she couldn't help it. She turned in its prism, in its prison. Words!

Sourly, she thought they would observe the blessing, agree it had been lovely, oh the beautiful singing, thank Vivian, get in Colin's car, drive home and—what?

In the weeks following that first call with Vivian, Mary had tried to sort it all out.

She didn't think it was to do with Will. Not really. Will was a means to an end. It was to do with Shaun Anderson, who'd needed to reconcile the various parts of his life, about which she knew nothing, and who had finally found something, that aspect of himself which had been lost, stripped from him, no doubt. He was damaged by this. Of course he was. Somehow he'd survived. Now it was about reconnection. Good. Good for him. Mary understood all this. Stories like it were appearing constantly. She read the newspaper, watched TV. And yes, it was long overdue. Even way back then in the police, you had to have been a special kind of ignorant not to notice you were locking up a lot of Māori men. Disproportionate was the word now. And you had to have been resolutely blind to certain facts not to wonder whether there might be other things going on. In the system as kids, in the homes and foster care, then on the streets, then in the courts. Gangs. There was a pattern, yes. But it turned out it was very easy to be ignorant and blind. The world she'd policed depended on it. She'd seen it clearly only when she stepped outside it. When you were in the middle of it, you were just getting through the day.

When DI Steve Harwood became Tipene Harwood, she scoffed like everyone else.

Was it really about all that? Had they come, far too late, to witness the new world? And why resent it? Vivian, she believed, was a decent person—and a good daughter. It was a generous thing she was doing. Sure, Mary couldn't help feeling managed by her. Yet here they all were—not present by force but by invitation. She just didn't see her son in it.

She hadn't shared her thoughts with Pete. Or with Colin, who she felt might have been quite receptive to them. This last notion also made her doubt herself once again. Colin liked to tell them how good people were missing out on getting into medical school because of quotas. He and Pete would argue about it. Funny, she couldn't imagine Will being friends with his cousin as adults. Not that she knew for sure how he would have turned out. Guesses—it was all guesses.

Her mind was rubbishy and ancient.

What to do? What to do? What to do? She walked rhythmically to the question in her head.

The bush got thicker, and she pulled off her stupid hat. She realised she'd pushed on ahead, leaving Pete with Ross. Colin was somewhere in front. At the densest part of the bush, the temperature dropped substantially. She felt the sudden cold on her bare arms.

A large tree had fallen close to the track. Emerald moss grew on it and crown ferns pressed around it. A small pool of water was collecting slow drips from the damp bank of earth. She stopped and looked into the pool. Nothing appeared to be moving, but then she noticed that the surface of the water was pricked occasionally by tiny darting insects touching down and taking off. In their landings they left scribbles. She stared, trying to read what the insects were writing on the pool. She turned to face back along the track. She'd been about to call to Will, that he should look here, look at what she'd found.

Of course, it was Pete and Ross who were walking towards her. She heard their voices before she saw them. She moved off quickly.

She found Colin sitting on a log, eating a banana. Sunlight arrowed through the canopy and just touched the top of his white hair. 'There you are!' she said. 'You look like a little boy. Like a choir boy.' Her mind was still on Will.

'Would you like something to eat?'

She shook her head. 'Drink please.'

He passed across her water bottle. Pete had written 'Mary' on a label and stuck it to the bottle. Each of them had their own labelled bottle. His librarian feel for catalogue and order came through from time to time.

Colin took his bottle from the pack and pointed at the name. 'Good old Pete.'

She grinned. Actually, she thought she had this in common with Pete: an organising impulse. They both liked lists. They thought their son was very different—from others and from them. But as Will got older, she'd recognised a lot of her own traits. Pete's too. Their son wasn't an alien at all. Her hand hardly shook as she put the bottle to her lips and drank.

She said, 'What do you remember from that time, Colin?'

'What time?'

'With Will.'

'With Will, I just remember all the good times we spent together.'

'You liked coming around to the house.'

'Yeah. Up in his room. Or being outdoors. All his projects.'

'You were a good friend to him, a good cousin.' She took another drink. 'Did he speak about us?'

'What do you mean?'

She felt foolish. Why did she need any assurances? It was the trip, coming here. 'I don't know. Did he say, "Oh god, I have to put up with Mum, or Dad's being a real pain," stuff like that?'

'Boys don't think about their parents. We were too busy, you know.'

'Of course.'

They heard the men coming. Pete called out, 'Ahoy! Is that the official rest stop?'

When they emerged from the bush, cloud had moved in. Above the hills to the north the sky was luminously dark. Ross gestured in that direction and said, 'Rain in a couple of hours.' Mary almost laughed. He looked like an ancient wise figure from a movie, pointing at the sky. Where was his cloak and his staff?

A small group of people were gathered at the far side of the grassy expanse. Someone was waving. Pete raised his hand.

In the car Ross had told them that he'd attended a number of police events after he retired and had got to know the police kaumātua. Mary missed the word at first. 'The what?'

Pete had asked him about his Māori knowledge. 'I have almost none,' Ross said. But then he mentioned the kaumātua's name and how good it was to see that position established. He also had a granddaughter who was almost fluent. Mary felt herself flinching. 'Impressive,' she said. She was hoping no one was about to say how Māori had a much more enlightened attitude to death. Pete was capable of it. Ross probably had stories of attending tangi. No doubt it was true. Why not wail for days if you felt like it?

It was childish of her, this antagonism. She was a remnant.

'I'm hopeless,' Colin had said on their way here. 'I don't have an ear for languages at all. That's my excuse anyway.'

'Your mother was a great mimic,' said Mary. She saw her chance to divert the conversation. 'She could do anyone.'

'That's different,' said Colin.

'Maybe.'

He sounded dismissive, as if he didn't care to have his mother in the picture then; she was the wrong person.

Mary was remembering the old Czech neighbour they had, a very kind man who gave them silverbeet he'd grown. He'd hand it over the fence. Claire loved to imitate him. *Kill ze slugs before you cook.* Mary felt she couldn't add these details.

Ross and Colin had started walking over to the group. Mary was aware that Pete hadn't moved.

'You good?' she asked him.

He nodded. 'I think it's hit me.'

She didn't feel like hugging him. It was too warm. More than that, she wished he wasn't fading in this moment. He looked pale. She touched his arm. Not now, she thought. She felt she was heartless. Why had Pete stayed with her? She was heartless as her sister had been heartless. That was where the mimicry came in. Other people were always fair game. Their old Czech neighbour had fled the Nazis. Don't be cruel, you girls, their mother always said. Their cousin Louise was cruel too—it was how Claire bonded with her. She saw it in Colin as well. They had a shorthand. One time he'd said to her that a lot of his patients, women, were basically either hypochondriacs or malingerers. He could be very unlikeable. Whereas Pete was kind. He said nice things about people. He put up with Colin. He put up with her. He walked the old dogs of people who were ill. No wonder his heart was giving up the ghost. It had had to work so hard to accommodate them.

'Come on then,' she said.

Vivian was in her fifties and taller than Mary expected. Whatever had given her the idea about her height from one phone call and some emails, she didn't know. Anyway, Vivian was a tall, athletic-looking woman in a black skirt and a white blouse. She had bare feet. Should Mary also take off her shoes? No, that was only if you were entering a house. She was instantly back in Claire's apartment when her sister was dying and Rina had arrived. Actually, she would have loved to take off her shoes now and feel the grass in her toes, but it was too late.

A sudden image came to her—Pete's mother when she was in care. All the trouble she had with her feet. The swelling, the tenderness, the recalcitrant toenails. It was one task Mary took on, attacking those nails. How much of Margaret's thinking settled on her feet. She wanted you to know everything. The pain and bother as well as the little triumphs. Her feet were adversaries, ugly and foreign. Oh, chop them off, will you, she'd once told Mary who was holding the nail scissors. Don't be shy about it. Use those implements and let's be done with them. Up to the point Margaret had gone into care, the idea of her feet would never have occurred to them, would have been off-limits.

The feet, however, were a red herring, Mary thought. Or

they were a sign. Margaret now wore her inside on the outside. What did she mean? Her interior was walking around, using these crippled and crippling feet. Her toes weren't toes, they were her ideas, her self.

Like Will! Mary suddenly saw this—after all this time. Dead Will existed as his inside, which was inside them.

She could barely follow her own explanation. Where was Colin with the water bottles?

Vivian was carrying a small leafy branch. She came towards Mary quickly and they were embracing. It all happened too fast to think about properly.

Stepping back, Mary said, 'This is Pete.'

'Tēnā koe Pete,' said Vivian. She kissed him on the cheek.

'Hello,' he said. 'Kia ora.'

Vivian led them to where the two men were standing. They were dressed similarly to Vivian, in black suit trousers and white shirts. She introduced them as her uncle and her cousin. 'Dad's brother and his nephew,' she said. They kissed Mary on the cheek.

Pete stepped forward with his hand out, and Shaun Anderson's brother drew him into a hongi. The nephew did the same. And then it was Ross and Colin's turn.

After that, there was a silence. Mary was aware for the first time of the sound of water. She walked a few paces and saw the river. She was not ready for it. She stopped. Having prepared herself for everything, she was unprepared for this basic fact. The river! She was also not prepared for being unprepared. Mary was always prepared. *Enter the Scene.*

The river was fuller and faster-flowing than she remembered. In her mind it had all been stones and shallows, with deeper pools in places. Reeds lined the banks. Further upstream was an old bent tree, one long branch almost touching the water. She imagined children jumping off it. There was no sign of the bridge. Maybe this was a different spot altogether. It didn't really matter. It was the same river. You could step into the same river twice.

'Where's the bridge?' said Pete. He sounded disappointed.

'The bridge was removed a long time ago,' said the brother. 'They built one further down, in a better spot.'

Yes, of course. The bridge was a hazard. They knew that from the court case. It should have been removed before the accident. Perhaps Pete had forgotten or buried that detail. And there it was again, in the police file Dave Monk had magicked up.

Mary was troubled by a burst of doubt. Had she got this all wrong? Had she got Shaun Anderson terribly wrong? Was she wronging his family now?

They'd tried not to think about Shaun Anderson for all this time. They'd pushed his presence out with such deliberateness, banishing his name, and what had happened? He had swollen to take over all their thoughts. He'd always been there, at three times his size, four times. A monster. Big enough to blot out everything else. He seemed to be approaching them now in human size and shape. Mary felt him in the people here: the brother, the nephew, the daughter. He was like them, of them.

Vivian said, 'Have you got a photo?'

Colin reached into the pack and took it out. He offered it to Vivian.

'No,' she said. 'He can stay with you.'

Despite what she'd said on the phone about being terrified, Vivian seemed calm and in charge.

Colin took a quick look at Will's face in the photo and held it against his chest, turned outwards. Colin was rigid with—what? Seriousness. Of course it was serious. The situation, he knew, was beyond his expertise. Mary saw that he was making himself into a statue of readiness, with no idea what to be ready for.

She saw Pete glance at their son and look away. He brought his hand to his face, shielding it. The photo had been taken on a beach holiday. Will had been absorbed in something by the sea's edge. Pete took the photo in the moment Will looked up at him, unaware he was being photographed. He looked quizzical, beautiful, open. They'd enlarged the photo after he died and had it in their bedroom, first in the family home and then in the next house. They were very used to it, seeing it every day. They hadn't yet put it out in the village place.

Then Mary felt her breath catch. The photo was new suddenly. In this setting, Will was remade. He looked out at them, at the river. *Who put the river there? Where did it flow to? What life did it contain?* He was curious all over again. Alive. Wanting to know. He was in the outdoors. He would have investigated this world. Perhaps he had—during the first days of the camp.

She imagined him walking near them, his fine bare feet. If he had a prickle in his foot, he would always get it out himself. Even when he was very small. She saw him sitting down, intent, his tongue stuck between his lips in concentration, working at the task. Often he seemed not to need them. That was why they'd urged him, cajoled him, forced him to go to the school camp—because they felt he would be fine, in the end. He would be able to cope. He didn't need them.

She began to cry soundlessly. A tear ran down her cheek.

'My uncle will do the karakia now,' said Vivian.

Mary felt her body become enormously heavy. Her knees

wanted to fold. Was this where praying came from? You think you can stand but you need to sink to the earth?

Shaun Anderson's brother began to intone.

Everyone had bowed their heads, she saw. And she did too.

They drove back in almost total silence. They were all exhausted. At different times the three passengers fell asleep. Mary had a dream in which she was swimming and she became so tired that she felt the beginnings of panic. At the point when she felt she might be in real danger, she'd stood up and discovered the water was only ankle deep.

How odd for Colin, the youngest, to drop the three old people off at the village, as if he was their parent returning the children to their boarding school after a day's outing. Pete asked if either Colin or Ross wanted to stop in at their place for a drink or a quick bite to eat. It was almost dinnertime, and surely drinks time, he said. But no, they both said they couldn't. It had been such a long day.

'Thank you for coming,' Mary said to Ross, after Colin had driven away.

'Ah dear Mary,' he said, taking her hands in his. He looked directly into her eyes, and in that instant she thought he was going to say something. Something about that time, and how he'd let her down, abandoned her. But of course he didn't. It was the past, and she was only a small figure in his past and now a small figure in his present. His wife had died. He had clever grandchildren. He gave her hands a little shake and let them go. He turned and walked in the direction of the main buildings, leaning on his stick a little more than he had during the day.

Poor Ross, she thought. He'd come with them from

interest, from a sense of connection and rightness; he'd also come because it was an outing. He'd used up one more day.

In the carpark, they'd had afternoon tea. The uncle did the prayer and then Shaun Anderson's daughter played mum, pouring them milky tea from a couple of thermoses, going around the group with a plastic pottle of sugar and a Tupperware container of bought biscuits. Was Mary criticising the biscuits now? No.

Vivian's matter-of-fact kindness seemed to cure them—of what? Mary felt they'd moved back from an edge.

Behind all of Vivian's actions, her uncle was somehow the unobtrusive guide. They exchanged glances, nods, one or two whispered words. The thing flowed.

They stood around the picnic table. The men talked about fishing. Shaun Anderson's brother ran a charter boat somewhere up north. Ross knew someone who the brother said he knew. It grew into a jolly conversation, Mary saw. Ross had always been good at connections. This mutual acquaintance was a real character. They laughed about his exploits. Pete took another biscuit. He was grinning too. Vivian stood off to one side, drinking her tea. Mary approached her. They smiled at each other.

'Sit down, eh,' said Vivian, gesturing at the bench by the picnic table.

'I'm good,' said Mary. She was very tired and she wanted no one to see it. 'I'll be sitting for hours in the car soon.'

'Shouldn't be too busy going home.'

'No.'

Vivian looked up at the sky, which was even darker now. 'Timed it about right.'

Ahead of the day, Mary had been afraid that she and Pete

would somehow be dragged into something. They would be asked something. She didn't know what that thing was. 'Yes,' she said. It wasn't as though they'd felt like extras, extraneous. Only that they were not in the spotlight. She should have been thankful. Still, weren't there things they had to say to each other, Vivian and her? If there were, they seemed to have been put somewhere, elsewhere. In the river perhaps. Was that what had happened through the ceremony? It was biscuits and jokes now. It was okay.

What did she want to ask? If Vivian had children. And what sort of person her father was. No, not that. They were past him somehow. What her job was. Actually, Mary realised, their subjects weren't obvious and Vivian, cleverly, knew this. The idea that they would have some heart-to-heart right there in the carpark was ridiculous. The thread connecting their lives was too fine to pull on. With each movement, they stepped carefully over it and around it, making it and pretending they weren't.

Who knew what it might mean, this connection. Most likely it would dissolve. Had it already been carried away, like the stick in the river? She liked Vivian and her uncle.

Next, Mary found herself helping Vivian collect the cups, tidy up. The men watched, chatting about nothing.

Packing things into Vivian's car, Mary said, 'You did really well. Not that I'm an expert.'

'Nah,' said Vivian.

'I know you said you were terrified.'

'I was!'

'It didn't seem like that.'

'Okay. Covered it up well.'

'It was fine.'

'I was all right once it began. Maybe it was all right.'

'I think it was all right.'

'Yeah. For a first time.' She laughed.

'How many times are you planning on doing this sort of thing?'

'I don't know. Depends on how many people Dad needs to . . .'

Needed to what? Mary wondered as Vivian trailed off. Had she been about to say 'apologise to'? But that wouldn't have been right. It was not what Mary and Pete expected or needed, and it was not finally what was on offer.

Vivian laughed again. 'I think my uncle was auditioning me.'

'Thank you anyway,' said Mary. Then she added, truthfully, 'We're so glad to be here. I'm sorry about your father.' Sorry that he'd died before this day? Yes. Sorry she'd waited months to call them? That too. Also, it seemed, another kind of sorry. Sorry for the life he'd not been given? The one denied him? Snatched from him with violence? Could she, Mary, stand in for that much sorry? It was too grand. She felt unsteady. Could Pete come now? This was much more his area. She felt like a pretender.

Vivian smiled. 'Thanks, Mary. I would have really liked to meet Will.' Tears came to her eyes as she smiled at her.

Mary said, 'You know there's something I didn't tell you before, about the accident.'

'That's all right, we don't need to go back over all of that. It's really painful for you, I know.'

'No, it's fine. Because you need to know.' She'd not rehearsed this bit. Even now, this far in, she could probably leave it, pretend it was nothing. Say their goodbyes. There was time. She didn't feel well at all. 'The bridge was a hazard. It was condemned and should never have been in operation.

The council just hadn't got around to removing it or even putting up a warning sign. "Don't Use." That would have done it. The bridge's condition was likely to have played a part in the accident. They couldn't be certain, but they think that maybe your father's vehicle hit some decayed or damaged part of the surface of the bridge and this could have made it all a lot worse than it might have been. There'd been an accident before on the same bridge, maybe more than one. That was raised in the court case. A likely contributing factor. It's all in the police file. So that's something you should know.'

'Thank you, Mary. Thank you for saying that.'

'I'm not saying it. It was part of the proceedings.'

'I understand.' Vivian reached across and held Mary's arm with a light though definite pressure for a moment, and then released it. 'Dad's here,' she said.

Mary was startled. Shaun Anderson had come? She might have turned around to check if she hadn't had the presence of mind to take a deep breath. Wait. Think.

'Will is here too,' she said finally.

Mary lay in bed in the dark, Pete beside her. Both were awake. She was thinking again of the moment when Vivian had stepped towards the river and sprinkled water from a plastic bottle into it. Water on water. She had thrown her branch into the river, which grabbed it at once and took it away. The stick was gone in the current before you could see it again.

'I thought we might have been invited to say something,' said Pete. 'But we weren't.'

'What did you say?'

He turned on his side and repeated himself directly into her ear.

'Probably a good thing,' she said.

'Probably.'

'What would you have said?'

'I don't know. I don't know if I would have been able to speak.'

'Me neither,' she said. 'When she threw the branch in the river . . . That was a hard moment.'

'I know.'

They were silent, listening to the quiet, dead house.

He said, 'I wish I'd had the courage to speak.'

She reached for his hand and held it.

He said, 'Did Vivian say anything to you?'

'About what?'

'Her father, I don't know.'

'No,' she said. 'I didn't ask.'

It was so dark. Behind the curtains, the stars were too high up to make a difference. The birds were asleep. The sea was asleep.

She drifted above them for a moment. Looking down, she wondered, What are these two people thinking at this moment? It was hard to say. Maybe that by the river their son had been put back into the world, not as a person but as a question. What was the question?

'Actually,' said Pete, 'it's funny. It wasn't really about Will.'

'Exactly!' said Mary. She came down with a bump. 'That's what I thought too.'

'And that's what made it good.'

She didn't immediately like what Pete was saying. She couldn't bring it into focus. Could he be right? Will had been there—that was true. And Shaun Anderson—his daughter had felt it. Others too. Pete's mother. She was trying to remember what she'd thought about his mother's feet the moment she saw Vivian's bare feet. The feeling in her brain was a bit like dehydration, though she'd had plenty of liquid. She felt vaguely poisoned, or as though she was recovering from an illness, a voyage. She sensed the other side of it coming through, getting better.

Pete sat up suddenly. 'Where's the photo?'

'Damn, it must still be in Colin's pack. We'll ask him to drop it off.'

'Or he can hang on to it for a while.'

'Okay, yes. It's not our only photo of him.'

'We have others.'

'If we ever get around to unpacking.'

Pete lay back down again. 'This place is terrible.'

A subject she was sure about! She felt a burst of love for this person beside her. She said, 'Agreed.'

There was another long silence, then Pete said, 'I don't want to learn to play bowls.'

After a while, Mary said, 'I don't want to be here. Can we leave?'

'Dig a tunnel?'

'We'll hide the dirt in our pockets.'

'We could leave.'

'How?'

'Not sure.'

'But how?'

The idea of digging must have penetrated her dozing mind. A boy was digging, though not in the earth. He was digging in his pack, searching for something, getting desperate. There were shouts from outside: Come on! Come on! We're leaving! The boy continued to hunt through his pack, tossing clothes on the floor of the bunkroom. Where was it?

Finally, he found what he was looking for. He shook a pile of clothes and it fell on the floor. His torch! He'd wrapped it in a sock. How had he forgotten that?

I'm coming! he shouted. Wait for me! Then he ran from the room into the darkness.

There was the sound of cheering, and then the engine starting, revving, and the boys shouting with joy as they were thrown together when the ute took off and they were away. The boy shone his torch into the night sky where its light disappeared.

Seventeen

The weeks of unhappiness continued.

There was always a lot on. Flyers appeared daily in their letterbox. *Post.* Nearly all the mail was internal. Invitations and notices and schedules. Activities and trips. To the orchestra, to the art gallery. And none of it was compulsory. People said that to them. They could choose to take part or not. The other residents were very considerate and gentle. Would they like to come over for drinks? Mary and Pete felt ungrateful. Sometimes this feeling made them accept an invitation. Would this be the time their deep objections faded out? A single moment of joining would help them see the light.

They sang Happy Birthday to a woman called Joan, two doors down. They and a dozen others ate her birthday cake and looked at her family photographs. People's cats were remembered. A poodle sniffed the crumbs at Mary's foot. There was a rule that you could bring your dog to the village but you couldn't get a new one. The dogs of the village were the last dogs. They walked liked gods among them. Even the tiniest ones seemed massively significant, aware of their own importance.

Mary and Pete felt wretched. In larger groups Mary's hearing aids struggled. She found herself sitting back, nodding and pretending, full of rage. It was too late to make new friends, or too early. They'd never really needed them up to this point.

An ancient figure sat in an armchair in the corner of Joan's house, smiling. It wasn't clear if he could speak. He'd been a High Court judge. Mary recalled the name. One of the pre-eminent jurists of the last century, someone whispered loudly. What was whispered about them, about her and Pete? Mary wondered. *A bit stand-offish. Hard work.*

A few party attendees had a go at getting the cork out of the bottle of bubbles. It was no good. Wrist strength. They'd have to get help. The bottle went around until finally Pete offered. The cork went off with a good pop and the poodle barked once. Everyone laughed. *Calm down, Freddie.* We'll invite you again, they said to Pete. They weren't so sure about Mary, Mary felt.

Someone asked if Rita was coming. No, she wasn't. There was some dark talk about Rita's ongoing resistance to re-entering their group. People shook their heads sadly. It's time, everyone agreed. It's gone on long enough.

Finally, Mary asked, 'What's wrong with her?'

'Nothing,' said Joan.

Then someone explained that Rita's husband had died a few months ago. If you didn't watch it, grief, they explained, could become your identity.

'She's sad,' said Joan, 'but we're all sad.'

'Are you?' said Mary. The question came out more harshly than she'd meant. Was she doubting them all? A ripple of affront paused the party. Everyone was looking at Mary, even Freddie the poodle. She felt the dog's resentment. Pete was staring at the floor. Mary wanted to leave. How soon could they make their excuses?

From the corner, the old judge said sternly, 'I'm not. I'm very happy!'

Mary missed it and turned to him. 'I'm sorry, what was that?'

'Eh?' said the judge, craning forward.

'He's *happy*,' said Joan, who now looked unhappy. 'He said he's very happy.'

Mary raised her glass of bubbles. 'Good for you!'

Then one afternoon, Trent was at the door.

Mary couldn't think who it was at first. Someone from the village come to fix something, inspect something. Men arrived regularly. *Sorry to bother you.*

Trent had to point to himself and say his name. He must have thought they were crackers.

'Trent!' said Mary. 'Come in. Pete, it's Trent.'

'Who is it?'

'Trent. From next door at the old place.'

'Trent!'

He looked the same. The black clothes, headphones around his neck. He said he was sorry to turn up unannounced, did they have a few minutes?

It was a great shock to see him in their place. They'd seldom got this close to him, and apart from the time he'd knocked on their door to ask about his lost cat, they'd never actually talked to him, seen his mouth move, watched his face as he spoke. It was like witnessing Pinocchio come to life, Mary thought.

'Something's happened,' he said. 'My sister said I should tell you.' It sounded immediately grudging. 'Like in case you saw it and thought, Hello, what's this?'

'Saw what?' said Mary.

'I'm putting your house back on the market.'

Your house. 'Sorry?' said Mary.

'What are you doing?' said Pete.

'My sister's plans changed. She got pregnant and her wife just scored a great job in London. Sort of her dream position, apparently. She wasn't even going for it. Anyway, they were all, Can we do this? Can we not do this? Kid on the way. The wife's family is all there. Yadda yadda.'

Pete looked from Trent to Mary and back again. What is he doing? Someone is pregnant?

'Your sister—' said Mary.

'Yeah. Crazy,' said Trent. 'Anyway, basically my sister needs to sell.'

Pete raised his hand. 'She needs to sell? She's selling our house?'

'Yep.'

'Gosh,' said Mary. Still she didn't trust her hearing. If words came too quickly, she couldn't distinguish them. Slow down, she often said to Pete now.

'And she says, "Don't leave them thinking there was anything wrong with the house."'

Pete said, 'What's happened to the house?'

'Nothing,' said Trent. 'Well, how would we know? Haven't even moved in.'

Mary and Pete were staring at him. He carried on talking.

Mary didn't think he was their son. He was definitely nothing like their son. But they regarded him as if he were an apparition. Not a visitor, a visitation.

Finally, she interrupted him. 'It's just been empty?'

'Yeah. I mean I've been inside. I had to do the inspection after you moved out. But she told me she didn't want me squatting or putting my shit in there, my stuff in there.'

The information came at them in sudden bursts. It was still hard to follow.

Pete said, 'You came to tell us because—'

'Maybe you'd think we were flicking it on for some huge profit, ha ha, having owned it for five seconds. Nope. She needs to ditch it pronto. It's been a lot of hassle for me. Plus living next door to sis, I wasn't sure. Sounded good. But . . .' He was starting to move to the door. 'But this is a nice place, eh.'

They were not going to let him leave. Not this soon.

Pete said, 'Mary, are you hearing all this?'

'I am. I am.' She stepped into the apparition's path, blocking his exit. 'Trent,' she said. 'Trent. When will you sell it?'

'Yes,' said Pete. 'What sort of timeframe are we talking about?'

'Like soon as. Off to the agent's now. You were on the way. Handy.'

'Trent, do you mean today?' said Pete.

Trent nodded.

'Mary,' said Pete, 'Trent is on a mission.'

'It's urgent, Trent, is it?' she said.

Trent laughed. 'What do they call it? Highly motivated vendor.'

'Your sister,' said Pete.

Mary smiled. 'I can see her dilemma.'

It was a private sale. They bought the house back for the same price Trent's sister had paid for it, plus her and their lawyers' fees. She wouldn't have to pay the agent's fee. Selling their village place was also straightforward since there was a waiting list. They took a bath on it, of course—Colin was correct—but they were all right. Pete cashed in a superannuation scheme they'd been keeping for a rainy day. They'd need to watch their expenses.

Trent was confused. He probably thought they were crazy. But he liked the ease of it.

Maureen the manager wasn't even that surprised. Some people find it's not for them, she said. How many, Mary wondered. Surely not a large number. They were a special kind of fool, weren't they? They felt their own expendability in the brief moment they had with Maureen in the office with the children's artworks. They didn't tell her they were moving back to their old house. It was still embarrassing. It was a joke.

At the door to her office, Maureen said, 'It's a shame that Ross, your old friend, is not here to say goodbye.'

They asked where he was, and she said he was in hospital. He'd had a stroke. She thought they would have known.

'How is he?' asked Mary.

'Oh, he's coming right. Says he'll be back.'

'Good,' said Mary.

They were moving back in with about half their stuff. Sure, they'd need to get a couple more armchairs and a sofa, a bed for the spare room (people might stay!), other bits and pieces. Generally, they agreed they could live with less. They liked the idea of more spartan spaces. Fewer trip hazards, said Pete. They liked the idea of their reconditioned wood burner. They were sort of starting again. And if they fell down the stairs they'd relocate to the spare room. These mysterious guests could have the great views of the island. And if they began to struggle up the path there were such things as little cable cars. A two-seater quietly moving up through the trees. Pete had done some research years before, when they'd been wondering how to future-proof the place. On a still night, imagine taking a ride—just for the fun of it, just to hear the frogs and all the creatures who moved among the grass and the leaves.

They were ecstatic and chastened. They were ashamed and glad. They were home. They were delirious.

Mary also thought of the rat she'd seen the day Pete had had his last heart episode. The rat wasn't Will and, she now supposed, it wasn't Shaun Anderson either. Anderson was Vivian's dad and not some haunting creature. Who, then? She was afraid and she didn't know what her fear consisted of. Many things, no doubt.

She remembered the time she'd collected Will from Pete's parents' house. Will was playing in their garden with some of Margaret's birds. 'He's very content by himself,' Margaret had said to her.

'Yes,' said Mary, 'should we be worried?'

'Why? It's a tremendous skill to develop.' She had reached out and held Mary's arm. 'The other thing is one should never interrupt a child's game or try to join in when they're playing. It breaks the spell. It's confusing. He knows we think the birds aren't real. But they are real.'

Shortly after they moved back, Mary met Colin at a nice café in town for their Claire lunch. He brought the shoebox of his mother's letters and documents. He repeated what he'd said the day he'd come around to their house when it was filled with the furniture for the sale. That his mother's handwriting was almost illegible and there didn't seem to be anything of significance in the box. It was more or less random what she'd saved. Once Mary had looked, she could put it in the rubbish. He said he had enough keepsakes and reminders already.

'Are you sure, Col?' she said.

'Totally. It's yours.'

The shoebox was in a supermarket bag which Colin now placed beside Mary on the bench seat. They were sitting at the back of the café and luckily there was no one at the next table. Mary disliked the way most cafés and restaurants jammed you in. The last time she and Pete had gone out to dinner, they'd been able to hear the entire conversation of the couple beside them. They may as well have been at the same table. When Mary complained to him about it later, Pete thought she was overdoing it; he really hadn't been bothered. Truthfully, she hadn't been able to hear exactly what they were saying, but the low babble of their voices had made it hard to hear Pete. She couldn't tune the others out.

Colin ordered a bottle of wine—as he always did—and she chose their food, as was the custom. It had begun as a little joke between them years ago: the aunt was helping the young nephew new to dining out. Somehow it remained the pattern.

They talked for a while about what Colin called 'la rentrée'. He'd been flabbergasted (his word again) by the whole performance. And even though it went against all his advice, she sensed he was sort of impressed by their madness.

'Was it so terrible in the village?' he asked. He'd never had the chance to visit them properly.

'No,' said Mary. 'It was all right. It just wasn't us. We're not ready.'

'Possibly you're the only people who have ever bought the same house twice.'

'Do you think?'

'Oh, there might be hordes of you! At least now you know what it'll be like when the time comes.'

'The other thing, Colin, is that we're massively in denial.'

The wine came and Colin raised his glass. 'To denial!'

'To denial!' said Mary.

He drank the first glass very quickly. She'd barely tasted hers and he was topping himself up. She couldn't drink without food.

'If you get into any sort of trouble,' Colin said, 'just be aware that I can help you out, financially.'

'Colin, we're absolutely fine. But it's very nice of you.'

'But if you want to do more than just potter around, living off your super or whatever, I can help. I want you and Uncle Pete to know that.' He took another large gulp of wine. 'You've always been there for me, and I want you to know . . .'

'It's so kind but not necessary. We're really okay.'

Their food arrived and Colin ate hungrily. He was an unselfconscious eater, seemingly always starving. His body shape hadn't really changed since he was at university, when he'd come back to stay with them for a few days during holidays. Time to feed you up, they'd tell him. Mary remembered how they used to worry about him. Wasn't a student supposed to put on the beer weight? They'd asked him if he was playing sport to stay so skinny. He'd laughed and said it was too cold down there. She saw that he had her sister's constitution. Lean, nervy, quick.

Soon he was pushing his plate to the side, finished.

'Sorry,' she said. 'I'm slow.'

He poured more wine into her glass even though she'd barely had any, and then filled his own. He seemed more pumped than usual, working himself up to something. She knew the pattern. He said, 'In the storage place was all sorts of other stuff. Things of mine from ages ago. When I was at med school.'

He'd read her mind. 'I was thinking of you just then back in those days.'

'Really? I don't know what I would have done without you and Uncle Pete.'

'You did extremely well off the back of your own talents and resources, Col.'

'Partly,' he said.

'You were a force.'

'When Will died, I was pretty useless. I was better when Mum died. I'd had some practice, I guess.'

'Oh Col, you were so young!'

The bottle of wine was empty. Colin lifted it to check. It wasn't that she liked him best when he was morose or anything like that, but it did mean that he trusted her, and she valued the fact that he could show that side of himself. In this way he was a bit like their child.

'We love having you in our lives,' she said. 'That's what you've done for us.'

Mary finished eating and their plates were cleared.

Colin said, 'One item I found, which I'd kept, was a photo you sent me.'

'What was it?'

'Remember when all the ivy outside Mum's bedroom window came down?'

'I do.'

'You sent me a photo of that.'

'Did I?'

'Yeah. It was really hard to look at that photo.'

She didn't hear at first what was in his voice—a sort of accusation. Pain certainly. 'In what way?'

'Maybe you don't remember, but Mum hated that ivy with a passion.'

'I remember. She used to get you to bang on it with a broom so the birds wouldn't sleep there.'

'Right. Right. And when I was a bit older, I said to her, No, no, I am not going to do that!'

'She told me.'

'I always think that in her last days she had to look out the window and see the ivy. All those little sparrows returning at night, waking in the morning. They made a racket. I could sort of see her point. And they made a mess everywhere. I had to hose that down.'

'It was a real bugbear for her.' Mary recalled how the apartment Claire and Colin had lived in was rented out for a year while the estate was settled and the question of where Colin would live was addressed. He'd ended up with his father and then gone away to university after that. An agency managed the apartment, while Mary was the contact person and attended to body corporate matters. The agency must have sent the photo to her. They'd needed to tidy it all up, remove the ivy, so it would have been in connection to that. She explained this to Colin.

'That's it,' he said. 'Such a terrifying photo, Auntie Mary.'

'I'm sorry.'

'The ivy had half peeled off the wall and was hanging there, with all the roots exposed. I think a gale or something had caused it. It was like skin or whatever. It was all hanging off. I don't know why that made things more horrible, but it did.'

'Col, I'm so sorry. That was thoughtless of me. I don't know why I even thought it would have been a good idea to send it to you.'

'Oh, who cares now! You put a note in it. You wrote, Just updating you. The note said, All those poor birds without a home but your mother would have been quite pleased.'

'Oh dear.'

'No, it was all true. Mum dreamed of something like that happening. You weren't wrong.' He tried to drink the last drop from his glass but it was gone. 'It was funny seeing that photo again.' He was looking around for the waiter. 'Will we have something sweet?'

'Yes,' she said.

On getting home after the lunch, Mary immediately opened the box he'd given her. Colin was right—Claire's handwriting was appalling.

There was a journal Claire had started when she was travelling through Europe in her twenties. Mary flicked through some pages. Claire accidentally overpaying the old woman guarding the toilets in Rome and then being too embarrassed to ask for the money back. Trying to make herself understood at a bakery in Paris. Helping a fellow traveller back to the hostel in Dublin after a big night. Deciphering it took time and, in the end, Mary gave up. Sorry, Claire! She said this aloud. The journal ran out after a month of entries, picked up again after a missed month, then stopped again for good. Her sister, bored with writing, had begun filling the margins with doodles. In a few places a line of doodle would stretch out, become the tail of a cat walking across the top of the page. Somehow this cat stood in for Claire more than the words. It was sleek, evasive, knowing. She was powerfully there, and Mary, upset, had to stop reading and return the journal to the shoebox.

It was easier to throw away the documents which had got mixed up with the personal things. There were various warranties, old loan agreements, employment offers.

*

She came across a letter their mother had sent Claire when she was in London. The date told Mary that this was the year after she had finished university. Their mother wrote about various things happening around the house and about people Mary didn't know. The weather had been nice. She hoped it wasn't too miserable over there. She asked if Claire had received the package she'd sent. She wasn't going to tell her what was in it—that was a surprise but 'your sister will be jealous when she hears'.

Mary felt a flicker of anguish to see herself mentioned.

'M & P came to dinner last week,' their mother wrote. 'He's quiet and Mary talked ten to the dozen. I wonder if they'll last. She still wants to join the police. No matter what we say, she's determined. Why are you girls so pig-headed? Family tradition I suppose. Grandchildren seem a long way off and that suits me fine though I also wouldn't complain.'

Finally, there was a letter from their mother to one of her sisters, Louise's mother, written around the time Claire and Mary were young girls. Their mother would have had her hands full. The letter was three pages of densely packed writing. Patricia wrote to her sister in a state of distress about their mother, Mary's grandmother. It must have come to Claire from Louise, perhaps, after her mother died. Mary had been only vaguely aware of what happened at the end of her grandmother's life. She had dementia, was taken away to live with another relative, went into hospital briefly and then died.

Mary remembered going to her grandparents' place on Sundays. Nana was a fantastic baker and there was always a choice of cakes and slices wheeled in on a trolley. Louise cake, lemon slice, cupcakes in paper wrappers. Nana, she recalled, was a very private person, quite stern, always very neat and formal, her silver hair combed immaculately. A tidy, stiff house of doilies and heavy placemats. The great fear you had as a child was to leave a ring mark from your glass on one of the many small side tables.

Patricia wrote about visiting her mother after a period when she'd been away. She was horrified by the change.

'Nana is constantly cold and the heaters are always on in her room. She is confused. I wanted her to find some sticking plaster that I had given her the day before. She hunted frantically through her drawer and offered me in turn, hopefully, a tin of pins, a packet of needles, and some coins. I rejected them all. One could almost say she is neglected. I went yesterday to take her to the Post Office. She knew I was coming. She was sitting asleep in her chair. She was wearing her cardigan, inside out, a singlet, a jumper inside out and back to front, her petticoat and then another singlet, next to her skin. I didn't even check if she had her shoes on the wrong feet. She wasn't even very interested in changing the singlet. She would just put her coat on and no one would know. One element on the stove was on. The day before when I arrived the oven was on and she said she had to turn it off three times already that day.'

She wrote that there were waiting lists at all the local rest homes. Did her sister have any suggestions? She didn't know what to do.

Mary was astonished by the letter. Their mother had never spoken about this time, aside from some jokey comments about 'when I lose my marbles'. But here she was, as a busy mother, having to deal with her own mother and despairing of finding a solution.

She'd taken Nana to a doctor, she wrote—'a strange pipe-smoking creature'—who examined her and said that she was badly constipated and that Patricia was to administer some mini enemas. There was no need for the District Nurse to do it, he said. It was very straightforward.

Patricia 'screwed up her courage' and did this. Later that day she was rung by the District Nurse, who hadn't managed to visit her mother but had spoken on the phone to her. Was she always this confused? Anyway, the nurse said, her mother sounded quite cheerful and had had a good motion.

'The next morning,' Patricia wrote, 'I had a call from Daddy, very excited, who launched into his story right away, with a preamble that it was lucky he had been in the army and been on latrine duty because when he got up that morning there was shit from one end of the house to the other and Nana was covered in shit and would I come over and give her a bath. I asked him how Nana was and he said, Good, she's very cheerful. That word again! Well I rushed down there and when I arrived I found Nana as white as a ghost and looking absolutely ghastly. I couldn't give her a bath because she couldn't stand on her feet without support and I simply couldn't have got her into the bath. I got a basin and put her feet in some warm water and gradually got all the shit out from between her toes. Daddy had been at work with a knife scraping it away from the carpet and the mats. He had even used an old toothbrush which he said worked quite well.

'I got Nana into a chair in the kitchen and wrapped her in a rug and there she stayed all day. The District Nurse turned up in the afternoon but she was unable to do anything to help and she is going to get the other Nurse—Stebbins—to come tomorrow and assess the situation. Daddy was fairly shaken by the whole thing and whereas before he was lukewarm on the necessity for a Home, he has now said to go straight ahead. He says he will stay in the house and continue with his gardening, his golf, and he'll visit Nana. Whatever Home we choose will need to be close enough for him to visit. But will we have much choice?

'I'm writing late at night and I need to go to bed. I'm exhausted. The girls wake so early.

'Daddy has promised to keep the doors open when he goes to bed tonight and Nana said she will bang with her stick when she needs help. I wonder how they will manage. We will meet Nurse Stebbins in the morning. Pray for us, my darling.'

Mary put her mother's letter back into the shoebox and put the lid on it. She presumed Colin hadn't got to it; the pages had almost been stuck together, and she'd had to separate them carefully so as not to tear the paper.

It was agonising that she couldn't phone her sister and talk about the letter. Had Claire herself ever read it? If she had, she would surely have spoken to Mary about it. They would have talked about their poor Nana and all the things they didn't know about her life and their mother's life. They would have mentioned the toothbrush!

The letter, however, wasn't just about the past. It was about the future. Together they would have stared into their futures. When I'm ga-ga, Claire would have said, will you come and put a rug over me? Will you turn off the oven? I'm older than you and I'll be first. She remembered the conversation she'd had with Pete, standing in the sea on the hottest day of the year, in the depths of their unhappiness, joking about her end. What had he seen to bring it up?

Mary had sent Colin the awful photo of the ivy coming

unstuck from the wall, and now Colin, through Claire, had given her this letter. Were they even?

They'd need a place for the shoebox. For now it could go on the top shelf in the cupboard in the spare room. One day someone would find it and throw it out. Colin, probably.

No. Better to save him the trouble. They didn't need to collect any more stuff. She took it to the wood burner and tipped its contents inside, along with the shoebox. Then she found some matches in the kitchen drawer and lit the fire. The old dry paper took instantly. Even before she closed the door of the wood burner, the pile was roaring.

In a flash she remembered going through ashes. There'd been a few cases in her time. People generally overestimated the power of incineration to dispose of evidence. Objects were stubborn. They wanted their stories told. *What have we here?*

She stood at their open front door, looking down the steps to where Pete was beginning to carry the firewood to the pallets they'd set up years ago in the old carport. The load had been dumped on their lawn the day before. Mary suggested they should get some help in to stack it—use Student Job Search or one of the local kids. Not that they knew any of the local kids. Pete made an agreeing sound, but he'd said this morning he might just make a start anyway, see how he went.

She watched him bending, gathering a few pieces in his arms, pausing and then walking to the pallets, out of view. She'd noticed he was more energetic than he'd been in ages. She hoped he wasn't just trying to prove something. Well, so what if he was? Everyone was always trying to prove something, she supposed. *I'm not done yet, bucko.*

When he walked back, he looked up the path and saw

her. 'Are you coming down, love?' he called to her. 'We can make a dent in it.'

'What's that?' she said.

'Come down, come down, Mary! Light of my life!'

'All right,' she said. 'You don't have to shout. I'll just change. Be there in a minute.'

In the upstairs bathroom she put sun cream on her face, her neck and the backs of her hands. Behind her, in the mirror, was the porthole window and today a clear view of the island. She took the tub of sun cream down with her for Pete. He always forgot.

Walking down the steps, she heard birds taking off from the branches above her head, but it was too bright to look up and she didn't want to lose her footing. She held on to the handrail they'd installed when they first bought the house and were thinking of their parents visiting.

As she got closer, the firewood smelled very woody, almost smoky in the morning sun, as if it was already alight.

She'd wanted to tell Pete something about the night of the needle, when Claire had called them and she'd taken her sister to the ED. How Colin had spoken about it the last time he'd visited the house. It had come to her now why she remembered the night so vividly. Nursing her sister's foot in the hospital, waiting to be seen by the doctor, Mary had felt somehow that it was her own foot which carried the needle. She had stepped on the needle, not Claire. She'd felt this powerfully, the pain and also the comfort of her sister's hands cradling the foot. They were entwined, sharing, unaware of which part belonged to which sister. Did it matter? They were together and it was late. She'd planned to tell Pete about this, but by the time she reached him she'd forgotten it again. In its place was just a sensation. It was pleasant but also like an ache. Moving her body helped. She'd tell Pete what she'd told Vivian at the river about the hazardous bridge. She'd wait a bit. She'd tell him over morning tea. Sitting down. She picked up three pieces of firewood. In the wood she felt the day's early warmth. She followed him to the small stack he'd started and which she would mess up and he would neaten and she would mess up again, working on like that until they'd earned a rest. It seemed like they had been away for years, minutes. They were home and everything was different.

Author's Note

The text of the letter which appears in the final chapter of this novel is from a letter written by my mother to her sister. The circumstances surrounding the discovery of the letter and the characters of the novel are all invented. However, my mother is also the source of many of the best stories Margaret tells.

Acknowledgements

Many thanks to Rose Grigor for the conversation about police work; and also to Keri and Tony for their help.

I'm grateful to Anna and Paul for the writing space.

To Madeleine and Joseph, much love and admiration.

To Susanna for sending me my mother's letter to her amazing mother, darling Patricia.

To my siblings, absent from the parts of this story you will recognise, you are the reason I've been able to write this book.